"I have to live with the idea that some perfect stranger came into my house to bug my phone while I was sleeping,"

Jessica whispered. "That he could come again, anytime he wants. That maybe next time . . ." She buried her face against Arlen's shoulder, her hands clenched into fists. "I don't think I can stand it," she said tautly.

"You won't be alone," he promised. "Jessie, I swear you won't be alone."

She pulled back from him. "You told me there was no danger in being a double agent, Arlen. This doesn't qualify as danger?"

"I told you, the Bureau would protect you."

An eternity passed during the moments while Jessica stared unblinkingly at him. Well, you couldn't get much clearer than that. The Bureau would protect her. Arlen would protect her— but only because it was his job.

Dear Reader,

Once again, Silhouette Intimate Moments has prepared a stellar list of books for your reading pleasure. So go ahead, sit in the sun (or the shade, if you prefer) and treat yourself to a few hours of enjoyment.

First up, Kristin James finishes her trilogy called "The Marshalls" with *The Letter of the Law,* featuring James Marshall, the last of the brothers to have his story told. And don't forget—if you missed *A Very Special Favor,* the first of the series, you'll be able to find it in bookstores in September. Rachel Lee made her first appearance as part of the "February Frolics" new-author promotion, and you won't want to miss her second novel, *Serious Risks.* It's a wonderful blend of romance and white-knuckle suspense. I think you'll love it. Dee Holmes spins a warm tale (despite its wintry setting) in *Maybe This Time,* a story proving that love can, indeed, conquer all. Finally, one of your favorite authors, Kathleen Korbel, is back with *A Rose for Maggie.* I don't want to give anything away about this one, so I'll satisfy myself with saying that this is truly one of those books that will bring tears to your eyes as you share the very special love of this family in the making.

As usual, we're keeping an eye on the future as well as the present, and you can count on seeing more of your favorite writers in months to come. To name only a few, look for Nora Roberts (next month!), Emilie Richards and Marilyn Pappano. And also next month, look for Judith Duncan—a name that many of you may recognize—to make her first (but not her last) appearance in the line.

As always—enjoy!

Leslie Wainger
Senior Editor and Editorial Coordinator

RACHEL LEE

Serious Risks

SILHOUETTE·INTIMATE·MOMENTS®

Published by Silhouette Books New York

America's Publisher of Contemporary Romance

For
Markey—who believed
Gil—who is my hero
Bob—who shored me up when I got scared
Aaron—who is my biggest fan
Heather—who shares my excitement
And
All the men and women who perform the thankless task of
protecting the nation's security.
I feel privileged to have worked with you.

SILHOUETTE BOOKS
300 East 42nd St., New York, N.Y. 10017

SERIOUS RISKS

ISBN: 0-373-07394-1

First Silhouette Books printing August 1991

Books by Rachel Lee

Silhouette Intimate Moments

An Officer and a Gentleman #370
Serious Risks #394

RACHEL LEE

wrote her first play in the third grade for a school assembly, and by the age of twelve she was hooked on writing. She's lived all over the United States, on both the East and West coasts, and now resides in Texas with her husband and two teenage children.

Having held jobs as a waitress, real estate agent, optician and military wife—"Yes, that's a job!"—she uses these, as well as her natural flair for creativity, to write stories that are undeniably romantic. "After all, life is the biggest romantic adventure of all—and if you're open and aware, the most marvelous things are just waiting to be discovered."

A Note From The Author:

As the Assistant Facility Security Officer for a defense contractor, I was responsible for the protection of a great deal of classified information, and I often wondered what would happen if I or one of my co-workers ever discovered evidence of espionage. The FBI answered that question for me at one of the Counterintelligence Awareness Seminars they give to defense contractors around the country.

If circumstances warrant, the FBI will ask civilians to act as double agents. Although that sounds dangerous and brings to mind all kinds of frightening images, the fact is, being a double agent for the FBI isn't dangerous. As the agent leading our seminar said, "Up until now, no American on American soil has ever been harmed by a foreign intelligence operation."

How disappointing! But the phrase "up until now" is where my imagination took off, and where this book began.

Chapter 1

"Somebody stole a classified document from my safe last night."

The breathless, nervous claim over the telephone brought Special Agent Arlen Coulter upright in his chair and banished every other thought from his head. A perfectly routine afternoon of reviewing case reports from his agents lost the last vestige of ordinariness. Swiftly reaching across his desk, he pulled over a legal pad and a pen.

"What's your name?" he asked the woman. "And where are you calling from?"

"My name is Jessica Kilmer, and I'm calling from a pay phone on the interstate."

"Give me the number in case we get disconnected." He made her recite it twice to be sure he got it right. In the background he could hear the whiz and roar of the late-afternoon traffic. "Okay, Ms. Kilmer," he said. "Tell me about it."

There was a shuddery breath from the other end of the phone. "I work for MTI—Military Technologies, Inc. We do a lot of defense work."

"I'm familiar with MTI," Arlen said. Indeed he was. MTI ranked as the area's second-largest defense contractor. "Go on, ma'am."

"Someone took a classified document from my safe during the night," she repeated unsteadily, as if she couldn't quite believe her own words. "I'm the only one who has the combination, except for the copy that security keeps in their vault."

Arlen leaned forward tensely. Possibilities were already flitting through his head, not the least of them that this was a crank call. In the past he had worked in counterintelligence in the Washington, D.C., area, so he knew just how common espionage was. Nevertheless, this was the first hint of it that he had gotten during his entire six years in Austin, Texas. Still, the woman knew things that only someone engaged in classified work would know, such as the fact that security would have the only other combination to a classified safe. "You're sure the document is missing?"

"Oh, yes." She expelled the words on another unsteady breath. "I went through every folder in the safe, in case it was misfiled."

"It couldn't have been left out by accident?" Arlen kept his voice calm, nonaccusatory. Once a witness was put on the defensive, you could forget any hope of getting a straight story.

"No. I haven't had it out of the safe in several weeks. It was there last night when I filed the document that comes just before it. I *know* it was there!"

The rising tone of her voice conveyed her frustration and concern as no words could have. Arlen felt a small twinge of sympathy for her, but he put it firmly aside. He couldn't afford to allow his mind or his judgment to be clouded by sympathy.

"I believe you, Ms. Kilmer," he said soothingly. "Have you told anyone else about the theft?"

"I reported it to security," she answered, and now her tone was indignant. "They're insisting *I* must have mislaid it or misfiled it or loaned it to someone, because I'm the only one with the combination to the safe. That's the whole point, and they're missing it. That's why I'm calling you!

he point is, *someone opened that safe last night.* Some-
ne *else* has the combination!"

Arlen didn't need to have the ramifications of that state-
ent spelled out. If someone else had the combination,
ere was no telling how often that person had gained ac-
ss to Jessica Kilmer's safe. There was no way to know
w many other safes at MTI this supposed spy might have
mbinations for, or how often he might have invaded
em. Or how many classified documents he might have
olen, photographed, copied—the list of potential abuses
as catastrophic.

Arlen addressed Jessica Kilmer. "Are you going back to
ork?"

She gave a shaky, mirthless laugh. "Hardly. By the time
ey got through grilling me and insinuating that I have the
Q of an insect, I had a splitting headache. I'm going
me."

"Just a few more questions, Ms. Kilmer, if you're up to
"

"Yes, of course."

"Does anyone know you're calling the FBI? The secu-
ty people at your company, perhaps?"

"No, no one knows." Jessica Kilmer sighed heavily. Even
er the phone, her weariness and frustration were appar-
t to Arlen. "The security people aren't planning to tell
yone about this just yet. They're evidently convinced that
e report will show up and that they'll be able to explain
e whole thing in some fashion that won't reflect badly on
em or the company."

"And you don't believe that."

"How can I? I know that document was there when I
cked my safe last night, and I know it was gone when I
ened it this morning. There's no way that can be ex-
ained as carelessness or an accident."

No, indeed, Arlen thought. He glanced at his watch and
ted that it was nearly five. "Ms. Kilmer, we need to dis-
ss this in more detail. Can we get together somewhere this
ening, say a restaurant?"

There was a brief, hesitant silence. "Wouldn't it be more
nvenient for you if I came to your office?"

Arlen couldn't suppress a smile, and he was sure she must be able to hear it in his voice. "There's no question it would be more convenient, Ms. Kilmer, but until we get some idea of the size of this mess and who might be involved, I don't want anyone to know you've contacted the Bureau. Our offices are in the busiest part of downtown, and there's always the unwelcome possibility that someone who knows you might see you come in here."

"Meeting at a restaurant just seems a little irregular, I guess."

He understood her trepidation and tried to tease her out of it. "Believe me, Ms. Kilmer, I've questioned people in places that are a lot more irregular than any restaurant could ever be."

There was another very brief silence, and then Jessica Kilmer laughed, a genuinely amused sound. When he heard that, Arlen knew he'd taken the first step to establishing a rapport with the lady, a rapport that would be absolutely essential if it should turn out that they had to work together. And if she was right about this document, they would unquestionably wind up spending a lot of time together.

"Actually, ma'am, we're not so very different from your local police force. When you call to report something, we generally visit you to get the information. It would be just as easy for me to come to your home, if that would be more convenient for you. My only requirement is that we meet in a place where I can question you without interruption. It's very important that you don't get distracted and forget to tell me something."

"All right, all right," Jessica said with a laugh. "Let me give you my address." She rattled off a street and number, then added, "I just moved in a couple of weeks ago, so I'm still neck-deep in packing boxes."

"Don't worry about it," he said. "I'll never notice."

"What time should I expect you?"

"Say around seven, if that's okay by you."

"That's just fine."

"And, Ms. Kilmer? Don't tell anyone at all that you called the FBI. I realize that sounds cloak-and-daggerish,

ut secrecy is essential. You wouldn't want word of this
onversation to get back to the wrong person.''

How could she possibly tell anyone what she couldn't
uite believe herself? Jessica wondered as she climbed back
nto her car. She'd actually called the FBI! Her stomach,
hich had been sinking all day anyway, sank further at the
gnificance of that realization. She forced herself to ig-
ore the sensation, just as she had all day long. Other than
read and worry, the only other feeling she'd had today had
een indignation.

And frustration. She had always believed the facility se-
urity officer to be a reasonably intelligent man, but now
he seriously wondered. Was she the only person with the
it to understand the gravity of what she'd been saying all
ay: that *someone else* had the combination to her safe?

Mr. Coulter had apparently understood, she reminded
erself, and felt reassured that her decision to call the FBI
as correct. Correct? Of course it was correct! The com-
any's own *Security Practice Procedures Manual* said that
e FBI should be informed if espionage was suspected,
referably from a pay phone off-site so there was no chance
f being overheard. And Jessica most definitely suspected
spionage.

By the time she arrived at home, however, she was re-
embering the suspicion with which her every statement
ad been heard by the security officer. Barron obviously
ought Jessica was making everything up to conceal her
wn negligence. What if Coulter suspected the same thing?

Usually when Jessica stepped into the antique elegance
f her two-story Victorian house she experienced the pride
f her new ownership, the thrill of at last having a real
ome of her own. Tonight, however, all she felt was the
eight of the mortgage, reminding her that she couldn't
fford job trouble. Not now. Not as long as she owed that
ayment every month. Not as long as most of her hard-
rned savings, accumulated by scrimping for five long
ars, were tied up in the house.

What if Barron managed to hang the missing document
n her?

As seven o'clock drew closer, Jessica grew edgier. She'd never been questioned by the FBI before—or any policeman, for that matter—and she found herself wondering why she hadn't just let MTI security handle it. They couldn't prove she had taken the document, no matter how much they might want to believe it. What if this FBI agent wanted to believe the same thing? What if he thought her call to him was all a smoke screen?

What if he got *rough?*

"Oh, for heaven's sake, Jessica!" she said disgustedly to her reflection in the bathroom mirror as she finished brushing her teeth. "He's an FBI agent! They don't get rough except with criminals." And spies?

"I am not a spy!"

She knew it, and so did the small, pale face staring back at her from the mirror. Pushing her eyeglasses up her nose, Jessica gazed into her own wide, worried brown eyes and thought she looked exactly, *exactly,* like a small brown mouse pinned by an eagle's eye.

A few strands of dark hair had escaped from the confines of her chignon, and she smoothed them back into place. Outwardly, at least, there was no nonsense about Jessica Kilmer. She might have the world's most inventive, overactive imagination, but no one would ever guess it by looking at her.

On the other hand, she thought with a sigh, she wasn't quite passing as her usual businesslike self, not with worry stamped all over her face. "Mouse" was the kindest description she could give herself.

The front doorbell sounded, and Jessica's stomach plunged instantly in response. *Oh, God, the FBI is here!*

A real, honest-to-gosh FBI agent.

"Cut it out," she told her reflection with more conviction than she really felt. "He puts his pants on one leg at a time, just like anybody else."

She headed downstairs, drew a deep breath, expelled it and opened the door.

And looked into the grayest eyes she'd ever seen. Not the pallid color that might be blue or green depending on the light, but gray like flannel, and fringed in thick, dark lashes. His hair was a rich, very dark brown, threaded with silver, and a little longer than she'd expected. Evidently FBI agents didn't have to wear military-style haircuts anymore.

He was tall, over six feet to her five foot two, broad shouldered, narrow hipped. Elegant looking, especially in a gray suit, white shirt and dark tie. He wasn't, thank goodness, handsome. Handsome would have been too much to handle. No, he was simply attractive. His face was at best pleasant, regular featured.

But nothing in her life prepared her for this man's total impact. The term *sex appeal* took on a whole new meaning for her in that instant, an understanding that might have frightened her except that there was nothing wolfish in his expression or posture. In fact, he was giving her a very pleasant smile and holding out his hand.

"Ms. Kilmer? I'm Arlen Coulter."

Jessica felt her hand swallowed in his firm, warm grip and heard herself say something courteous in response, and tried not to notice the very acute and observant way his gaze measured her.

Arlen recognized her nervousness, but it hardly surprised him. Most people were nervous at the prospect of dealing with the FBI. He saw past the nervousness, though, past the no-nonsense hairstyle and the high-collared white blouse and neatly pressed gray slacks. Behind the armor here was waiflike vulnerability. It peeped uncertainly out at him from the depths of astonishingly bright brown eyes, and, to him at least, it would have been much less obvious had she not gone to such great lengths to hide it.

"A pleasure, Ms. Kilmer," he said, releasing her hand. In order to seem less threatening, he plunged his hands into the front pockets of his slacks and waited for her invitation to enter. She continued to look uncertainly up at him, and then color rose from the neck of her blouse to meet the roots of her hair. Where did that blush start? he wondered, and felt an unexpected stirring of his body.

Jessica licked her dry lips, unaware that the small, nervous gesture had an electric effect on the tall man who stood so casually before her in a conservative gray suit. "I, um I, don't mean to be offensive, but can I see your badge, or whatever?''

Arlen's smile broadened a shade, and he reached into the inside breast pocket of his suit jacket. Handing her the slim leather wallet, he said, ''I'm not offended. The whole reason I have ID is so people can ask to see it. All you've done is show me you're not gullible, Ms. Kilmer.''

Jessica, who wouldn't have recognized a valid FBI identity card or badge if it had stood up and bitten her, stared at the contents of the wallet and registered the words *Arlen V. Coulter, Special Agent, Federal Bureau of Investigation.* Her blush deepening, she passed the wallet back.

''Please come in, Mr. Coulter. Or do I call you Agent Coulter?''

''If you insist,'' he said with a smile as he followed her through the gleaming entry hall and into a living room where packing boxes still occupied quite a bit of space. ''I'd prefer it if you'd just call me Arlen. We're probably going to be seeing quite a bit of one another.''

Jessica smiled shyly as she offered him a seat. ''You can call me Jessica. Would you like some coffee?''

''Not just now, thanks. Maybe later.''

Jessica settled onto the couch, facing the armchair where she'd seated Arlen, and watched as he pulled a pad and pen out of his breast pocket. He had blunt-fingered, large hands, competent, capable-looking hands. Their movements were calm, controlled. As was he, she realized. Everything about him was controlled, even his smile.

''I'll probably need to get an official statement from you later, but for the moment, why don't we just go over what happened?'' He offered what he hoped was a reassuring smile. ''The questions may get a little repetitious, but I need to be sure you aren't inadvertently overlooking something. All right?''

Jessica nodded and clasped her hands tightly, wondering why the living room suddenly seemed small. She'd considered it a pleasantly large room until Arlen Coulter entered it, but he seemed to fill it completely.

And there was a wedding ring on his left hand. She noticed the gold band with an unexpected stab of disappointment and wondered why it should matter.

Arlen spoke. "Jessica, why don't you tell me a little bit about your job and the kind of classified information you work with."

"I'm a programmer," she explained. "I work on software for Department of Defense applications. Right now I'm designing a package that's intended to be able to pick out planes and incoming missiles from all the electronic countermeasures that are available to confuse radar."

Arlen was impressed. "Can it?"

"It's too soon to tell yet, but in theory it should work."

"How long have you been working on defense applications?"

"Six years."

In answer to his prompting, she described some of the other programs she'd worked on over the years. Listening to her, watching her, Arlen realized a couple of things. This lady was very bright, and she loved her work. As she spoke, she grew animated, using her hands and smiling, and her eyes sparkled with enthusiasm. At this new glimpse of the woman behind the uptight, severe facade, Arlen wondered what had happened to her to make her want to hide her vitality. Not that it mattered, he reminded himself. He was here as an agent to do a job, not to wonder about a woman who was young enough to be his daughter.

Eventually he brought her back to the events of the past day. Her animation faded, to be replaced by the nervous worry he'd seen when he first arrived.

"At the end of the day," Jessica explained, "I lock up everything I work with—my files, my hard drive from the computer, any paper I've scribbled on or written on. I don't bother sorting at night, because I'm tired and might make a mistake. In the morning I'll decide which stuff needs to be burned, but in the evening I just lump it all into an envelope and file it in my safe."

"What kind of safe do you have?"

"It's a GSA-approved four-drawer cabinet." All safes used for the storage of classified information had to be approved by the General Services Administration, or GSA, an indication that the safe met certain standards.

Arlen nodded. "What level material do you keep in it?"

"Just Secret and Confidential. If I need to use Top Secret or special-access information, like Secret Compartmented Information, I check them out of the vault downstairs and return them at the end of the day."

"And last night you followed your usual procedure."

Jessica nodded, clasping her hands together so tightly that Arlen saw her knuckles turn white.

"Why don't you run through it again for me? Just so I can be sure I have it right."

Jessica nodded again. "I take my hard disk out—"

"Just a second," Arlen interrupted. "You take your computer apart every night?"

Jessica shook her head. "I have an external, removable hard disk. It's designed for this kind of thing. I can take it off my system in just a minute, and I always store it in the top drawer of my safe, unless for some reason there's material of a higher classification on it. Then I take it to the vault."

"Okay. You put your hard disk in the top drawer. Then what?"

"Then I pick up any documents I've pulled, and I file them in their proper folders in the other drawers. When that's done, I pick up whatever scraps of paper there are that I've scribbled on, doodled on or whatever, put them in a manila envelope and file them in the suspense folder I keep at the front of the second drawer." Seeing the question form on his lips, she hastened to explain. "The suspense file just means the stuff in it is suspended, set aside to deal with later."

He nodded. "And that's how you know the missing document was there last night?"

"That's right." Realizing suddenly that her fingers were aching from the tight way she had folded her hands, Jessica unlaced them and wiggled them to relax them. "I always put the suspense file right in front of it."

Arlen watched her wiggle her fingers, pursing his lips thoughtfully. "And you're sure it was there?"

Jessica's eyes snapped to his face. "Yes." She said it with conviction.

Arlen's gray eyes lifted from her hands to her eyes, and they no longer held any of the warmth and friendliness she'd seen in them earlier. "I have to ask these questions, Jessica. They're not intended to be offensive. How is it you're sure the document was there? Usually when we do things in certain ways they become so habitual that we don't really notice. Did you really see that document last night, or do you just think you saw it?"

Her hands knotted into fists on her lap. "I *saw* it," she said flatly. "The folder it was in is red, and the three folders behind it are blue. If that folder was gone, I'd have noticed it instantly, the way I noticed it was missing this morning."

Arlen nodded and wrote in his notebook. "Okay," he said pleasantly. "I believe you. The folder was there last night. You filed the suspense file in front of it?"

"Yes."

"And then?"

"I closed the drawer and locked the safe."

"How did you lock the safe?"

Jessica sighed. "I turned the dial four full rotations and tested the lever. It was locked."

"And it was still locked when you came to work this morning?"

Jessica opened her mouth to respond, and then hesitated, her brown eyes widening. "I don't know," she said after a moment. "I always turn the dial four times before I start to work the combination. And I never try the lever before I enter the combination."

"So it could have been closed but unlocked this morning."

She nodded. "But I don't see—"

"Don't you find it odd that the entire folder was missing?" Arlen asked her.

Jessica's reply was tart. "To tell you the truth, I haven't been allowed any time today to think about anything, least of all whether what happened was odd. Of course it was odd. It was odd that *anything* disappeared overnight. I still don't see.''

"Well, if you were going to steal classified information, would *you* leave such an obvious footprint? Wouldn't it make more sense to photograph the document and put it back? Or photocopy it and replace it?''

"Well, yes, of course," Jessica agreed. "But if you didn't have time—'' Her eyes widened. "Oh!" she said on a breath. "Oh!"

"Exactly." Arlen smiled faintly. "Did you come to work early this morning, by any chance?''

The expression on her face answered the question even before she spoke. "I was a half hour early because I wanted to check out something I thought of last night.''

Arlen spread his hands, as if to say, "See?" "Could I take you up on that coffee now, Jessica?''

"Yes, of course." She went to the kitchen to get it, impressed with how quickly Arlen Coulter had picked up on something she'd entirely missed, something even the security officer, Dave Barron, had entirely missed, in spite of all the questioning she'd endured today.

She was also uncomfortably impressed with a few other things, like how good Arlen Coulter looked. Few men her own age and younger looked half as good as Arlen did, and he must be somewhere over forty. He also made her uncomfortably aware of him. And of herself. She was most definitely *not* accustomed to such feelings, and she supposed she should be grateful that he was a married man and therefore could be no more than a passing and temporary ripple in her tranquility. She would get used to how good he looked, and that would be that.

An expression of determination on her face, she marched back into the living room with a tray bearing two cups of coffee, the sugar bowl and creamer. Setting the tray on the cherry coffee table between them, she asked, "Cream or sugar?''

"Black, thank you." Arlen looked at the dainty china cups and saucers with their delicate pattern of roses and wondered when was the last time he had seen anyone serve coffee in anything but a mug. Aunt Celeste, he remembered. His wife's great-aunt had always served coffee in bone china teacups. It wasn't until Andrew was born that Celeste had astonished Arlen one day by handing him a large mug with his name painted on its side. "You've accommodated to our family customs a great deal, my boy," she'd said in her stentorian voice, "and I thought it was high time we accommodated to one of yours." Until she died at the age of ninety, Celeste had made sure that Arlen's coffee was always served in a mug whenever he visited any of his wife's relatives. Damn, he still missed the warm, wonderful, tough old lady.

"These are lovely cups," he said now to Jessica, compelled by his memory of the elderly woman. Celeste had taught him whatever drawing-room manners he could claim, and Lord knew there were few enough.

Jessica smiled with pleasure. "Thank you. I found them in an antique shop a few months ago. The entire set, in fact, without a chip or a missing piece." They'd cost dearly, but they were an essential part of the home she was trying to create.

"They remind me of some dishes my wife's aunt used to have," Arlen remarked. "I've been terrified of breaking the darn things ever since the first time I ate dinner at Aunt Celeste's." He gave Jessica a rueful smile. "She was a wonderful old lady, but her blasted dishes have haunted my entire adult life. They must be a hundred years old, and every time they get passed on to a new generation, they just take on more sentimental value. Aunt Celeste got them as a wedding gift from her husband. Then, when she passed on, they went to my wife, and now my daughter has them."

His daughter had them? Jessica felt she had missed something somewhere. "Your daughter has them?" she repeated questioningly.

Arlen looked up from the cup, his gray eyes unfocused. "I'm afraid my wife is gone."

"Gone?"

Jessica's eyes strayed to his ring, and Arlen followed the direction of her gaze.

"I haven't been able to bring myself to take it off," he admitted. "She died over three years ago."

Jessica hardly knew how to respond to that. "I'm sorry," she said hesitantly.

Arlen shook his head, giving her another rueful smile. "My fault for wearing the ring." Lifting one of the delicate cups, he took a sip of coffee. "The coffee is delicious, Jessica."

"Thank you." A widower who still wore his wedding ring after three years was as safe as a married man, she figured. Maybe safer. And probably a whole lot safer when he was an FBI agent.

"Okay." Arlen picked up his pad again and made a quick note. "Let's get back to this morning, Jessica. What exactly did you do when you arrived at MTI? Start in the parking lot."

So she took him step-by-step through a day that had grown more frustrating with each passing minute. From the parking lot she had entered the building through the main entrance. Most mornings security waved her through on sight, because the day shift recognized her well after six years. This morning, however, she'd arrived before the shift change and had had to stop to display her identification. It had been a small, routine matter, and she had taken the opportunity to clip her badge on her collar, where it would have to stay the rest of the day anyhow.

The empty elevator had carried her up to the second floor corridor, and a brief walk had brought her to the locked door of the controlled area that held her office, along with a dozen others. There she had keyed in her code on the alphanumeric keypad beside the door, and the door had unlocked for her.

Once in her office, she had opened her safe to remove the items she needed for work: first the hard disk, which she installed in the drive case attached to the side of her computer. Then she had pulled out the second drawer of the safe, and it was as she was removing the suspense envelope that she noted the conspicuous absence of the red folder that contained a Secret NATO document.

Her first thought, of course, was that she was mistaken, that somehow the hanging file folder had come off the tracks and slipped down between the other folders to the bottom of the drawer. Item by item she had examined the contents of the drawer, checking every red folder twice, finally examining each and every one of the blue folders and their Confidential documents, as well.

"And that's when you called security?" Arlen asked.

"No." Jessica flushed faintly. "I decided I must have been mistaken about where the folder was last night. So I looked through the bottom drawers, too. Document by document. That's when I called security."

Arlen's pen made faint noises as it moved quickly across a fresh page in his notebook. "You said you were sure the document was there last night."

"I was. I *am*. It's just that when I couldn't find it this morning, the last thought that occurred to me was that somebody had gotten into my safe overnight. It was easier to believe I was mistaken."

He looked up, and his expression was reassuring. "I know. But I have to ask."

And he kept on asking. At some point or other, Jessica started to feel immune to the implications of some of the questions and found herself more aware of Arlen. The longer she was with him, the more she became cognizant of his magnetism.

"Jessica?"

Her gaze focused on Arlen, and a painful blush crept into her face.

"You're tired," he said kindly. "Just a few more questions, if you think you can stand it."

Her cheeks felt as if they were on fire, and she had to remind herself that Arlen Coulter couldn't read her mind. "Sure," she managed to say. "I'm not all that tired."

"Did you change the combination on your safe today?"

Jessica shook her head. "I don't know how to do it. Security always does that, and since they don't believe that somebody got into my safe last night, I don't think they're going to change it."

Arlen slapped his notebook closed and hooked his pen onto the cover. "I'll tell you what I think is going to happen tomorrow. I may be wrong, but if I'm right, I want you prepared to carry it off."

Jessica leaned forward a little, fixing her gaze attentively on his face. There was a faint, jagged scar under his lower lip, running diagonally from the corner of his mouth to the center of his chin. That must be what gave his smile that interesting lopsidedness.

"I think," Arlen said slowly, watching her from intent gray eyes, "the missing document will turn up sometime tomorrow."

Jessica's eyes widened behind her glasses, and her lips parted on a breath. "Why?"

Did she, Arlen wondered, have the least idea what that expression did to a man, even one as old and abused as he was? Probably not, he decided. If she had, she would have saved it for someone worth spending it on.

"Because," he replied, forcing his attention back to business, "the only way to minimize the damage that was caused by your discovery of the document's disappearance is to put it back in a way that makes it look as if you mislaid it."

Jessica blinked and straightened with indignation. "Frame me, you mean!"

"I figured that would be your reaction," Arlen said soothingly. "Just listen for a moment."

Jessica's eyes were snapping, but she sat back, compressed her lips and gave him a short nod.

Arlen managed to smother a smile. "Okay," he said. "The document will turn up, and it'll be pinned on you as carelessness or forgetfulness. Security will believe it, because they can get out of this with a decision that nothing's been compromised, and a reprimand to you will close the entire matter. They'll write their letter to the Defense Investigative Service explaining the events and the actions taken, and the worst that will happen is that DIS will pull an unannounced inspection to ensure that MTI's security is up to snuff."

"And I'll have a written security reprimand in my personnel file," Jessica reminded him sharply.

"Only temporarily," Arlen said. "Only until we get this mess settled. I promise you I'll personally see to clearing your record with the company. In the meantime, Jessica, how would you like to work with the FBI?''

"But I *have* a job." At least for now, she added to herself.

"And you'll keep it. No, I want you to work with me on this case. You'll be my inside contact at MTI. For the moment, I don't want anyone over there to know you've called the Bureau, but I still need to know what's happening. Can you do that for me?"

Her chin sank a little, but her eyes lifted to his with a kind of wondering shyness and pleasure that gave him some inkling of how little she thought of herself. "You mean you think I can help you?"

"Absolutely," he said firmly. "Not only that, but I don't think I'll get very far without your help. Until I get a better idea of who's who and who makes a good suspect, I can't risk trusting anyone else at MTI. Will you help?"

"Of course I will."

Arlen smiled. "Good. The first thing is that when that document turns up tomorrow, and I'm positive it will, you can't argue too hard with the idea that you mislaid it. I'm not saying you should be thrilled with the possibility, but you should be just as relieved as everyone else when it shows up, and only a little more reluctant to believe that you were responsible."

Jessica wasn't happy with that, but she nodded her agreement. "I get the idea."

"I know it hurts," Arlen said sympathetically, "but try to look at it from another perspective. This uproar has undoubtedly scared somebody, and if he stays scared, we'll never get our hands on him. It's essential that we catch him, so we can stop him, so we can find out how long and how much he's been compromising us, and who he's working for."

He came around the coffee table to stand right beside Jessica, and touched her shoulder lightly with his fingers. "Maybe it'll help if you think of yourself as an agent working under cover. That's what you'll be, you know. In a very real sense."

Jessica tilted her head, looking dubiously up at him. "Just by pretending to believe I mislaid that document?"

"That's part of it." Arlen squatted, resting his elbows on his knees, bringing his face level with Jessica's. "I also want you to start paying close attention to the people around you. Notice whether any of them seem to be seriously troubled, or disgruntled with MTI. Notice if any of them seem to be living too well, or drinking too much—anything that might indicate they're not entirely trustworthy."

That idea didn't sit well with her, Arlen could tell. Most people didn't like the idea of spying on their co-workers or friends.

"Jessica, I'm not asking you to *spy* on people. I'm just asking you to pay attention to your impressions of people. See if anyone's attitude makes you genuinely uneasy about what they might do. You have to remember what's at stake here."

He was right, of course, Jessica thought. They were talking about national security. If she had evidence that would convict a murderer, would she withhold it? Of course not. This was a crime, too, potentially as serious as murder to soldiers who might someday depend on the efficacy of MTI-supplied equipment and software to protect them in the field.

Turning, Jessica looked Arlen right in the eye. "I'll do it," she said firmly. "What about you? What will you be doing?"

"Well," he said, standing up, "I'll start by calling DIS—Defense Investigative Service—and getting a complete report on the security arrangements at MTI. For example, I imagine the vault you referred to is patrolled by armed guards round the clock."

"Well, yes, I think so. Guards are necessary for the protection of Top Secret information. That's why I can't keep it in my safe."

"Exactly. DIS can give me a complete rundown. They had to approve all the arrangements to begin with, and I imagine they inspect things pretty thoroughly every few months."

Jessica nodded. When the DIS inspectors came in they usually managed to spend a few minutes talking to each and every one of the employees who were cleared for access to classified information.

"And tomorrow," Arlen continued, "I'll initiate background checks on all the people who have access to your controlled area. Maybe we can find someone who's in financial trouble, or who's vulnerable to blackmail. Maybe we can close this out quickly."

Looking down at her, he shrugged and gave her a crooked, rueful smile. "But don't hold your breath. I used to work in the Foreign Counterintelligence Division of the Bureau in the Washington area. It can take months to gather enough evidence to prosecute."

Jessica sighed and looked down at her hands. "So it'll probably drag on."

"Probably. But look at the bright side."

"Is there one?" She gave him a doubtful smile.

"Sure. We get to become acquainted. Really well acquainted. In fact, I guarantee you'll be sick of the sight of me before this is over."

Jessica shook her head, laughing. "I can't imagine that," she said, the words slipping out before she knew they were coming.

Arlen watched the brilliant color flood her face, saw the dawning of her shocked embarrassment. Her reaction gave more weight to her words than he would otherwise have assigned them. If she hadn't blushed, he would have thought she was teasing. Because she'd blushed, he knew she wasn't.

And he was astonished how good that little slip of the tongue made him feel. Not since Lucy's death had anyone said anything that made him feel good. Angry, maybe. Irritated, yes. But not good. Good feelings seemed to have left his life along with Lucy. And, to be quite honest, he wasn't sure he wanted them back. Those feelings had a price, and he'd paid it once.

So, knowing she wasn't teasing, he acted as if she was. "You think you won't only because you haven't had to look at me every day for a week or a month," he said, chuckling and turning away as if he hadn't seen her blush.

"I'll let you get some rest now, Jessica," he continued, heading for the door. "Call me if you have any questions."

He paused suddenly and turned back, patting his pockets. "I must have my card here somewhere. Although maybe it's better if you don't carry it around with you."

"I can reach you at the FBI office, can't I?" she asked, her embarrassment fading as he seemed to notice nothing remarkable about her comment. "I don't really need your card."

"You can reach me at home, too," he told her. "And I really don't mind if you call. The number's in the book. And if I need to get hold of you, what's your office number?"

He pulled the pen and pad from his pocket, but Jessica forestalled him with *her* business card. Arlen's gray eyes twinkled down at her.

"You're better prepared than I am," he confessed. "If something comes up, I'll call."

He took his leave almost with a sense of relief. Damn it, Arlen, he thought, the lady's young enough to be your daughter, and you're too damn old and wise to get tangled up with her.

And maybe, he thought a few minutes later, she wasn't as young as she looked. Maybe he was going to start feeling again whether he wanted to or not. Three years was a long time. Maybe even dead feelings came back to life after enough time passed. Maybe, no matter how much you wanted them to stay gone, they just came back anyhow.

Chapter 2

Arlen arrived at the Bureau offices in the morning to find things in an uproar. One of the agents, Ted Wilson, was cooperating with the Secret Service in a sting operation, and overnight they'd rounded up five major drug dealers who were selling crack and coke for food stamps. The Drug Enforcement Administration had gotten involved somewhere along the way, and as near as Arlen could tell they had U.S. marshals, DEA agents, Secret Service agents and even, unless he was mistaken, a Customs agent, in the hallways and offices of the Bureau. They lacked only a U.S. Attorney, and it wasn't more than a couple of minutes before one showed up. Carolyn Granger came downstairs with a tape recorder, warning everyone that unless somebody gave her some good reasons to use with the judge, the dealers would be out on bail in a couple of hours.

Arlen paused at Ted Wilson's office door and leaned in to congratulate the young agent. Wilson, looking tired and rumpled in jeans and an FBI windbreaker, grinned up at him. "Thanks, Chief. It feels pretty good."

"What's all the congregation for?"

"Well, they're painting all the Treasury offices, which means the Secret Service guys and the Customs guys are grabbing any excuse to stay out of there. I think DEA's just curious.''

"Arlen?" The voice of his secretary, Donna, rose above the din and reached him down the length of the hall.

"Yo!" Twisting his head and leaning backward into the hall, he could just see her.

"It's someone named Jessica on the phone."

"Tell her I'll be there in just a minute." He looked back at Ted. "We *do* have some other work to accomplish here today."

"Sure thing, boss." Ted's grin broadened. "I think it'll calm down pretty quick. These guys were supposed to be at their desks ten minutes ago, anyway."

It was impossible not to grin back. This was Ted's first bust, and Arlen had no trouble remembering the exhilaration he'd felt his own first time. Walking down the hall, he edged around similarly jubilant men and escaped into the quiet of his own office.

Three of the lines on his phone were lit, so he buzzed Donna and found out that Jessica was on two.

"Jessica," he said pleasantly into the phone, swiveling his chair to look up at the gray sky that promised rain before the morning was out. For years he'd worked in an office without a window, and the nicest part of his current assignment, he sometimes thought, was the window, with its view of the sky. "Are you calling from work?"

"Yes, I—"

He interrupted her quickly, but kept his tone casual. "Don't tell me you're canceling our lunch date."

At the other end of the line, Jessica drew a total blank. Lunch date? She didn't remember making a lunch date with Arlen. "I was just going to—"

"I can change the time if that'll make it easier for you to meet me," he said smoothly. "Noon instead of one o'clock? Would that be better?"

"I—I guess." Flabbergasted, she didn't know what else to say.

"Good! I'll pick you up out front at noon, then. I'm sorry I can't talk, but you know how it is at work. I'm already late for a meeting. See you at noon."

At her own desk on the other side of town, Jessica listened to the hum of the empty phone line as she looked down into the safe drawer. The document was back, all right, stuffed down beneath the other folders so that it lay on the bottom of the drawer. If Arlen hadn't predicted it, she would probably be thinking she was losing her mind. There was no way she could have missed it in her search yesterday, and yet she would have wondered anyway.

And for some reason Arlen didn't want to discuss the matter over the phone while she was at work. At least, that was the only conclusion she could draw from their crazy conversation. But she'd wanted to ask him what to do, because it had occurred to her that the red folder or the pages of the document might have fingerprints on them. If she called security first, they would probably send someone up to check things out and ruin all the prints. If there were any.

Troubled, she closed the safe and sat back in her chair. Well, she could wait until after lunch to tell security she had the document. It would make her look even dippier, but what the heck. There was evidently no way she was going to come out of this looking good.

In the meantime, she had a great deal of work still to accomplish on her design for this new software project.

And someone had been in her safe again last night. The idea sent chills racing up and down her spine. In that safe were highly classified details about the Western world's electronic countermeasures systems. There were threat estimates and survivability estimates, all of which would be very useful to America's enemies.

In defense work, there were three main levels of classification. Confidential, the lowest, was given to information that could cause serious damage to national security if it fell into the wrong hands. Secret, the next highest, was given to information that could cause grave damage. Those were the levels in her safe. Quite a serious problem, to have someone rummaging around in those documents.

But what if that someone also had access to the guarded vault downstairs? That was where the Top Secret documents were kept, documents that by definition could cause exceptionally grave damage to national security, or even provoke war. It was downright scary even to think about.

And whoever had the combination to her safe probably *did* have access to the vault, because that was where copies of the combinations for every safe in the building were kept. Somehow this person must have gotten to that copy. And that meant everything in the building was open to him.

It was not yet nine in the morning, but Jessica found herself rubbing her temples to ease a growing throb. Take some aspirin and forget it, Jess, she told herself. Just focus your mind on work.

"Hey, Jessica." Bob Harrow stood in her office door, looking his usual seedy self, with his hair standing up wildly and a stain of some kind on the front of his T-shirt. "Did you finish your part of the design yet?" As project director, Bob had the unenviable task of trying to keep the team on track.

"Not yet, Bob. Sorry. Yesterday blew me out of the water."

Bob looked sympathetic. "You don't look any too great this morning, kiddo. Don't beat yourself over the head about it, Jessica. You won't be the first programmer up here who's spaced something out and found it two days later. Why do you think they put the digital locks on the door? I keep waiting for them to come up with retina identification equipment so they don't have to worry about one of us scribbling the door code on our pants leg or something."

But Jessica's mind caught on something he said. "You mean other people have mislaid things up here? When did that happen?"

"It happens all the time." Bob shrugged. "Well, not every day, but it was . . . oh, maybe a month ago that Jerry couldn't find some report or other on some NATO test. It turned up under a stack of papers on his desk the next day. If you ask me, the only mistake you made was telling security about it. Those guys are completely useless. Did they find it for you? Nope. They just drove you crazy, and yet they're perfectly convinced it'll turn up today or tomorrow under some papers somewhere. And it will, Jessica. Believe me. Quit worrying about it.''

Jessica summoned a smile. ''You wouldn't really write the door code on your jeans leg, would you?''

''Well, *I* wouldn't, but it wouldn't surprise me if Mike or Carl did something stupid like that. I swear, neither one of them can think except in assembly language. Well, don't let me keep you from working. And, Jessica, if this has still got you upset, don't worry about the design. We've got a little slack and can wait a little longer.''

Alone again, Jessica took two aspirin and forced her attention to her work. Work, she'd discovered a long time ago, was solace.

Arlen pulled his car up under the overhang in front of MTI's main entrance to wait for Jessica. He left the engine running and the defroster blowing to keep the windows clear. The day had turned unexpectedly cold and miserably wet. He was glad he had an old umbrella in the back seat, because he suspected Jessica had probably misjudged the weather this morning just as he had.

Jessica. He'd been thinking about her a little too often for his own peace of mind. Such a severe little mouse of a woman, he told himself, and then remembered the unusual brilliance of her brown eyes and the soft shell pink of her full lips. Or the fact that her loosely cut gray slacks and high-necked white blouse had hinted at a figure that was better than average.

Well, better than average if you liked women with some meat on them, Arlen thought wryly. He guessed he did, to judge by his reaction to the lady. It hadn't been something he'd really thought about before.

He'd dated Lucy all the way through high school, over her family's ceaseless objections, and married her a week after graduation. Then had come an eighteen-month separation while he went to Vietnam with the marines. He'd returned from Southeast Asia with a couple of medals to rejoin his bride and meet his eleven-month-old daughter, Melanie. And nine months after that, Andrew had been born. Two years later, he was out of the marines and in college on the GI Bill, both him and Lucy working to support the kids. The hard times had paid off in a big way when he fulfilled his life's dream of joining the FBI.

Sighing, he looked back with a kind of nostalgic sadness. How young and invulnerable he and Lucy had been then, both of them sure that the hard times were over. Life had a hell of a way of grinding out the smugness of youth.

Exiting the building through the electronically controlled glass doors, Jessica caught sight of Arlen just moments before he spied her. In that instant she thought he looked sad. Alone. The way she felt inside all too often. Did she look like that to others?

But he smiled as he climbed out of the car and came around to open the door for her. That lopsided smile of his was infectious, she realized as she felt her own lips stretch and lift in response. Today he wore another, darker, gray wool suit, and he once again looked very much like the FBI agents of her imaginings. Very neat, very correct. Very tall and very imposing. Strange, nervous little tickles danced through her stomach.

But Arlen didn't act like her image of an agent. As she slipped past him to get into the car, he bent without warning and kissed her lightly on the cheek. When she looked up at him in astonishment, he further confounded her by laughing and dropping a kiss on the tip of her nose.

"Climb in, honey. It's cold out here." Still smiling, he urged her into the car.

Honey? Surely he couldn't be one of those awful men who called every woman *honey*. Awful as that thought was, she was even more astounded to realize that some fugitive part of her wished he really meant it. She couldn't help thinking that it must be really nice to have someone in your life who called you "honey" and surprised you with kisses.

But a very long time ago Jessica had decided it was wisest to avoid men. The boys in high school had scorned her because she was too poor, too plump, too smart and wore glasses. She was one of the very few girls who didn't go to her senior prom.

Things like that had hurt, of course, but nothing had prepared her for the anguish she discovered in college.

Prince Charming had arrived in her freshman year in the guise of a premed student. To this day Jessica considered herself fortunate to have discovered that he was more interested in having her do his programming assignments than he was in her love, and that wooing her had been just a way of buying her brains.

And to this day she could still writhe with embarrassment when she recalled her own eager stupidity and readiness to believe in magic. Lord, the whole world had turned bright and shining for her in those two short months. She had believed the sun rose and set on Chuck Meyers, had done any and everything he had asked her to, and all because he took her out to a couple of movies and spent his evenings in her dorm room. Making her believe he liked being with her. Teasing her with little kisses and then laughing at her blushes.

Fool that she was, she had thought he was laughing because he thought she was cute. And then he would hand her his math book or his computer science assignments and say, "Hey, Jess, I don't exactly understand this. Help me, huh?" And she would do his whole damn assignment because he gave her those little kisses and made her feel like a million dollars.

Stupid, stupid sixteen-year-old Jessica. How crushed she had been the day after she finished his final program, the one that had guaranteed him an A for the course. How stupid and crushed and humiliated when she learned that Chuck thought they'd had a fair trade. "You had your fantasy, and I got my A," he had said bluntly. "What's the big deal, Jess? It isn't like I even slept with you." He hadn't even had the moral decency to understand what the big deal was. She'd been a fool, all right, and she had plumbed the true meaning of despair. She'd also learned what it meant to be used, and while she might risk the heartbreak, she would never again risk the humiliation and the sense of worthlessness that went with knowing you had been taken advantage of.

Sitting next to Arlen as he pulled out of the MTI parking lot, Jessica realized she wasn't as immune as she'd believed these past years. For the first time in a very long time she found herself acutely, femininely aware of a man. She found herself noticing the way his thigh muscles flexed as he drove. The easy competence with which his large, lean hands held the wheel. The faint shadow of the morning's beard growth on his cheeks and chin. The muted scent of a man, just barely noticeable in the closed confines of the car. The things that make men different, and that make them attractive to women.

And she found herself wondering what it would be like to lean over and rest her cheek against the wool that covered his shoulder. What would it be like to have his arm close around her shoulders and hold her? Just hold her. Dear heaven, was it possible to ache just to be held? Startled by a need she had never recognized before, she simply stared at him.

Arlen glanced her way as he eased into the heavy noon-hour traffic and caught her staring at him. Before Jessica's blush became visible, he'd once again fixed his eyes on the road.

"I guess I owe you a whole pack of apologies, Jessica," he said. "You probably think I've gone off the deep end. But the simple fact is, if somebody notices us together, whether it's someone who recognizes me or someone who recognizes you, I'll be a whole lot more comfortable if they assume we have some kind of personal relationship."

"Why?" And then it dawned on her. Her scalp prickled as she realized that Arlen actually thought someone might be watching her.

"After your report to security yesterday," he continued, "somebody might be interested in your actions for the next couple of days. It's better all around if they don't get wind that you've talked to the FBI."

"Is that why you wouldn't let me talk on the phone this morning?"

He nodded and glanced at her. "You never know who might be listening. It's just a precaution. Why *did* you call?"

"Because you were right. The missing document was back in my safe this morning, tucked at the bottom of the drawer as if it had slipped down. I wanted to ask you how to handle it, because it occurred to me there might be fingerprints on it.''

Arlen steered the car into the parking lot of a popular restaurant. Only when he'd pulled into a slot and switched off the ignition did he speak. Turning a little on the seat, he faced her.

"Well, now," he said, "that's a good question. I sure as hell can't come up there to lift the prints, and you sure as hell can't bring the document out to me."

"Are you so sure security wouldn't be helpful if you talked to them?" Jessica asked. It bothered her that he seemed so determined to circumvent the company's security.

"I'm sure they'd be real helpful. The problem is, I can't be sure one of them isn't involved. When somebody is able to access classified stuff, you have to suspect everybody who can get the necessary combinations. That means your facility security officer and all his people."

Jessica nodded slowly and looked out at the drizzly day. A soft, small sigh escaped her. "Bob Harrow—he's my project chief—mentioned this morning that my document isn't the first one to turn up missing temporarily."

Beside her, Arlen stiffened. "Really."

Jessica looked at him. "It shook me. And he mentioned it so casually! Like it's just the dumb kind of thing you expect a programmer to do—mislay classified documents overnight. I mean, I couldn't believe it, but I could see Bob's point, too. They always turn up, there's always an explanation for how they got to be where they are, and besides, there's a digital combination lock on the door to the whole section, so the documents are as good as locked in a safe even when they're left on a desk."

She looked down at her hands. "Except, of course, that the cleaning people come in during the night, and they shouldn't be able to get their hands on the material. And security comes through at five for the burn bags, and while they're cleared to take out the classified trash, they have no need to see anything else. And that's the whole basis of the protection program, isn't it? That clearance alone isn't

enough to gain access. A person has to have a verified need
to know, as well.''

"You have a better understanding of security than most
people," Arlen remarked. "Most people don't begin to
understand the concept of 'need to know.'"

"Well, it makes sense to me," Jessica said. "And I'll tell
you what's really got me so upset this morning. Someone
was in my safe again last night. I don't know how to change
the combination, and I don't know how I can convince security to change it. So all that information is essentially
unprotected. Mine and probably everybody else's. There's
got to be some way to put a stop to this, Arlen!"

It was refreshing, he found himself thinking, to meet
someone these days who actually cared. So many people
were cynical, or at least pretended to be.

"Actually, Jess," he said, "the plug is going to be pulled
this afternoon."

Her bright brown eyes widened behind her glasses, and
Arlen spared a moment to wonder just how bad her vision
was. "The Defense Investigative Service is going to pull an
unannounced inspection at your plant this afternoon. One
way or another, they're going to ensure that information is
protected."

"But how?"

Arlen shrugged. "They're going in looking for an opportunity, and they won't quit until they find it. They'll
make your folks change all the combinations. They understand the situation as well as anyone, Jessica. That information won't go unprotected another night."

"But you said it's as important to find out *what* has been
compromised as it is to prevent further compromises. If
they change all the combinations, won't that prevent the
spy from doing anything? How will you find him?"

Arlen shook his head. "For a novice, you're good at
thinking these things out, Jessica, but you're not considering motivation here. This person isn't stealing these documents because it's easy. He's motivated by *something*. The
most common motivation is greed, even though it's a fact
that spies generally don't make huge sums of money. Still,
if someone is motivated to steal defense secrets in order to

get money, he's not likely to stop just because there's a set-back. Same goes with other motivations, from revenge to blackmail. Whatever is driving this character, he's likely to lie low for a couple of days or weeks, then try to get his hands on the new combinations."

Jessica's slow nod indicated her understanding. "And you'll be ready."

"Believe it." He smiled, then utterly deprived her of breath by the simple expedient of reaching out and running the tip of his index finger along her cheek.

In that instant Arlen experienced an overload of sensations. All at once he was aware of the satin texture of Jessica's skin beneath his finger, of the way her breath caught and held, of her faint feminine fragrance. He saw, too, the way her eyes darkened and her lips parted, just a little, an unconscious betrayal of her reaction to his touch. His own body clenched in response, a sharp, hungry stab of wanting.

Abruptly, he drew his hand back. "I promised you lunch," he said briskly. "We'd better get inside before your break is over."

Feeling slightly dazed, Jessica didn't move until he opened her car door. She wasn't used to such courtesy, and as often as she'd gone out with men for lunch, this was the first time in her life one actually tucked her arm through his, holding it snugly to his side as he guided her around puddles and held an umbrella over her with gentlemanly concern. Being unaccustomed to it, she wasn't sure whether she liked it, but it certainly made her feel ladylike.

It also made her aware of two other things: how large he was beside her, and that he was wearing a gun. The first unsettled her, but the second unnerved her, causing her to miss her step. Arlen steadied her immediately, looking down with quick concern.

"Are you all right?"

Feeling foolishly naive—of *course* an FBI agent wore a gun—she responded tartly to cover her embarrassment. "I'm just not accustomed to rubbing elbows with a gun."

Gray eyes looked down at her steadily for an interminable moment. When he spoke, his voice was absolutely level. "Does it bother you?"

Jessica had the inexplicable feeling that she was being tested in some way, though she had no idea what kind of response he wanted. She could only tell the truth. "Actually," she said, and felt her blush rising again, "it caught me by surprise. I wasn't expecting it, that's all. And I *wish* I could learn to stop blushing!"

Arlen looked startled, and then he chuckled, asking, "How old are you, anyway?"

Her color deepened even more. "I'm twenty-six. Are you laughing at me?"

"Not at all." He shook his head solemnly, but his eyes were dancing. He urged her toward the restaurant door. "Twenty-six? And you've been with MTI for six years, you said? You must have graduated from college young." Twenty-six was no child, he found himself thinking, and then wondered why that relieved him.

"I was a little accelerated," she admitted, reluctant to discuss this. People, especially men, seemed to be put off when they learned that she'd graduated from high school at sixteen and completed her undergraduate work and her masters by the age of twenty.

"I was your age when I graduated," Arlen volunteered. He collapsed the umbrella and opened the door for her. "Vietnam slowed me down."

The restaurant was less crowded than usual at that hour, probably because the weather had dampened a few appetites. Jessica ordered the crab salad that was her favorite lunch, and Arlen ordered the vegetarian plate.

"I'm not a vegetarian," he remarked as he handed the menus to the waitress, "but on my job I wind up eating a lot of greasy fast food. Every so often I throw a sop to my conscience."

Jessica laughed.

"I think," he said, returning to business, "I'd like to hear from you tonight about the DIS inspection this afternoon."

"I won't know much about what's going on," Jessica told him. "When they've come other times, they spent a couple of minutes asking me whether I have any problems or questions, or whether I've had any unusual or suspicious contacts, but that's the extent of my involvement."

He nodded and leaned back to allow the waitress to serve them. "But you might pick up on people's reactions to what's happening. This is going to be a different inspection from most, Jessica. It's going to be harder, tougher and longer. This time DIS isn't going in with the assumption that everything's on the up-and-up. This time they know something's seriously wrong, and they're going to dig for any sign or symptom of it. It's certainly apt to irritate people, and it should make anyone with a guilty conscience just a little uneasy. People get incautious when they're worried, and you just might pick up on something." He shrugged and lifted his fork. "I just want you to be alert and then share your impressions with me. Maybe you'll get something, maybe you won't."

"Well, I can do that much," Jessica readily promised, and then laughed. "I have to admit, though, when they ask me if I've had any suspicious contacts, you're definitely going to be the picture that pops into my mind."

Arlen laughed, too. "Just try not to look guilty."

"Did you bring one of your cards for me today?" Jessica asked. "It doesn't really matter, but last night I realized that I never knew FBI agents carried business cards. And then I got to wondering what it looks like."

"Just a regular card. No bells or whistles or anything fancy." He patted his pockets until he found the one holding his card case. "I don't know why it is," he said, "but I can never remember where I keep these damn things. Here you go. But I'd really be a lot happier if you didn't carry this around with you."

"I'll give it right back, then." She accepted the white card, studying it with an interest she didn't bother to hide. Embossed in gold with an FBI badge in one corner, it identified Arlen as Special Agent in Charge of the local field office.

"Special Agent in Charge?" she read questioningly.

"We call it SAC. It means I get to do a lot of extra paperwork and stand on the firing line for a lot of extra flak."

She handed the card back and smiled at him. "You're just being modest."

"I'm never modest. It's the plain truth. I also get to work twice as many hours as anyone else when we have multiple operations going."

At that moment his pocket beeper tweeted at him. Looking rueful, he switched it off and spread his hands apologetically. "It also means I can't enjoy an uninterrupted lunch with a lady. Will you excuse me?"

He crossed the room to the pay phone near the exit, weaving among tables with a grace that could only come from peak physical conditioning. A gun and a pocket pager. Shaking her head ruefully, Jessica lifted a forkful of crabmeat to her mouth. No sane woman would be attracted to a man who wore a gun under his coat on one side and a pager in the pocket on the other side. Neither object promised a tranquil existence, and that kind of excitement was not what she wanted.

But he hinted at other kinds of excitement, too, she found herself thinking wistfully. Excitement of a kind she'd never thought she might experience—and in all honesty still didn't think she ever would.

With a sigh, she forced her thoughts back to the safer area of espionage. That was Arlen Coulter's sole interest in her, and she would do well to remember it.

And then, like the proverbial bolt out of the blue, she remembered something that had happened just the week before last. No, maybe it had been a little longer ago than that. Closing her eyes, she tried to remember exactly when it had happened.

"Sorry I was gone so long," Arlen said, sliding into his chair. And then he noticed her frown of concentration. "Jessica? Are you all right?"

"I'm fine. I just remembered something." She looked at him, eyes troubled behind her lenses. "I suddenly remembered something that happened a couple of weeks ago. Someone I met. I was just trying to remember exactly when."

Arlen leaned toward her intently. "You had a suspicious contact?"

"I don't know. It wasn't any big deal. It's just that something didn't feel right about it, and I was trying to pinpoint it. I don't know how familiar you are with MTI, but a lot of us graduated from the local university, and many of us still have social and professional contacts there. I keep in touch with a lot of the professors from the computer science and engineering departments, and sometimes I brainstorm with them."

Arlen nodded encouragingly. "Go on."

"Well, on one of those visits Professor Kostermeyer in engineering introduced me to a couple of his graduate students. One of them was Chinese."

"From Taiwan or the People's Republic?"

"I don't know. It never occurred to me to wonder."

Arlen nodded again. "What happened?"

"Nothing, really, but even just thinking about it bothers me. I was in the supermarket two weeks ago, the one near my house."

He nodded. "I know the one. Corbett's."

"Right. An awful long way from the university. And I ran into the Chinese grad student Kostermeyer introduced me to. The thing is, I really didn't remember him until he reminded me, and then it struck me as really odd that he would remember me well enough to recognize me and call me by name several months later." She watched him, half hoping he would reassure her somehow, maybe tell her that it wasn't odd at all.

The back of Arlen's neck was prickling overtime, a sure sign that this was important. It was an instinct that had never failed him yet. "Well, some people do have really amazing memories for faces and names. They're also about as rare as ice at the equator. It's exactly the kind of contact you're supposed to report to your security officer. This is a classic type of recruitment approach. What exactly happened?"

"Well, he suggested we have lunch together, and I said I was busy. Then he suggested we do it another time, but I managed to keep it vague and left. It was just now, sitting

here, that I really started thinking about it." She shrugged.
"Maybe I'm just getting paranoid because of this other
stuff?"

"Did he by any chance offer to pick up the tab when he
made the suggestion?" Students were usually too tight on
money to do more than pick up their own tabs, especially
foreign students, who were often living on very restricted
stipends. If this fellow had offered to buy lunch, the contact would be even more suspicious.

She looked down, trying to remember exactly how the
invitation had been worded. "I'm not sure about that,
either. I just wasn't paying enough attention, Arlen." She
raised eyes that asked for his understanding. "The whole
thing seemed more like a slightly uncomfortable nuisance,
if you want the truth. I figured he wanted some help getting a job at MTI. And I was vaguely worried that he might
be persistent about it."

"That may be all he wants," Arlen agreed. "I've seen
recruitments start out exactly like this, though." Reaching
out, he startled her once again by briefly covering her hand
with his. Almost as soon as she registered the dry warmth
of his skin, he withdrew his touch.

"Let me tell you a story, Jessica."

She nodded, pushing her salad aside and giving him her
full attention.

"A number of years ago, a university student knocked
on his neighbor's door and complained that the volume of
the man's stereo was disturbing his studying. The neighbor, a Bulgarian student, apologized and promptly turned
his stereo down. A few days later, the Bulgarian invited the
American over for a drink, and the American accepted to
show there were no hard feelings. With me so far?"

Jessica nodded. "Is this true?"

"Absolutely. Anyhow, while he was having a drink with
the Bulgarian, the American was introduced to a friend of
the Bulgarian's, a man who was identified as a cultural attaché at the Bulgarian embassy. The attaché talked to the
American for a while, ascertained that the student, like
most students, could use some extra money, and offered to
hire him to do some economic research."

"I think I can guess the rest," Jessica said.

Arlen shook his head. "I doubt it. This student happened to see a program about espionage on a local public television station right about that time and, wonder of wonders, he called the local FBI field office. The Bulgarian attaché turned out to be an officer in the KGB, and we successfully ran the American student for two years as a double agent." Arlen smiled faintly. "The student had a yen to be James Bond. He loved every minute of it. And we got five or six very important arrests out of it, not to mention all the disinformation we passed to the Soviets."

"So my student might have been making an approach." Jessica watched him, hoping he would deny it.

"He might have been. The thing a lot of people don't understand about students from some less-than-friendly nations is that they're not spies exactly, but they're expected to report back to their embassies about every person they meet. So say this student reported his brief meeting with you, as he's reported a hundred others, but this one caught the eye of somebody in intelligence. So he was told to make a further contact with you. If he can manage to become just slightly acquainted with you, then he can introduce someone else to you without arousing your suspicions."

Jessica nodded unhappily. "Then if it really wasn't an accidental meeting, I can expect to run into him again sometime."

"Absolutely. And if you do, I want you to go along with his suggestions."

Jessica's eyes widened, and she drew a sharp, disbelieving breath. "You're kidding! Tell me you're kidding!" But from the expression on his face she knew he wasn't. The unease she'd felt over the missing document was nothing compared to the nervous fluttering in her stomach right now. "Arlen, I don't have the nerves for this!"

"No nerves are required," he said calmly. "The man asks you to lunch, and you go. He may or may not introduce you to someone else. At each stage, you're always free to continue or bow out. Nothing commits you for the long haul, Jessica."

"But—but—" How could she adequately express the terror she felt? "I'd be too scared to do it."

"There's nothing to be scared of. Nobody who's been a double agent for us has ever, *ever,* been harmed. In fact, a few have found the KGB protects them as carefully from the FBI as we try to protect our double agents from them."

"We're not talking about the KGB here, Arlen."

"It doesn't matter. I'll look after you. The whole damn Bureau will look after you. And if the opposition tumbles to the fact that you're a double agent, all they'll do is skedaddle so fast your head'll spin. They would have absolutely nothing to gain by harming you, and everything to lose."

Jessica shook her head, frantically trying to find an objection that would convince him.

"Look." Reaching out, he caught one of her hands in each of his and stilled their nervous motions. "Just think about it, Jessica. You don't have to answer right now. Just think about it and how important it is."

He saw the fear in her bright brown eyes and felt guilty for what he was doing. He was positive she wouldn't be hurt in any way, or he wouldn't be suggesting it. It was important that she do this, damn it, but not important enough to put her life at risk. The problem was, people's heads were full of Hollywood notions of espionage, notions that had little to do with reality, particularly the reality of domestic espionage. In fact, Hollywood aside, foreign intelligence operations had more to lose than they could ever gain if they even once harmed an American citizen who was working for either them or the FBI.

Her fingers felt so small and fragile within the confines of his large hands, and her skin was so smooth and satiny. Her wrists were small and delicate, certainly less than half the size of his. She would be small and soft and satiny, hot and tight and—

He abruptly released her hands, schooling his thoughts to less inflammatory paths. What a damnable time for his libido to resurrect itself!

"Just think about it," he said, relieved to find he sounded natural. "I promise I won't pressure you."

That was fair, Jessica thought with relief. She understood the importance of what he'd asked her to do, but she seriously doubted she had steady enough nerves for anything of the sort. In many ways, she was simply a mouse. Still, she thought wistfully, she might almost consider it— if he would hold her hands again. She had known so little caring physical contact in her life.

"I'd better be getting you back," Arlen said, signaling the waitress. "I'll come by this evening, unless that will interfere with your plans."

"To ask me about what happens this afternoon?"

He nodded and gave her a reassuring smile. "And that's all, I promise. Unless *you* want to talk about something more."

"All right." She tried to look indifferent. "I'll just be trying to straighten up the place. Someday I hope to have all those boxes emptied."

When they were driving back toward MTI through the steady rain, Jessica thought to ask, "What do you want me to do about that document?"

Arlen braked for a stoplight and rubbed his chin before glancing at her. "Leave it undiscovered until tomorrow," he said after a moment. "Tonight I'll give you a crash course in how to lift a fingerprint. I'm willing to bet, though, that the prints will be wiped off. Anyone with half a brain would have thought of that once the hue and cry was raised over that document."

"But if I find one?"

"It may be yours. Whatever you find, you can bring it out to me tomorrow. Why don't I meet you for lunch again?"

Jessica looked sideways at him. "Is your expense account up to this?"

He chuckled. "When it starts complaining, I'll let you know."

When he pulled up before MTI's main entrance, he set the car in park and turned to her. "Take care, Jess," he said and bent forward, giving her the lightest, gentlest kiss on her lips. "See you tonight," he added in a husky murmur.

It was all for show, but it didn't feel like playacting, not to Jessica. Her heart stopped in her throat, and electric sparks shot out from that brief, light caress, dazing her.

Somehow she climbed out of the car. It was only as she was stepping into the lobby that she realized someone *had* been watching. Bob Harrow, her project chief, stood just inside the doors, grinning like the Cheshire cat.

"Something wrong, Bob?" she asked him, feeling annoyed that he'd seen the gesture. That in fact he'd probably precipitated it.

"Not a thing," he said, suddenly all innocence. "Not a thing, Jessica." But there was a knowing glint in his eye as he rode the elevator upstairs with her.

Chapter 3

Bob Harrow hadn't been the only one to notice Jessica's lunch date. Frank Winkowski, another of the project's programmers, had seen her departure and Arlen's kiss on her cheek. Before the afternoon was over she had endured some merciless teasing, and naturally she made it worse by insisting that Arlen was just a good friend.

She wasn't entirely comfortable with teasing. She'd been an only child, raised by a mother and grandmother who'd had little use for her. Since coming to work at MTI, she'd seen a lot of teasing among her co-workers, and on occasion she'd been the gentle butt of some of it. It was easier to handle now, but she couldn't take it as casually as others did.

The teasing, however, had taken her mind off other things, and she got through the entire afternoon with only occasional thoughts of the document in her drawer or the security inspection that surely had begun somewhere in the building.

Unannounced inspections were permitted by the terms of the security agreement a defense contractor had with the government, so the Defense Investigative Service needed to give no excuse for showing up. No one knew that this inspection was a direct result of Jessica's report to the FBI, and Arlen had assured her that DIS would be careful not to draw any attention to her. She would be treated exactly like everyone else, and since these inspections always took at least three days, she didn't really expect to see an inspector for another day or so.

When she got home she changed into jeans and a sweat-shirt, ate a quick salad for dinner and dug into the packing boxes that still waited all over the house. She'd accumulated quite a few possessions over the years since she left college. Most of them had been bought by chance when she stumbled on some item that she knew would be perfect for the home she dreamed of owning someday. Now she owned the home, and she was a little surprised to find how much of the furnishing and bric-a-brac she'd already acquired.

She had just dragged the last of a series of boxes to the foot of the stairs to be carried up when the doorbell rang. *Arlen.* This time she didn't imagine herself slinking away. This time a swift image flashed across her mind that left her aching. Giving herself a mental scolding, she dusted her hands against her jeans and went to open the door.

If she'd been jolted by his charisma last night, tonight she came close to being stunned. Tonight he wore snug, faded jeans and a black sweater that awoke swashbuckling images in Jessica's hyperactive imagination. She wouldn't have thought that a man who could look so elegant and conservative in banker's gray could look like an outlaw in a pair of jeans.

"Hello, Jessica." He smiled, deepening the creases at the corners of his eyes. Unaware of the effect that expression had on her pulse rate, he scanned her from head to foot. Her jeans, unlike last night's slacks, were worn from many washings and were a closer fit. Her sweatshirt, also worn thin from many washings, hugged her breasts with more familiarity than he suspected she realized. This lady was womanly. She would fill a man's hands and arms; she would cradle him in softness and surround him in heated satin. And he sure as hell shouldn't be thinking about things like that when he was supposed to be working.

Jessica stepped back, achieving a smile despite her heart's hammering—the way he'd looked at her!—and invited him in.

"This isn't a bad time, is it?" he asked as he stepped into her foyer. Immediately he noticed the boxes lined up at the foot of the stairs. "Do you need those carried up? Let me do that for you."

"Oh, I couldn't really—"

Turning, he smiled down at her. "Sure you can. You're helping me, and I'd like to do something in return."

Jessica's knees rubberized instantly. That crooked, warmly intimate smile did things to her insides, tweaking, pulling, tingling. Before she could gather her wits to respond, he squatted and hefted the first box. His sweater pulled up in the back, exposing a band of smooth skin and the fact that he wore no belt on his jeans. Why did the absence of a belt cause a deep, slow pulsing inside her?

"Where upstairs?" Arlen asked as he began climbing.

"First room on the right." Was that really her voice, sounding so husky?

Arlen set the box out of the way against the wall in the designated room. As he straightened, he knew with sudden, deep certainty that this was Jessica's room. It was, he supposed, prying, but nevertheless he looked around him with interest, noting the ruffled dotted swiss curtains on the tall windows, the white satin comforter and white dust ruffle on the maple four-poster. Embroidered linen doilies decorated the top of her maple dresser, and dotted swiss skirted a dressing table with a matching mirror. The only colors in the room were the bright area rugs scattered around the polished wood floor.

Virginal, he thought. The room of a sixteen-year-old. He started to turn away, wondering what had arrested Jessica's development, when he suddenly had the most erotic image of bare skin on white satin and dark hair that tumbled to her waist. How long *was* her hair? he wondered, then shook himself and headed downstairs for the next box. *Damn it, Coulter, this is business!*

Five boxes later, he'd seen the other two bedrooms, one of which held a desk, bookcase and personal computer with all the necessary peripherals. And he was still as randy as the old goat he was beginning to feel like. Bare skin on white satin. He cursed the randomly firing brain cell that had brought that image to mind.

Jessica awaited him at the foot of the stairs. "Coffee's ready," she said brightly.

"Great." He descended the last few stairs wondering what she would do if he pulled her into his arms and kissed her. By the time he reached the bottom she'd started to move into the living room, unwittingly giving him a view of her gently swaying rear that only compounded his problem.

Once again she served coffee in the delicately patterned china cups. Seated in an armchair, Arlen gave himself a few minutes to savor her really excellent coffee and to bank some of his unwanted urges.

"How'd it go at work this afternoon?" he asked finally.

"Like always." She flushed. "Well, not exactly. It seems you were right that we might be observed. Two of the guys I work with saw us, and I got teased about it."

One corner of his mouth lifted. "But I bet they didn't ask who I was."

"Of course not. They had that all figured out." Her voice was tart, and then she laughed softly. "You were right. Once they saw you kiss me, they filled in all the blanks. Nobody even asked your name."

"It's an old magician's technique. Misdirect the attention of the audience. Works every time." His smile broadened. "What about the inspection?"

"It never got anywhere near our section today. The grapevine didn't even get the word to us until almost quitting time. The only thing different that I noticed was that the security stations were performing random briefcase checks for the first time in an age."

Arlen nodded. "I expected that. Just like I expect that tomorrow you'll have to show your ID to get past the front desk, even if it's a security crew that knows you."

He sipped coffee and let his head rest against the chair back. "This chair is too comfortable, Jess. You may never get rid of me." Heavy lidded, his eyes watched her lazily.

"I've got the fingerprint kit out in my car. I suppose I should get it."

"There's no rush," she said. "I'm not going anywhere."

They sat for a while in companionable silence, and he began to feel more relaxed than he could remember feeling in quite a while.

"Arlen?"

"Hm?"

"How can I carry fingerprints out of the building tomorrow if they're doing briefcase checks?"

He rolled his head a fraction so that he could look at her. "There's no law that says you can't carry fingerprints around with you."

"But what if they ask?" Her small face was worried.

"Tell them your boyfriend's a cop, and they're his. Or tell them you're taking a night school course in criminology. Relax, Jess. They probably won't even look in your briefcase tomorrow, but if they do, they'll know better than to bother you about things that are none of their business. They don't want any trouble with their bosses."

He spoke lazily, his eyelids still drooping, and Jessica's wild imagination suddenly presented her with the image of a panther lazing in the sun, deceptively sleepy but very much alert.

"Where are you from originally?" she asked him abruptly.

Arlen heard the shortness of her tone and wondered if he'd said something to disturb her. No, he was sure he hadn't. And then coiling through him like liquid heat was the memory of the way her lips had parted at his touch earlier in the day. Could she be bothered by the same impulses that were troubling him? Turning his head a little more, he looked at her fully.

"I hate to admit this," he said, "but I'm a damn Yankee from New York."

Jessica's lips curved. "New York? Do you miss it?"

"Hardly. One of the Bureau's rules is that you can't be stationed anywhere too close to home. I knew when I signed on that I'd never go back."

"How long have you been here?"

"Long enough to know you Texans have the same opinion about Yankees in general and New Yorkers in particular that the rest of the country has about Texans."

Jessica laughed. "So you're a big-city boy?"

"Oh, I'm not from the city," he said. "I'm from a sleepy little dairy-farming community upstate. What about you? Did you grow up right here?"

She shook her head. "No, I'm a hayseed, too. From a little town in West Texas where we had a lot more dust storms than we had rainstorms. Let me get some more coffee."

At the door she paused and looked back. "Are you hungry? I think I have some coffee cake in the freezer. It'd take only a minute to zap it in the microwave." Actually, she more than *thought* the coffee cake was there. She had bought it on the way home this afternoon just so she could offer it to him.

"Sounds good," he admitted. He'd stayed late at work tonight, and by the time he got away he'd decided on fast food so he wouldn't arrive at Jessica's too late. The food had been tasteless, though, so he'd ditched his dinner, stopped by his apartment just long enough to change, then dashed over here. Coffee cake sounded very good. In fact, relaxing sounded very good. It was Thursday evening, and so far he'd worked every night this week, not to mention last Sunday, when he'd had to help one of the agents iron out some wrinkles in a bribery investigation.

"Do you work all the time?"

The soft question caused him to look up at Jessica. She was standing beside him, holding out a plate with one hand and his freshly filled cup with the other.

"Thank you." Smiling, he took both from her and set them on the coffee table.

"Do you?" she asked as she resumed her seat on the couch.

"Do I what?"

"Work all the time."

He shrugged. "Sometimes it seems that way. Aren't you having any cake?" His plate held a large piece. She had no plate at all.

"I can't afford the calories. Don't worry about me."

She said it as if she'd been saying it for a very long time and had come to accept it, and somehow Arlen found that utterly intolerable. "Are you trying to lose weight?"

"Of course." She smiled faintly. "All the time."

"Why?"

She gaped at him. "Why?" she repeated stupidly. "Why?" Anybody could see that just by looking at her.

"Yes. Why?" And somewhere between images of pink satin skin on a white satin bed and the understanding that he was being driven out of his mind by the sexual appeal of a woman who believed she didn't have any, Arlen lost the first iron layer of his self-control. Having been, for more than four years, unable to hold and love a woman probably added considerably to the stress of the moment. Since Lucy had become too ill to love, he hadn't wanted to love. Not until this plump little partridge entered his life. And here she was trying to waste away the very charms that were driving him wild.

"You have no idea," he said flatly, "just how beautiful your healthiness is. How attractive you are—just the way you are."

Jessica's hand fluttered to her throat, and she stared at him disbelievingly. "I, um, t-that's very kind of you to say," she squeaked. Her heart was hammering so hard there was no room in her chest for air. He was just being nice, she told herself. But, oh, how she wished . . .

The wish was plain on her face, and Arlen was just tired enough, just pushed enough, just frustrated enough, to forget he was an agent on a case. Rising, he walked with a deliberate tread around the coffee table and just as deliberately sat beside Jessica on the sofa. Her head had turned as her eyes followed him, and now she looked at him with wide, wondering brown eyes. Bright eyes, he noticed, that were far more hopeful than fearful.

"I'm going to kiss you, Jessie," he said huskily as he reached up and removed her glasses, setting them aside on the table. She blinked uncertainly at him while he noticed that her eyes were even larger without the lenses in front of them. And her lashes were long and silky.

Gently, he cupped her face between his hands. "I'm going to kiss you because I've been wanting to for the last half hour," he told her, stroking her cheeks lightly with his thumbs. "I'm going to kiss you because you're so damn sexy, and because those soft pink lips of yours are just begging for it."

She seemed to have stopped breathing, but now she drew a shaky breath and her eyelids fluttered down. Arlen smiled as he saw her consent. The hunger in him was strong, but gentleness tempered it. This woman needed gentleness as surely as she needed to be desired.

Bowing his head, he brushed his lips lightly against hers, gently questing like a bee seeking nectar, again and again, the lightest brush of lips against lips, his breath as much a caress as his touch. It had been so long since he'd kissed a woman for the first time that he wasn't really sure he remembered how. He was coaxing because she seemed to be as uncertain as he was. His tongue touched her upper lip, stroking its length enticingly. Next her lower lip, a sweep to incite.

Arlen heard her swift intake of breath, felt her lips part beneath his. And then, so good, her arms wound around his back and reached upward to cling to him, to embrace him. Ah, God, it had been so long!

To Jessica the moment was a miracle. She simply didn't know what pleased her more, the strength of his muscular back beneath her hands or the sinuous, sinful enticements of his tongue as he plundered the depths of her mouth. She'd never dreamed there were so many sensitive nerve endings there, nerves that were mysteriously linked to other parts of her. Her entire body felt as if it were being kissed. *This* was what she had believed she could live without?

Arlen lifted his head a fraction, looking down into her hazy eyes. His voice was a husky whisper. "More, Jessie?"

She nodded, dazed by the sensations he was evoking in her. "Please," she whispered.

Her head had fallen back, bespeaking her surrender to the moment. He moved, cradling the back of her head in one hand, wrapping the other arm around her back as he lowered her to the sofa cushions and stretched out beside her.

"More, Jess," he said roughly, a statement this time.

And this time, when he took her mouth in a kiss, he took it deeply, with a rhythm so primitive that her very cells responded to it. She opened her mouth wider to receive the bold thrusts of his tongue and responded in kind with a need she didn't even know how to name.

Her hand somehow found its way to his hair and combed into the dark silk, finding the warmth of his scalp. His mouth slanted to a new angle over hers, giving her a chance to catch her breath a little, giving her a moment to feel her whole body pulse in time to his kiss. Giving her a moment to feel his pelvis rock against her hip. Giving her a moment to feel the evidence of his desire.

A new thrill trickled through her, the thrill of being wanted, but the trickle was accompanied by a stronger thrill of fear. She'd met this man only last night. A chill clamped over the throbbing ache in her body, cleared the fog from her brain. What was she doing?

Sensing her mood change even through the hazy red layers of his hunger, Arlen clamped down on his needs and began, by gentle stages, to withdraw himself without causing embarrassment. Damn! he thought. He'd been celibate for too long if he could lose control like this.

Before long Jessica sensed his intent, and her fear dissipated, leaving her with a dissatisfied ache and a dawning sense of wonder. He had wanted her! She'd felt the proof of it.

Arlen raised them both to a sitting position and cradled Jessica's cheek against his shoulder, his arm around her. It was exactly the embrace she'd fantasized about on the way to lunch that day, and it was so much better than her imaginings. His shoulder was firm beneath her cheek, his distantly sensed heartbeat a steady, somehow reassuring thud. Even the faint scratchiness of his sweater was somehow stimulating. And the weight of his arm around her shoulders—there just weren't words to adequately describe how *good* it felt.

"Are you all right, Jessie?" he asked presently, touching her cheek with gentle fingertips.

"Yes." The word sounded lost and breathless against his shoulder.

"I'm sorry," he said. "I shouldn't have done that."

A long moment passed before she could find her voice. "Why not?"

"Any number of reasons." His voice had returned to normal, and his heart rate was coming into line. "In the first place, it wasn't very professional. I don't think there's a specific rule against it, since you're not a suspect, but I still don't think an agent is supposed to be kissing someone who's involved in his case."

"I won't tell," Jessica murmured, still too swamped by emotions to speak cautiously.

Arlen smiled and tightened his arm around her just a little. "And I won't do it again, Jessica."

It was on the tip of her tongue to protest, but her mind was swinging into action again, and she caught the words before she could speak them. She didn't know this man, and if she were to think about it she would probably be shocked that she had fallen into his arms so easily after an acquaintance of a mere day. After all, she'd never before fallen into anyone's arms.

Jessica tilted her head back and looked up at him. He was close enough at the moment that she could see him clearly without her glasses. "How old are you, Arlen?"

"Forty-two."

His smile, she thought, looked a little sad somehow. "That's part of the problem, isn't it?" She didn't mention the wedding ring he still wore, which she suspected was the biggest part of the problem.

He didn't ask what she meant. He knew. "I have a daughter who's nearly your age, Jessie. She's twenty-three and expecting her first child. My first grandchild. And I have a son who's twenty-one."

"You started young." It wasn't a question.

"I was eighteen when Lucy and I married. Right out of high school and right over everyone's objections."

"Were you right, or were they?"

He closed his eyes, and his smile broadened just a shade. "We were," he said. And he brought his other arm around Jessica, giving her a little hug. "I had a good marriage, Jessie. A very good marriage. Once in a lifetime is all anyone has a right to expect."

Eventually, because their embrace was still too intimate both for their respective roles and for his conscience, Arlen stirred. Releasing Jessica, he handed her back her spectacles.

"I'll go get that fingerprint kit," he said, rising from the sofa.

She slipped her glasses onto her nose and looked up at him. "Okay," she managed to say brightly. "I think I'll make some more coffee. Do you want any?"

He looked down with a smile that didn't reach his gray eyes. "I'll pass, thanks. I need to get some sleep tonight."

So did she, thought Jessica, but she seriously doubted she was going to get it, coffee or no coffee.

It was a night for memories, Arlen thought. It was late, and his apartment seemed emptier than usual, though not as empty as the house he'd shared with Lucy had seemed after her death. The only keepsakes he hadn't put into storage were an eight-by-ten photo of Lucy and a slew of photographs of the children. Everything else had been put away, because a man his age had no choice but to move on.

But sometimes he remembered, and tonight, with a glass of bourbon to keep him company, he held Lucy's photo and looked back.

He hadn't been kidding. It *had* been a good marriage. Not a perfect marriage, but a good one. A comfortable one. A hell of a lot better by far than most marriages he knew about. Part of him had died with Lucy, had expired with her last breath as he held her in his arms that one final time. Afterward, he had figured he would go on as father, friend and government agent, but never again as lover or spouse. That part was gone.

Evidently, he found himself thinking as he looked down at Lucy's smiling face, he'd been a little naive in his expectations. The feelings hadn't died but had merely gone into hibernation. That created a whole mess of interesting problems he wasn't sure he cared to deal with at this stage in his life.

First of all, he was about to become a grandfather. He had certain images of that role that didn't jibe with the memory he had of himself and Jessica on her couch this evening. It also meant he was too damn old to be rolling around with a girl her age. His children were grown, and she was the right age to be having children. Damn, Jessica was only a few years older than his daughter! That realization kept drawing him up short and hard, like a yanked rein.

Setting Lucy's picture aside, he carried his drink into the kitchen and dumped it down the sink. He'd never been much for alcohol, and at a time like this he wanted his head to be perfectly clear.

Except how clear could it be when he kept imagining pink skin and white satin, and remembering just how right a certain young woman had felt in his arms? How perfectly she'd fitted against him and how passionately she'd responded to his kiss?

And what damn difference did it make? He was an agent on a case and had to remain professional. Whatever had gotten into him tonight had better not get into him again. That was the beginning, middle and end of it right there.

She was too young for him, Jessica thought as she lay in the middle of her four-poster bed and stared up at the patterns made by the moonlight on her ceiling. Of course he would think so. How could he not? She and men had spent her entire life avoiding one another, so how could she possibly know the right things to say and do to make it clear that she didn't *feel* young? It had probably been that very inexperience that had caused him to draw back from her tonight. She didn't know how to kiss, how to please, how to entice. Discovering that, he'd naturally lost interest.

But, of course, it was all for the best. He still wore his wedding ring. Whether she felt young or not, Jessica definitely didn't feel up to dealing with the ghost of Arlen's wife. She had a very healthy respect for the power of ghosts. Hadn't she watched her mother languish and drink herself to an early grave over the death of Jessica's father? And, oh, what a slow death that had been, finally leaving the mother dependent on the daughter who was still only a child.

Arlen seemed to be holding up a lot better than her mother had, Jessica thought, but she knew too well what it meant to be invisible to grieving eyes.

Turning over onto her side, she looked out the window at the moon through the lacy tracery of tree branches. He had been in this room tonight. What had he thought of it? Did he think it childish? Probably. She knew as well as anyone just how childish it was. It was the room she had dreamed of having someday, a dream she could trace all the way back to the age of seven. That was the year after her father's death. That was when she'd finally realized there was no way to go back home.

And so she'd begun to dream of a home in the future. A lot of that dream had matured to more realistic proportions that could be embodied in this house she now owned. Tonight, however, it was strikingly obvious to her that she'd forgotten to include the most important part of any home: family.

Sighing heavily, her throat suddenly and inexplicably tight, she wrapped her arms around a pillow and hugged it. She'd been lonely for so long she'd ceased to be aware of it. Until tonight.

Damn Arlen Coulter for making her conscious of it.

Chapter 4

Dressed in her favorite dove-gray suit and black silk blouse, Jessica arrived at work forty-five minutes early the next morning. The extra time was essential if she was to try to lift fingerprints from the document. It wasn't so much that the process was complicated, because it wasn't, but she wanted ample time so she could move slowly and avoid errors.

Security, mindful of DIS inspectors, checked her identification thoroughly before waving her through. When she arrived in her own section she walked down the hall, assuring herself that all the other offices were empty. Only then did she return to her own office, close the door and start to open her safe.

"Talk about acting suspicious," she muttered to herself as she spun the dial first left, then right, then left and then right again. She felt the dial resist as she reached the last number and knew she'd worked the combination correctly. Pressing down the lever, she grabbed the drawer handle and pulled it open.

The document was still on the bottom of the drawer, apparently untouched since she'd found it there yesterday. When she'd emptied enough of the other documents to give herself unobstructed access to the red folder, she used the plastic gloves Arlen had given her to lift it out.

"It's not that your fingerprints will get you into trouble," he'd told her last night. "You just don't want your prints to destroy a good print by overlaying it."

Only there were no good prints. She knew that with certainty twenty minutes later, having dusted the entire folder and the document with dark powder. The powder adhered to nothing except some vague, blurry streaks. The spy had wiped the prints, just as Arlen had suspected.

Disappointed, she cleaned up the mess with exaggerated care and then went down the hall to wash her hands. Frank Winkowski was just entering the section when she came back down the hall from the rest room. He looked surprised to see her, then smiled.

"You're early, too," he said. "Brainstorm?" He was a pleasant-looking man with a round face and a tendency to softness around his waist.

Jessica shook her head. "Not really. I just woke up early this morning, and there didn't seem to be any point in hanging around the house. Besides, after all that uproar with security the other day, I need to do some catching up."

Frank nodded. "We'll all have to do some catching up, I think. From what I hear, this security inspection is turning into a real bear. Stan Watson—do you know him?"

"He's the guy heading up the Big Whistle project, isn't he?"

"Yeah." Frank shifted his briefcase from one hand to the other, as if it were heavy. "He said a team of two inspectors are shutting themselves up in a private office with each of his team members for an hour at a stretch."

"Oh boy." Jessica managed to sound surprised. "What's going on? What're they asking?"

Frank shrugged. "Dunno. The guys they questioned yesterday afternoon say they can't talk about it. Maybe there's been a leak from the project."

Jessica shook her head. "I can't imagine that. What does Stan think about it?"

"I think he's just plain furious. He also said that they're inspecting everyone's desk."

"I heard they can do that, but I never saw them inspect one."

"Me either." Frank shook his head. "I guess if you've got any embarrassing love letters in your desk from that guy you were with yesterday, you'd better dump 'em."

She saw the twinkle in his eye and decided not to let the comment bother her. "Thanks, Frank. If I ever get him to write an embarrassing love letter, you'll be the last to know."

"Thought so!" Laughing, he moved down the hall to his own office.

Back at her desk, Jessica installed her hard drive, booted up and resumed her work. She thought she was doing pretty well, too, until an hour later when Arlen called.

"Lunch at twelve?" he asked without preamble.

She sank back in her chair and pulled off her glasses, realizing suddenly that she had a tension headache. Rubbing impatiently at her forehead, she sighed. Arlen heard it.

"What's wrong?" he asked.

"Not a damn thing," she said, more sharply than she meant to. "What could possibly be wrong?" Other than espionage and an FBI agent who'd awakened her to things she was better off not knowing about. An FBI agent who called her, cool as you please, his tone the politely casual tone people used with strangers. His silence suggested to her that he was evaluating her response. Suddenly disturbed that he might draw conclusions, she said, "Sorry, Arlen. I've got a king-size headache."

"Have you taken aspirin?" It was the politely concerned question of an acquaintance.

Damn it, Jessica thought. Damn it. Back to business as usual. *Well, girl, are you going to let him get away with it?* The question drew her up short, creating as it did a whole new passel of questions she wasn't going to be able to answer without a lot of soul-searching.

"Jess?" His tone had lost a little of its distance.

"I'm here. Sorry. Noon is fine for lunch. I'll be waiting out front." If she didn't get swallowed up in the internal earthquake she felt herself verging on. "I don't have anything for you, though." As soon as she said it, she wanted to kick herself. He might cancel lunch.

But he didn't. "I figured you wouldn't. I've got a few things to talk to you about, anyway. Noon, then."

She took the aspirin, but it didn't answer the questions nor did it help her concentrate on her work. She found herself pacing her office, a not very large space that allowed her to take only three steps in one direction before forcing her to turn. Here it was, only the middle of the morning, and it looked as if she was done working for the day. Well, she could call security and tell them she'd found the document. If she wasn't going to work, anyway, there was no point in postponing it any longer.

But first she was going to think about that surprising question she'd asked herself. *Was she going to let Arlen get away with this?* On the other hand, how could she prevent him? She was no femme fatale to crook a finger and bring a man to his knees. In fact, the mere notion made her want to laugh.

Arlen had a lot of good reasons for wanting to keep matters between them on an impersonal footing, she thought. He was acting in a professional capacity when he was with her, and she supposed it wouldn't look very good to his superiors if they heard he was fooling around on the job. And if that wasn't enough, there was the biggest problem of all: the wedding band on his left hand.

On the other hand, there *she* was. She'd never felt anything approaching the feelings he'd stirred in her with a few kisses. All the rational arguments she could muster, either for herself or for him, meant absolutely nothing against the soul-deep yearning he'd unleashed.

So what was she going to do about it? *Could* she do anything about it? She had no feminine wiles that she was aware of, and even if she could have manufactured one, she would have been terrified of using it. Ten years later she could still hear the laughter of the premed student who had used her to do his homework. The scar was deep, and still very tender. Her lack of confidence in such matters had become an integral part of her nature.

Arlen had wanted her last night, but that could have arisen from any number of circumstances that had nothing to do with her, and she was painfully aware of it. She might not have a great deal of direct experience with human sexuality, but she prided herself on being well-read. A woman was wisest *not* to assume a man's response was a reaction to her in particular. Arlen might have been reacting more to protracted celibacy than to her.

It would have been almost possible to feel pleased with the objective way she was reviewing the situation, but the bottom line wasn't objective. She wanted—very much—to find herself in Arlen's arms again. In fact, someplace deep inside, she wanted to weep with the longing she felt to be there again.

Standing in the middle of her office, she wrapped her arms tightly around herself and closed her eyes, remembering what it had felt like for those few short minutes to be enveloped in a man's strong arms.

No, she thought, she wasn't going to let him get away with this. But what could she possibly do to beguile him?

There was no answer to that question. Feeling a sudden need to do something, anything, productive, she picked up the phone and dialed Security to tell them she had found the missing document. Dave Barron, the Facility Security Officer, was not in, however, and his assistant, Vicki Grier, was busy with the DIS inspectors. Having no idea who else she could discuss the matter with, Jessica decided to wait again. What was the rush, after all? This was almost like closing the barn door after the horse has gotten out.

Shortly after she finally managed to get her attention back on her work, a knock at the door distracted her. Sure it must be Bob, she called out for him to come in. It wasn't Bob, however. It was one of the plant security officers, and with him were two other men, one of whom Jessica remembered from the last security inspection.

"Ms. Kilmer," said the plant security officer, "these gentlemen are from the Defense Investigative Service, and they're conducting a routine inspection of security procedures. Maybe you remember Brian Earl from the last inspection?"

"Yes, I do, as a matter of fact." She shook hands with Earl, who was either the most forgettable guy on the face of the earth or one of the most memorable she had ever met, simply because he completely lacked personality. Until she met him, she would have believed that only brain damage of some kind could make a person so utterly and completely bland.

"And this is Dick Hartley, also with DIS," the security officer said.

Jessica shook the second man's hand and thought that he looked a lot more lively than Earl. At least he attempted a pleasant smile.

"I'll leave you now," the security officer said and walked out, closing the door securely behind him.

Jessica looked from the closed door to the two inspectors. Earl perched on the corner of her desk; Hartley took the single chair. Did they know about the document? Or had they just been sent out here with no more than a vague warning that something was rotten and had to be sniffed out?

"Isn't this unusual?" she asked them. "I don't remember plant security ever leaving you folks alone with me before."

"It is unusual, Ms. Kilmer," Earl said in his ponderous way. Jessica invariably found herself wanting to insert words for him just to speed him up a little. "This is what we call a Cadillac inspection." He gave her a smile that looked more practiced than natural. "Top of the line."

"Oh."

"Nothing to worry about," Earl continued, just as slowly and blandly. "It's just something we do from time to time to keep folks on their toes. Is your safe open right now? We'll start with the document check and then move on to other things."

"Not before I see your ID we won't," Jessica said.

"Very good," the other agent said, nodding in approval. "Very good. Most of your co-workers haven't asked for our credentials. You're very alert, Ms. Kilmer. Very security conscious."

An hour of that and she thought she was going to lose her mind. They went through her safe, checking every single document to ensure that they were properly classified and filed. They checked Document Control's list of the documents she was supposed to have against the actual contents of her safe, and she sent a hasty prayer of thanks that the missing folder was back in place. She had a feeling these guys didn't know what had precipitated this investigation but that they were out for blood.

They inspected her desk, as well, which really annoyed her, because she kept a number of personal things in there, like a box of tampons and a spare pair of hose. It was silly, she told herself. These were mature men; they knew about such things. It bothered her anyway, and then she discovered that Earl wasn't completely blank. He blushed when he saw the tampons. *That,* she thought wickedly, almost made it worthwhile.

And before they left the security officer rejoined them and changed the combination of Jessica's safe. It was such a relief to her to have that done at last that she almost forgot herself and thanked the officer. Now, for a short while at least, she wouldn't have to come in each morning wondering if something else would be missing. No longer would she have to live with the uneasy sensation that the back door had been left open and unguarded.

At noon she walked out of the building in the company of Bob Harrow and Carl Templeton. As soon as she saw Arlen she said goodbye to Bob and Carl and hurried forward with a smile.

Arlen was leaning against the side of his car, patiently waiting. One of the things he liked to tell young agents when they started to get restless was that the FBI offered the world's greatest education in patience. If you doubt it, he always said, try a stakeout. He had been on quite a few stakeouts that had lasted weeks at a stretch. Some of them had been spent outdoors in the rain and up to his neck in poison ivy. He had, eventually, learned to wait in perfect patience, particularly when the day was dry, the sky blue and the time frame set.

As Jessica approached he straightened and returned her smile with one of equal warmth. Mindful of her two colleagues in the background, both of whom were frankly watching, he prepared to give her a kiss on the cheek as he had yesterday.

Jessica, however, had different plans. Instead of trying to edge past him to get into the car, as she had before, she walked straight up to him. Clinging to the memory of how passionately he had kissed her last night, she screwed up every ounce of her courage. Halting mere inches from him, she tilted her head back and smiled up at him as she placed her hands on his chest.

"Hi," she said shyly, and slowly slid her hands up to his shoulders and thence to the back of his head. Tugging gently, she pulled his mouth down to hers.

Years spent with the Bureau, years spent raising kids, had made Arlen nearly unshakable, but Jessica came pretty close to rattling him then. Having prepared himself only for a brief contact with her, he had no defense against the alluring pressure of her full breasts against his chest, the warm hunger of the mouth that teased his so shyly, or the sheer pleasure of a woman's hands in his hair. Suddenly surrounded by enticing, sweet-smelling femininity, he almost forgot this was a pretense.

Kissing Jessica while standing was not likely to become a lengthy pastime; there was too much disparity in their heights. He had to bend not only at the neck but also at the waist to reach her. Some last vestige of sanity kept him from lifting her right off her feet and bringing her up to a more comfortable height.

Instead, wrapping both arms around her, he bent her backward, bringing her entire length into intimate contact with his hard contours. Breasts, hips, thighs, even her feminine mound, were delectably identifiable as he pressed her close.

Jessica had one last coherent thought before she was swamped in sensation: she was playing out of her league. Then Arlen took control of the kiss, and the rhythm of his thrusting tongue became a pagan drumbeat in her blood.

The kiss lasted no more than fifteen seconds. Though he came close, Arlen never quite forgot himself completely. Lifting his head, he looked down into Jessica's dazed, flushed face. At the moment, severe hairstyle and glasses notwithstanding, she looked adorable.

"Lunch, Jess?" he asked huskily.

She managed a nod, and a moment later she was in the car with no idea how she'd gotten there.

Arlen chose a restaurant farther from MTI this time. He wanted them out of the likely range of people they knew, because he didn't want to risk interruptions or eavesdropping. Traffic was heavy, demanding his attention. It gave Jessica time to think.

It was, she thought, almost a reprise of the humiliating events of her freshman year. This time, however, instead of shyly blushing and accepting his kisses, she'd brazenly walked up to the man and forced him to kiss her. Admittedly, Arlen hadn't laughed at her, but he'd obviously been unaffected, which was just as humiliating. Was it possible to die from mortification? She was beginning to hope so.

Arlen hid it better, but he was struggling with some pretty base impulses, any one of which would, he was sure, probably cause any inexperienced lady to reel with shock. Whatever experience Jessica might have, he didn't feel it was very much. Several miles passed before he felt that he'd clamped down on his imagination enough to be back in complete control.

Glancing over at Jessica, he caught her staring at him. In the split second before his eyes returned to the road he read her expression with skills honed by sixteen years with the Bureau. In that flash he got a fairly accurate notion of how she was feeling, and it was like another blow to his solar plexus. He wasn't trying to wound this woman, but it seemed as if he was bound to. Where the hell was some safe middle ground for them to deal on? And why did she have to be so damn vulnerable?

A light ahead flashed to yellow, and Arlen braked. When the car rolled to a complete stop, he turned and looked at Jessica. There wasn't a thing he could say that wouldn't make the situation worse, he realized. She was sitting there staring straight ahead, cheeks as crimson as if she were standing naked in public. And maybe that was precisely how she felt. Her lips were pursed primly, her hands folded on her lap, and he supposed that if he could see them her ankles would be properly crossed. Embarrassed, she'd retreated into the old-maid schoolteacher pose that he suspected was her defense, just as her hairstyle and glasses were intended to fool men into thinking she was homely.

Somebody, he thought, must have done a number on her sometime or other. And today she'd probably been making an attempt to step past that, and somehow he'd managed to humiliate her. Well, he certainly couldn't have made love to her on the pavement in front of her office building. So what the devil had he done wrong?

The light changed, and he accelerated, still wondering. Had she been embarrassed because he'd drawn her so close to him? Somehow that didn't fit with the way she'd walked up to him and tugged his head down to hers.

Maybe he ought to just ignore the whole thing and let it blow over on its own. The problem with that was that this lady innocently kept blowing his objectivity all to hell in the most devastating way. All his attempts to keep his distance and remind himself that he was an agent on a case just withered away when she got close. Somehow he knew, just knew, he wasn't going to let this blow over by itself.

"Can you be a little late back to work this afternoon?" he said abruptly.

Jessica started and glanced nervously at him. "That's no problem if it's important. I can call in and say something came up, and that I need to take the afternoon off."

"You won't get into trouble?"

"No." She looked doubtfully at him. "Is something wrong, Arlen? Has something happened?"

"That's the question I want to ask you." He turned the car suddenly, leaving a little rubber on the pavement as he cornered sharply. "We're going to my place for lunch. If you have any objections, holler now."

His place. She'd never gone alone to a man's home before. The whole idea sounded incredibly wicked. It was also an opportunity she found herself unable to pass up. "Is there a reason why I should object?" Only after she spoke did she hear the flirtatiousness of her words. Color mounted in her face.

"No," Arlen said. "But if you find any reasons for objection, I expect to hear them."

Another turn and they were heading across town in the general direction of the residential area where Jessica's house was.

"I live in an apartment complex only a mile from your house," he remarked.

Jessica had no idea how to respond to that. The only thought that came to her head was out before she could stop it. "I don't know why, but I imagined you living in a house."

"I used to. When Lucy was alive. Now I have a second bedroom for Andrew to use when he's home on semester break. And soon I won't even need that."

Jessica studied her fingers, hearing the sense of his words as much as their content. When she kissed this man, when she made her pathetic attempts to entice him, she was playing with real fire, and she might get seriously burned. In his heart he was still a married man, which meant there was no room for her. And he kept trying to tell her that. He kept trying to warn her, the way he was doing right now. When was she going to get smart and listen?

"Where does Andrew go to school?" she asked, trying to make it real for herself.

"The Colorado School of Mines. He wants to be a mining engineer and travel all over the world."

Jessica heard the pride in his voice, and her throat tightened. "Sounds exciting," she managed to say. "And your daughter?"

"Melanie's a highway engineer. Right now she's pretty busy on the improvements they're making to the interstate up north of here."

"You must be awfully proud of them both."

"I am." He glanced at her, long enough for her to see the truth of his words in his gray eyes.

His apartment was small, as much as a single person would need and little more. He hadn't wasted any time on decorating, had simply plopped the necessary pieces of furniture where they fit and left them. It *was* clean, however, and Jessica might have thought no one lived here, except for the photographs. After she called her office to explain that she wouldn't be back that afternoon, she turned her attention to the pictures.

Those photos were why he'd brought her here, she realized. On the wall over the sofa, facing the battered easy chair that she suspected was Arlen's favorite place to sit, were dozens of photographs of his children, beginning when they were newborns and continuing up to the present. Drawn forward, she picked out what must be a recent photo of his daughter. Melanie stood next to a huge piece of yellow road equipment. She was dressed in dusty khaki and a white hard hat, and her shirttails hung out. Turned sideways, she displayed her gently swollen womb and looked over her shoulder, laughing into the camera.

"Her husband took that last week," Arlen said as he came up beside her.

Jessica took the coffee mug he held out to her. "Thanks. She's lovely, Arlen."

"Yes." He looked at the photo for a moment and then glanced at Jessica with a smile. "Lunch won't be much, but I'll have it ready in a couple of minutes."

"There's no rush," she answered. "I'm taking time off, remember?"

It was hard to be nervous about being in a man's apartment when faced with a shrine to his family, like this wall. The sinking, butterfly-like feeling that had plagued her all the way here subsided. Turning, she decided to go to the kitchen and offer to help Arlen. She didn't quite make it.

On the table next to the easy chair was a framed color photograph of a smiling woman. Jessica didn't have even a moment's doubt: this was Lucy. Slowly she sank onto the edge of Arlen's chair and stared.

Lucy was lovely. Beautiful. All blond hair and blue eyes, photogenic cheekbones and perfect teeth. Even the faintest hint of crow's-feet at her eyes only added character and humor. Jessica had no trouble understanding how a young Arlen could have tumbled head over heels and married this woman as soon as he got out of high school. And she could understand why nobody else would ever measure up. Certainly not a brown mouse.

It hurt, but she was used to that particular pain. It had been part of her life all the way through high school and into college, and hadn't gone away until she'd convinced herself that she didn't want men any more than they wanted her. Now look at her. Disgusting.

Rising, she turned her back on Lucy Coulter and marched into the kitchen, her chin set with determination. "Can I help?" she asked as she rounded the corner.

Arlen had shed his suit jacket and tie, and rolled up the cuffs of his white shirt to reveal strong, bronzed forearms. A lock of dark hair fell across his forehead, and she resisted an impulse to brush it back. And he still wore his gun. As he turned a little, she came face-to-face with reality for the second time in just a few minutes. The man was an FBI agent. He wore a gun. He had a dangerous job. And she was just a part of that job.

"Thanks," he said, "but I'm just about done. Why don't you go sit at the table?"

Looking up with a faint smile, he saw the hollowness in her bright brown eyes. It seemed he'd gotten through, but the expected relief was missing. Instead he felt guilty, as if he'd just kicked her.

While they ate Arlen broached the subject of the espionage investigation that had been the whole point of meeting her for lunch today.

"Did you tell security that you'd found the missing document?" he asked her.

"I tried. They told me Dave Barron was out sick today, and Vicki Grier was tied up with the DIS investigators. I didn't know who else I should talk to about it, and then *I* got tied up myself with the inspection."

"Vicki Grier. She's the assistant facility security officer, right?"

Jessica nodded.

"Do you know much about her?"

"Not really. I don't have a whole lot to do with the security people, Arlen, and she's only been there a couple of months besides. I've seen her around, I'd recognize her on the street, but I wouldn't bet she'd recognize me."

"Okay." For a minute he didn't say anything, appearing absorbed in his sandwich. "All the safe combinations at MTI are going to be changed sometime today."

Jessica looked at him. "Mine was changed this morning. Did DIS find something to justify ordering the changes?"

"No." He sighed and pushed his plate aside. "You'll hear this, anyway, so I might as well tell you. Dave Barron committed suicide last night."

A cold wave of shock washed over Jessica. In the six years she'd worked at MTI, she had come to know the facility security officer well enough to feel horrified at this news. "You're sure?" she asked hoarsely. "Suicide?" She'd talked to the man for hours only two days before. It just didn't seem possible.

"It looks like suicide," Arlen replied. "We won't know for sure until the medical examiner's report is in."

"Was there a note? Does anybody know why?"

"No note, nobody has a guess." Arlen's gray eyes settled on her face. "Because of his position at MTI, the Bureau's taking over the investigation of his death. And because suicide indicates a dangerous emotional instability, DIS has the excuse it needed to see that all the safe combinations are changed."

Jessica looked at him uncertainly. "Do you think he was involved in the spying?"

Arlen shrugged. "It's anyone's guess. It's possible, I suppose, that he was, and that the intensity of the DIS inspection pushed him over the edge. It's even more possible that there was something else going on in his life. We'll investigate every possibility."

Jessica nodded. "Are you the one investigating?"

"No. Phil Harrigan and Ed Marcel are handling that. They'll keep me informed, but right now I'm staying very much in the background. I don't want anyone at MTI to discover you're hanging around with an agent."

Jessica's expression grew even more uncertain. "But why? I'm not important to anything that's going on. All I did was find out that a document was missing. You're just wasting your time with me, especially now that Dave's suicide gives the FBI a legitimate reason to conduct an investigation at MTI.''

''And you've also been targeted by the KGB.''

Jessica gasped. ''The—the—'' She couldn't even complete the words. ''Who—how—''

Without answering, Arlen pushed his chair back from the table and went to get the coffeepot. He filled both their mugs before returning the pot to the kitchen. By the time he resumed his seat across from her, Jessica had collected her wits.

''You're kidding,'' she said flatly.

''Nope.'' Settling back in his chair, he crossed his legs loosely, right ankle on left knee, and cradled his mug in both hands. ''We did a little investigating of Dr. Kostermeyer's grad students. The one who approached you was Greg Leong, right?''

Jessica nodded slowly. ''That's right.''

''Greg Leong is from Singapore, where he's a member of a Communist cell. He attended Patrice Lumumba University in Moscow before coming here. What most people don't know is that Patrice Lumumba is a recruiting ground for the KGB. Any student who has studied there is highly suspect. Combine that with his approach to you at the supermarket and there's an extremely high probability that he's making a planned contact with you.''

Jessica was having a hard time grasping that. ''How did you find out so much about him so fast?''

''We've been aware of him since he entered the country a year ago. This is the first indication we've had that he might be doing something other than studying here.''

Her eyes were wide as they met his. ''Then the meeting might have been just a coincidence. You can't be sure.''

''I can't be a hundred percent sure,'' Arlen agreed. ''But I wouldn't bet a plugged nickel that he ran into you by accident.''

But she continued to struggle with the idea. ''It's so unlikely, Arlen! Things like this don't happen in real life.''

Setting his mug aside, he uncrossed his legs and leaned forward. "Jessie, things like this happen *all the time* in real life. That's why the FBI has a counterintelligence division. That's why the Defense Investigative Service inspects contractor facilities and interviews employees all the time, and always asks if you've had any suspicious contacts. Most people think it's paranoia, but believe me, Jess, it's *not*. Approaches are so common in the Washington, D.C., area, that we tell people the only way they can avoid being targeted is never to leave their house. Out in the rest of the country it's not quite as bad, but it happens. It happens more than anyone would ever imagine. Hell, I was approached three times when I was stationed in Washington."

"Three times," Jessica repeated, trying to conceive of it. "But you're in the FBI!"

"That's why they approached me." He gave her a faint smile. "Nothing ventured, nothing gained. They use some minor bureaucrat who's about to go home to make the approach, and when it fails they ship him out of the country fast on his diplomatic passport. What you need to understand, Jess, is that it *can* happen and it *does*."

She'd been hearing this in security briefings for six years now. In the briefings, however, she'd never quite believed it could happen to her or someone she knew. It seemed so removed from daily life. Yet here was an FBI agent—the Special Agent in Charge of the local field office, no less—telling her that it might very well be happening to her.

"And I suppose," she said, "that you still want me to go along with it? If it happens."

"Yes. I do." His gaze was unwavering. "It's important, Jessica. We have to know who else might be involved. If there's an espionage operation in this town, and it appears there might well be, given your missing document, then we need to discover everyone who's in on it. Don't you see, Jess, your document and your grad student are probably only the tip of an iceberg. A potentially huge iceberg."

Jessica looked from him to her plate, and finally back at him again. "You promised you wouldn't pressure me on this, Arlen. I told you, I'm a mouse."

Leaning across the table, he covered her hand with his. "Trust me, Jessie. You won't be harmed. That's a promise."

She drew a shaky breath. "I'll think about it. I told you I'd think about it." But she hadn't been thinking about it. Once she got him to drop the subject, she'd dropped it herself. Jessica Kilmer, double agent. It didn't sound like her at all.

She looked down at his hand where it lay covering hers. It was a powerful, masculine hand, with a faint dusting of fair hairs, a tracework of strong veins and long, blunt fingers. And as she stared at them, those fingers curled around hers, holding them.

"Damn it, Jessie," Arlen said roughly, "haven't you realized how much I want you?"

Jessica's breath stuck in her throat, and she raised huge, disbelieving eyes. *Arlen.* Her lips framed his name, but no sound emerged. She would have sworn that her heart had stopped completely.

"I want you," he repeated, "but that's all I can offer you, Jessie. That's all I've got left to offer. So I'd be real grateful if you wouldn't kiss me again the way you did when I picked you up." There, he'd said it. It didn't ease his conscience in the least, but he'd said it. He'd warned her in no uncertain terms.

Her hand trembled beneath his, and then, with a violent tug, she pulled it away. Frantically she shoved her chair back, knocking it over as she stood. Arlen stared up at her in astonishment that was soon mixed with concern as he saw a tear sparkle on her eyelash.

She was breathing so hard that she could hardly form the words that were hammering for escape from her brain.

"You don't—you can't buy my cooperation with your b-body!" Turning, she fled, neither knowing nor caring where she would go, leaving Arlen stunned behind her.

What the hell . . . ?

She was fumbling blindly at the doorknob when he caught her.

"Jessie, I didn't mean—I never—Damn it, you misunderstood me!"

"D-don't t-touch me!"

What, he wondered, had scarred this woman so deeply? Why did she believe he must have an ulterior motive for wanting her? But this was clearly no time to ask about it.

He touched her. Gently but firmly, he turned her from the door and into his arms. She raised her fists in a gesture of self-protection, and her arms were caught between them as he held her snugly against his chest. One small fist made a vain attempt to strike at him, to shove him away, but he ignored it.

"Jessie. Shh." He pitched his voice soothingly and held her as she struggled against his hold, trying ineffectually to free herself. She didn't stand a chance against his training.

Finally a violent shudder ripped through her, and she sagged against him. Arlen didn't quite trust her surrender, so he continued to hold her, rocking gently from side to side, murmuring to her.

"It's all right, Jessie. It's okay." He'd missed this, too, he realized. He'd missed being able to offer comfort like this. "I didn't mean what you thought, Jessie. Honest to God, I didn't mean it the way you took it."

"How *did* you mean it?" Her voice was smothered but defiant, revealing her distrust.

"I meant it exactly the way I said it." Loosening his hold on her, he urged her to the couch. Drawing her down beside him, he tugged her back into his arms, holding her head on his shoulder. His weapon proved to be an immediate problem, so he released her for a moment so he could remove it.

Jessica watched dry-eyed, feeling as if something in her that had been about to take flight had died.

Arlen dropped his gun and holster on the coffee table and then turned to her. This time he didn't take her into his arms.

"Can you listen now, Jess?"

She nodded, refusing to meet his eyes.

"It's just what I told you," he said flatly. "I want you. Don't ask me to explain it, I just do. You're the first woman I've wanted since my wife, which is probably why I'm being so damn ham-handed about this. I don't know how to do it anymore. And I'm not at all sure I want to do it, anyhow, wanting aside.''

Jessica kept her eyes on her twisting fingers. "Why not?" she asked bravely.

"Because I'm forty-two and you're twenty-six. You ought to be getting involved with some guy your own age who wants marriage and children, not some burnt-out old guy like me who hasn't got anything to give you except a roll in the hay. I'm not in it for the long haul anymore, Jessie. I've had my kids. Now I'm looking forward to my grandkids.''

Slowly, very slowly, her eyes rose to meet his. "I understand that, Arlen." Whether she could have him for a few hours or just a few days didn't seem to matter somehow. She wanted, needed, not to miss this. Not to miss him. It was as if she knew somehow that if she didn't seize this opportunity she would regret it and wonder about it for the rest of her life.

"Do you?" He rubbed his chin and studied her. "Why the hell did you think I was—that I had an ulterior motive for what I said?''

Jessica shook her head and looked away from him, too embarrassed to explain.

"Whoever he was, he must've been a real bastard," Arlen said.

She didn't answer, but the way she flinched told him quite enough.

And she didn't really believe his reasons, Arlen realized. She was hearing them from a level of confidence that was so low that she heard his reasons as excuses. How could he possibly deal with that?

There was, he figured, only one way. He just hoped his self-control could handle it. He was being a fool for sure, but this was no noble sacrifice, either, however he rationalized it. He wanted this woman with an ache that went deeper than he dared to think about. When had he last ached like this? When had he last felt that he couldn't live without something? Too damn many years, that was how long.

"Come here, Jessie."

She darted him an uncertain look and didn't move an inch. Sighing, he reached out and took her by the shoulders.

"Come on, honey," he said gently. "Some things just have to be proved."

"Proved?" She squeaked the word as he lay back on the couch in one smooth movement and pulled her with him so that she stretched, breast-to-breast, thigh-to-thigh, on top of him. Shyness overwhelmed her at the unexpected intimacy of the contact, and she didn't know what to do. Closing her eyes as a red tide of color rushed into her face, she froze and felt Arlen remove her glasses.

"Proved," he repeated firmly. Catching her face between his hands, he drew her mouth down to his. "Come on, Jessie," he whispered, the husky sound sending electricity along her spine. "Kiss me."

He was already getting hard, an ability he'd begun to think he might have lost with the years. Every soft curve of her was pressed against him: full breasts, wide hips, soft thighs. Those hips were wide enough to cradle a man in softness, soft enough not to poke at him. As Jessica's mouth met his, Arlen ran his hands from her shoulders to her rump and quite brazenly pulled her hips harder against his.

"Feel that, Jessie," he whispered. "Feel what you do to me."

She shuddered with longing. The heat he'd been stirring in her from the moment of their meeting burst into instant conflagration. His mouth claimed hers, or hers claimed his. She couldn't tell and didn't care as their tongues dueled. Again and again Arlen broke the kiss to allow them both to gulp air, and again and again he tugged her mouth back to his, kissing her as if kissing were the end in itself, as if it were all he wanted and all he needed. Deeper he delved, until she pulsed to his rhythm and made heated little sounds, moving helplessly against him.

"God, Jessie!" Tearing his mouth from hers, he pressed her face to his shoulder, holding her as she rocked helplessly against him, inflaming him further as she responded to impulses and drives that were written in her genes.

And all kinds of thoughts that Arlen would have been sure must shock a lady came racing to the forefront of his mind as he realized that Jessie was a passionate woman. He told himself to resist, not to offend her or shock her, but somehow he moved her to the couch beside him anyway. Somehow he was raised on an elbow over her, and somehow they were both struggling to remove her suit jacket. And somehow his hand was touching the top button of her black blouse. No, not touching. Unfastening.

Jessica drew a sharp breath and held it as her heart stopped. Hearing the sound, Arlen looked up at her, his arm resting between her breasts, his fingers frozen on the second button.

Her face was flushed, her lips swollen, her eyes bright, very bright. "Arlen?" Her voice sounded far away, as if it came from someplace out among the stars that were beckoning to him. Her entire universe, however, had focused on the hand that hovered over that next button, on the ache in the breasts his arm lay between. Clothes constricted, suddenly a travesty of nature. Nerve endings sizzled with exquisite awareness. She felt as if she needed to turn inside out in order to satisfy her wild longings.

He meant to stop, to say something nice and hold her until they came back to earth and safety. He meant to stop before she had anything to remember that might embarrass her. He opened his mouth to say the nice, gallant thing, but what emerged was a man's hoarse plea.

"Let me, Jess," he said thickly. "Please let me."

Chapter 5

He was giving her a chance to draw a line, but Jessica didn't want to. Time hung suspended, and for an endless moment she honestly believed she would die if he didn't proceed. She had never imagined how overwhelming, how single-minded, such desire could be, but she was fully in its grip now.

A breath escaped her in a shuddery sigh, and her eyes fluttered closed. Thus encouraged, Arlen's fingers released the second button and then the third. Time continued to stand still for Jessica. A languorous expectancy filled her as her attention grew narrower and narrower. No one had undressed her since childhood, yet the anticipated shyness and embarrassment failed to materialize, held at bay by the profound, pulsing need that filled her.

The last button yielded, and this time it was Arlen who sucked in a deep breath. Drawing Jessica's head onto the arm on which he was propped, he bent and kissed her deeply, stoking the fires even as his free hand began to gently separate the silky black material.

And then his fingertips brushed against the bare skin of her midriff. Jessica stiffened and gasped, her mouth breaking from his, and Arlen raised his head.

"Easy, honey. Easy." He dropped a kiss on her cheek, then one on her chin and another on her throat, on the pulse that throbbed frantically there. Her arms lifted, her fingers clutched at him, helplessly beseeching. A pleading murmur escaped her.

"Yes, Jessie. Yes." His voice was a throaty whisper as he looked down at her and discovered she wore not the plain white nylon or cotton undergarment he expected, but instead wore shimmering black lace. It was a garment meant to entice, and it told Arlen a great deal about her. He hesitated only a moment before his own need drove him to reach for the front clasp. This and no more, he promised himself.

Her eyes flew open as he released the clasp and her breasts spilled free of their confinement. She saw him looking at her, but instead of embarrassment she felt a clenching thrill. "Arlen?"

The faint, ragged whisper drew his eyes to hers. "You're beautiful, Jessie," he said huskily.

The truth was plain in his eyes, and Jessica felt a smile of sheer pleasure tug the corners of her mouth upward.

"I want to touch you. Kiss you," he said roughly.

Oh, God, she thought she would die if he didn't! She'd never imagined her breasts could ache, actually ache, to be touched. "Please," she whispered, unable to find her voice. "Arlen, please."

Hardly daring to believe she meant it, he cupped one pale, pink-tipped mound in his large hand. A soft moan escaped her, and she turned into his touch, seeking more, much more.

"Like that?" he asked softly, wanting to make her feel what she was making him feel. She was so responsive, so eager, and he wanted to give her only good feelings, wonderful feelings, dizzying, marvelous, passionate feelings.

"Mmm." This time it was nearly a groan as she pressed herself harder against his hand. She didn't know how to ask for more, or for what she really wanted—if she was even sure what that was. All she knew was that the warmth of his callused palm cradling her breast was like a taste, a mere hint, of what she needed. "Arlen!"

The soft cry conveyed both her pleasure and her frustration. Hearing it, Arlen dared more. Boldly now, he rubbed her swelling nipple with his thumb, watching it engorge further, feeling Jessica's restless movements as her hunger grew. Her hand clutched at his shoulder, tugging, and he understood with a sense of wonder that this lady wanted what he wanted to give her. All thought of stopping fled as he drew her nipple into his mouth and sucked.

Jessica groaned deeply, and her hands clasped Arlen's head to her, encouraging, pleading. Wires that stretched from her aching breasts to her womb seemed to draw tighter each time he sucked on her, and soon she was rolling her hips helplessly, needing more, so much more, yet wanting him never to stop.

He moved to her other breast, teasing and tormenting her there, too. His hand slid downward, gliding beneath her skirt and drawing it up until he was able to slip a leg between hers, into the heated cradle of her thighs. Jessica's hips pitched against him, unleashing his own groan. When he felt her legs part even more in receptivity, he moved between them, resting on her, pelvis to pelvis. Only thin layers of material separated them.

What the hell was he doing?

The question penetrated the pleasurable haze that was absorbing him. He gasped, trying to gather himself to move away, when Jessica's eyelids fluttered and her hips gave a maddening upward roll against him.

No, he thought, not like this! Not like a kid in the back seat of a car. Hell, he hadn't even done this when he *had been* a kid! Both of them were clothed, but layers of fabric that should have been a barrier were merely a minor irritant at this point. He was lost already, his hips rocking slowly and deeply against hers, knotting his insides with aching hunger, causing him to moan as her hips moved in perfect counterpoint. Hungry. She was as hungry and needy as he, Arlen realized. He could have her, fully and completely, right now. All he had to do was strip away the last layers of their clothing. But, damn it, he wasn't going to do that. He wasn't going to take advantage of this woman's vulnerability.

"Arlen!" Jessica cried out in fright as strange, uncontrollable feelings of painful pleasure gripped her, clenching her insides in a vise.

He had more control than she, and he understood far better what was happening. Caught in the grip of a battle against his own mounting passion, he nevertheless heard her fear and understood it.

"It's okay, Jessie," he whispered on short gasps of air. "Let it happen. Just let it happen." Sliding a hand beneath her hips, he encouraged her movements against him. Whatever his self-denial cost him, he couldn't leave her hurting like this. "Raise your knees, Jessie."

She did, then cried out as the throbbing ache intensified even more pleasurably. She clutched at his shoulders, then at his head, holding him closer, closer, loving even the starchy rasp of his shirtfront against her swollen breasts. So good, so good, she thought dimly, and wondered fearfully if she would make it to the place her every cell seemed to be straining toward.

And then she found it in an explosion so intense that a keening cry escaped her.

Hearing it, he clutched her close and battered back his own passions, refusing to give in to himself. Not like this. No way. But damn! He felt as if he was going to explode. Drawing one deep, steadying breath after another, he held perfectly still, afraid the least movement would shatter the last thread of control. Forever. It took forever.

Arlen levered himself carefully off her. Reaching out, he drew her blouse closed over her breasts, then tugged her into the circle of his arms, tucking her head onto his shoulder. She lay there without resistance, a welcome soft warmth against him. From time to time an aftershock shook her, a small trembling that arched her slightly, pressing her breast and belly even closer.

Arlen held her close, inhaling her fresh fragrance, feeling the soft silk of her hair against his chin, guiltily savoring the physical closeness despite the torment it had cost him. He was finding it difficult to deal with the mental image he had of what had just happened. He was lying here, fully clothed including shoes, with a young woman whose blouse was unbuttoned, whose skirt was wrapped around her hips, and whose shoes were presumably still on her feet, too.

It sure as hell didn't fit with his idea of proper behavior for an agent on a case. And it made him grin with a kind of sheepish amusement. There must be life in the old boy yet if he could still carry on like a teenager.

Still, he felt he owed Jessica an apology for letting things get so out of hand. She was bound to feel embarrassed by what had happened. When her head stirred against his shoulder, he looked down at her and found her smiling shyly up at him.

In that moment he understood that she would be embarrassed only if he implied there was something wrong in what they'd done. The apology he'd formed died unspoken, and instead he bowed his head to gently kiss her swollen, smiling lips.

"How do you feel, Jessie?"

"Mmm." A sound like a purr passed her lips, and she snuggled closer, enjoying the intimacy of being held this way by Arlen. He smelled so good, soapy and musky, and felt so hard, warm and strong. Shyly she reached out and ran her palm over his shirtfront, stroking from the center of his chest to his stomach. Just as she reached his waist, Arlen caught her hand and held it.

"Witch," he said, surprising her with his warmly laughing tone. He turned and drew her even closer, confining her hand between their bodies. "You're going to start more trouble."

Jessica glanced at him from beneath her lashes, feeling more attractive and more like a woman than ever before in her life. "Is that so bad?"

That was when Arlen knew he was in real trouble. The rules had been broken, a line had been crossed, and there was no going back. The hell of it was, there was no going forward, either. Somehow he had to make Jessica understand that, and he had to do it without wounding her, a feat that would be even more difficult because of what they'd just done.

"Jessie..."

Jessica tensed. She heard it in his voice and knew he was once more going to tell her there was no future, that this never should have happened. She closed her eyes and thought of the wedding ring he still wore, of the photos on his wall and beside his chair. She thought of each of the things he used as a talisman against involvement and realized that he needed such defenses only because he had once been so devastated. To be desolated in such a way, a person had to be capable of great love.

He was afraid, she thought. Afraid of the pain and loneliness he'd suffered because of his wife's death. He simply didn't want to run the risk of going through that again. Having cobbled together some kind of a life on the ashes of his old one, he wanted to be left undisturbed in the peace he had managed to make for himself.

Jessica understood all too well. She, too, had managed to build herself a relatively safe and comfortable life, and she, too, was reluctant to risk it. Her insides fluttered fearfully at the mere thought. Intuitively, however, she understood that she would have to risk her tranquility and safety if she was to get anywhere at all with Arlen. She was the one who would have to step off the cliff first.

She opened her eyes and looked up at him, forestalling the difficult speech he was trying to formulate. "It's okay," she said. "You don't have to explain yourself all over again, Arlen. I understood the first time."

His gray eyes looked into hers penetratingly, as if he could see past iris and pupil to the thoughts behind. "Do you?" he asked roughly.

"Absolutely. I feel exactly the same way myself."

His hold on her relaxed a little, but his expression remained doubtful. "We need to talk about this, Jess."

"Why?" But she instinctively understood that, as well. Too much had happened. He simply couldn't let it lie any more than she could.

"We just do," he said firmly. "But not right now. Believe it or not, I'm supposed to be working. And I have to get back to the office before the afternoon is over."

He pushed himself to a sitting position and looked down at her, taking in her unbuttoned blouse and the wrinkled skirt that was still tangled around her upper thighs. In spite of himself, he ran his hand along the silky smoothness of her nylon-clad leg. His entire aching body responded in a flash. Idiot!

"I have to take you back to get your car," he said after a moment. "Is it all right if I come by your house this evening?"

"Of course." Suddenly, miserably embarrassed, she sat up, clutching at her blouse and tugging at her skirt. "But I'd really rather not get my car right now. I'll call a cab to take me over there tomorrow. I'm such a mess...."

Feeling like the worst kind of heel, he realized he had to do something or Jessie was going to leave here feeling used. Steeling himself against his body's inevitable reaction, he caught her face between his hands and leaned forward to kiss her gently on the lips. And then he uttered the truth. "You're damn near irresistible, Jessie Kilmer. What the hell am I going to do about you?"

Having the afternoon off gave Jessica an opportunity to finish straightening up the living room as well as time to unpack the boxes Arlen had carried upstairs—was it only *last night?*

She sat back on her heels and stared blindly at the box she had been unpacking. Was she losing her ever-loving mind? Was she actually trying to figure out how to hold a man she had known for less than forty-eight hours?

And what had happened this afternoon in his apartment...! Memory turned her cheeks crimson. She had heard kids talk about doing that in high school—she could even remember the term they had used—but she was *not* in high school. She was supposedly a mature adult!

A groan escaped her, and she pressed her palms to her hot cheeks. Her active imagination had little difficulty painting a vivid picture of the two of them on his couch a few short hours ago. Closing her eyes at the image, she nearly died from the embarrassment even as her body betrayed her by clenching pleasurably.

It was silly to feel embarrassed, she told herself. What they had done had just... happened. It had been a natural outcome of natural feelings. Arlen hadn't been embarrassed by it. Not at all. So *she* didn't need to feel embarrassed, either.

Besides, she thought as her lips curved upward in a shy but satisfied smile, she would never have imagined or even dreamed that it was possible to feel like that. She had certainly never before understood how it was possible to forget caution, modesty and good sense. And now that she had, she wanted to do it again. Soon. With Arlen.

In a burst of girlish exuberance, she threw herself back on the rug beside her bed and flung her arms wide.

All right, she told herself daringly, it was great. Fantastic. Embarrassment aside, she wouldn't have missed it for the world. She had liked all of it, especially being held. It felt *different* to be held by a man. There was a whole range of feelings to the experience that she struggled to find definitions for, feelings that were quite apart from the sexual arousal. And there were so many impressions to remember, sensations that had no words to adequately describe them.

With just the slightest effort, she was able to vividly remember the texture of his faintly scratchy cheek against hers. The way it had felt so right and comfortable to rest her head in the hollow of his shoulder, to rest within the shelter of his arms while she had been so—face it, Jessica—completely and utterly vulnerable. With just that gentle embrace he'd made her feel absolutely safe, as if she could without fear relax her guard and lower her barriers. As if she could safely bare her soul.

Somewhere, she found herself thinking, she'd missed the realization that a man could make her feel safe. On the rare occasions when she had noticed a man as a man, she had felt more threatened than anything. Somehow Arlen had never made her feel that way.

Of course, she told herself, staring up at the ceiling, maybe that was part of his training. Maybe FBI agents took a seminar called "How to Inspire Trust." The notion made her laugh. It was a fact, though, that government agents pretty much looked as if they sprang from the same mold. Six years with a major defense contractor had brought her into brief contact with inspectors from several different investigative branches. Arlen fit the mold in his conservative suit and neatly barbered hair. His restrained manner and politeness, too, were a copy of every other agent she'd met. Some had more personality than others—Arlen certainly had lots of personality—but otherwise you could almost always spot a government agent just by the way he looked and acted. Especially in this Texas city, where only bankers and federal agents actually wore suits. Around here, dressing up meant a white shirt with your jeans, or at best a sports jacket and slacks. It was as if government agents all strove very hard to present an inoffensive, pleasant, courteous exterior that would arouse dislike in no one.

However, Jessica thought, the blandness must be deceiving. People didn't join the FBI by accident. Agents obviously selected the career for a reason, and she suspected it wasn't to become another gray, faceless clone in an army of clones. That image, she thought, was a kind of camouflage. She would willingly have bet that beneath that facade there beat the heart of a James Bond.

What of it? What difference did that make? What mattered right now was that this particular agent had locked himself inside an emotional shell, a shell that she had no business disturbing for her own frivolous reasons. At this point, the only thing she had any right to want was a chance to get to know Arlen, and a chance for him to get to know her.

And he was probably going to make darn sure they never had the chance. That had certainly been part of the speech she had managed to forestall. In fact, something about the way he had looked at her when he dropped her off here made her think that he was going to find a way of avoiding her as much as possible. He was going to put a professional distance between them somehow, because what was happening between them was troubling his conscience.

Which brought Jessica around to something even more troublesome. After just two short days and a few very short meetings, she felt a peculiar hollowness in the vicinity of her breastbone when she thought of never seeing Arlen again.

She couldn't possibly feel an emotional attachment for a man she had just met—could she?

No, of course not. Love at first sight was a romantic myth based on hindsight, not foresight. An abiding love had to grow slowly, had to be nurtured gently. The first attraction was pure chemistry, nothing more.

But, oh, what chemistry!

Jessica sat up and crossed her legs, aware that her heart was beating a nervous tattoo in time with the butterflies flitting in her stomach. There was only one way to get the chance to know Arlen. Anything else would fail, she was sure. In her heart, she knew he was coming to see her tonight only so he could ask her one more time to act as a double agent if the opportunity arose. If she refused yet again, he would say goodbye and mean it. Arlen Coulter would turn and walk out of her life for good.

So what? she asked herself. Even if she did agree to become a double agent, even if Greg Leong actually asked her to pass classified information, what difference would it make? She would get to know Arlen better, and he would get to know her, but that wouldn't transform her from an ugly duckling into a swan. She had her share of good points, but none of them made her attractive as a woman. Arlen might come to actually like her—people *did* like her—but he wasn't about to fall madly in love with her. So why bother to take the risk in the first place?

Licking her suddenly dry lips, Jessica looked down at her hands and listened to the thunder of her heartbeat. It would be a double risk, really, being a double agent and exposing herself to the possibility of heartbreak. She didn't know which frightened her more.

But perhaps there came a time when sensible, cautious, *safe* alternatives no longer sufficed. Perhaps there were times when one had to accept a dare. Perhaps that was the only difference between living life and living death.

And that was why she was going to go after Arlen Coulter.

* * *

During his senior year in high school Arlen had spent every spare minute of his weekends and evenings repairing cars. He worked out of the back lot of the tenement where he lived with his father, charged a little less than established garages and built up a thriving business. By the August before his senior year he was able to afford his heart's desire: a Harley Davidson chopper, a marvelous chrome-and-black-metal machine that roared down the highways of upstate New York like a bat out of hell.

Motorcycles of any kind weren't a common sight in the small agricultural town where he grew up. A Harley inspired fear and anger in the older folks, including his alcoholic father and Lucy's parents. *Going to hell* was Lucy's father's opinion of Arlen after that, a downward step for Arlen, who up until that point had been ranked slightly above thieves and mass murderers.

Lucy had claimed to understand his love for his bike, but she would never get on it, and she begged him not to ride it anywhere her parents might see him. Within reason he'd complied, but after his return from Vietnam he'd given up riding it entirely. Somehow, when he looked at his tiny daughter or at his wife's stomach, swelling with their son, he had felt it was irresponsible to ride that bike. Irresponsible to take such unnecessary risks with his neck, his life and his livelihood. Two children and their mother depended on him, and in that moment of understanding he had shrugged off the last remnant of childhood.

Ever since, Arlen had cherished his bike the way a collector cherishes a priceless car. He moved it wherever the Bureau sent him, and kept it polished and in mint condition. Every couple of months he would pull it out of the garage, turn the engine over and listen to the full-throated roar. And then, after washing, waxing and tuning it up, he would wheel it back into the garage.

When Arlen arrived home that afternoon he was thinking it was time to take the Harley out again. Tomorrow morning, he decided. Maybe he would even ride it. If anything happened to him now, both Melanie and Andrew were capable of taking care of themselves. No more guilt on that score, Luce, he said silently to his wife's portrait as he tugged off his tie.

Turning toward the bedroom, he paused midstep and stared at the couch. Some traitorous part of his mind presented him with a clear picture of how Jessica Kilmer had looked lying there just a few short hours ago. No, damn it, he didn't feel guilty about that, either!

But he wouldn't risk the chance of a recurrence. And he would be damned if he was going to waste any more time reminding himself of all the reasons why he couldn't allow things to get out of hand again.

He changed into jeans and a black turtleneck pullover and tugged on his black boots. Maybe he would get the Harley out of storage tonight, he thought as he microwaved a frozen burrito. Maybe he'd ride it over to Jessica's. The evening was dry, cool but not too cool. A good night for a bike ride.

By the time he peeled out of the Texan Self-Store parking lot, the sky was a carpet of stars. The Harley growled powerfully beneath him, a primitive, potent throb. Arlen wished for open, empty roads stretching ahead like ribbons in the moonlight.

Instead he drove directly to Jessica's house, determined to make one more bid to convince her to act as a double agent if Greg Leong approached her again. He also, he thought uncomfortably, had to find a way to make sure that she didn't feel he had used her this afternoon. It certainly hadn't been his intent, but he could see how that might be difficult to believe. A man just shouldn't get that intimate with a lady unless he wanted a future with her.

Jessica was in her kitchen making a fresh pot of coffee when she heard the motorcycle pull up in the driveway just outside the kitchen door where she usually parked her car. She recognized the distinctive growl of a Harley immediately—her college roommate's boyfriend had owned one—and her first thought was to escape. She didn't know a soul right now who owned a motorcycle, and no well-intentioned stranger would pull up to her back door like this. Her head full of disconnected images of violence drawn from movies, she hesitated just long enough for Arlen to reach the back door. The inner door was open, and he peered in through the screen.

"Jessica?"

She whirled around, hand flying to her throat. "Arlen! My word, you scared me!"

"Scared you?"

He almost scared her now, she realized. The FBI agent had completely vanished. At her back door stood an outlaw in snug jeans, motorcycle boots and a leather bomber jacket. His neatly barbered hair was wind tossed and wild, and there was a strange silver gleam in his gray eyes.

"Jessie? What's wrong?" He pulled the screen door open and stepped into her kitchen, a frown knitting his brow. "What happened?"

"What happened?" she repeated. "What happened?" Indignation began to fill her breast, largely because she now felt foolish for being frightened. "I'll tell you what happened!" She crossed the kitchen and poked her index finger at the center of his chest, which was right on her nose level. "I was standing here, minding my own business, when suddenly a motorcycle pulled up to my back door. Not my front door, mind, where most guests arrive, but my back door. And who, I wondered, could possibly be pulling up to my back door, unless he meant something... something..."

"Unsavory?" Arlen suggested, beginning to grin. "Something violent and bloody right out of a horror film?"

"Yes!" She tipped her head back and glared up at him. "No one, absolutely no one, expects an FBI agent to arrive on a Harley Davidson!"

"I'll grant you that," he agreed, his grin broadening. "Used to be we had to drive four-door American sedans. These days they let us drive anything. Fools the KGB every time."

Jessica blinked, forgetting her annoyance. "What fools the KGB?"

Arlen moved before he could stop himself and brushed a stray tendril of silky dark hair back from her cheek. "The KGB thinks all FBI agents drive four-door American-made sedans. There was a time when that was true, but not anymore.

"Sometimes it works in our favor. A few years ago a colleague of mine stopped off at a convenience store on his way to work, some little place on the Virginia side of the Potomac. He noticed a car with Russian embassy plates in the parking lot and got suspicious, because it was well out of the usual stomping grounds for embassy personnel. He followed the car for miles, and the Russian never suspected he was being followed because my friend was driving a Honda hatchback. Turned out the Russian was going out to pick up a drop from a spy, and because of that little incident we got tipped to quite a large espionage operation."

Jessica searched his face. "You're not serious."

"I'm perfectly serious, Jessie. Truth is stranger than fiction. I've got loads of stories like that."

"Tell me another one," she suggested hopefully. She liked this side of him, she thought. She hadn't realized before that he was a man who could see the ridiculous side of a job he clearly believed to be important. He was smiling that crooked smile right now, and it reached all the way into the depths of his gray eyes, easing a tension there that she only recognized now that it was absent.

"Well, I can tell you about the two would-be spies who called the Secret Service in the middle of a Saturday night to announce they had possession of a Top Secret document that they would be quite happy to give to the Secret Service for the sum of twenty thousand dollars. Otherwise they'd sell it to the Russians."

Jessica's eyes were huge. "What happened?"

"The Secret Service agent argued that he couldn't possibly get twenty thousand dollars and talked them down to five thousand. Then he talked them into waiting until Monday to make the exchange, because he had to get to a bank for the money. The two guys agreed, and the agent called the FBI. We got the money and arrested the guys as soon as they made the exchange."

"Unbelievable!"

Arlen shook his head, still smiling. "I can tell you even less believable things. Take the CIA employee who worked in communications but really wanted to be a secret agent. The CIA didn't think he had what it took, so this fellow set out to prove he *did*. He sat down next to a perfect stranger in a Georgetown bar one night and offered to sell him a highly classified document."

Jessica was shaking her head in disbelief. "And?" she demanded.

"And the guy he spoke to was an FBI agent from the Criminal Investigations Division."

"No!" Jessica shook her head again. "No."

"Yes." Arlen chuckled. "Needless to say, the agent set up the exchange for the next day, and as soon as the document and money changed hands, we arrested the SOB."

Jessie looked cute, Arlen thought, as she stood there torn between disbelief and amusement. Finally her laughter won. It was when she laughed that he realized she wasn't wearing a bra under that loose red blouse. His groin tightened.

"I'm sorry I scared you," he said abruptly, his own humor fading. "I just never thought about it. I haven't ridden that damn bike in over twenty years, and tonight just seemed a perfect evening to try it out again."

Jessica moved around him and flicked on the back porch light so she could peer out through the screen at the huge black-and-chrome bike. "She's a beauty, Arlen," she told him sincerely. "Why haven't you ridden in so long? Have you kept that same bike all this time?"

"I've had that same bike since I was seventeen." He came to stand behind her and looked out at the Harley. "I haven't ridden it since I came back from Nam."

"Why not?" Jessica twisted her head to look up at him over her shoulder.

He shifted uneasily. Some things just weren't easy for a man to say out loud. "Riding a bike is a foolhardy risk for a man with a family."

"And now your family's grown," she remarked.

"That's right."

She spun around and looked shyly up at him from beneath her lashes, unaware of how flirtatious she looked. "What does a lady have to do to get a ride on that bike?" Her heart practically climbed into her throat, but she had promised herself she was going to take this chance, that she wasn't going to let this man walk away without at least putting up a fight to get his full attention. Darn, being a double agent couldn't possibly be half this nerve-racking!

For a moment he didn't answer. His eyes swept over her face, absorbing every detail, from the smooth, shell pink of her cheeks to the long, thick lashes shadowing her bright brown eyes. Wasn't he supposed to be restoring this relationship to a more businesslike level? Instead he felt he was entirely losing his grip on matters.

Finally he answered. "A lady needs a helmet," he said, and immediately wanted to kick himself as his mind filled with a lush image of Jessica clinging to his waist from behind, her thighs pressed against his, her breasts crushed against his back as they roared down the road.

"You couldn't be persuaded to overlook the helmet just once?" she asked.

Arlen shook his head, his eyes locked on hers. "Sorry. The law says you have to have a helmet, and I wouldn't take the risk with you, anyway, Jessie. No way."

She sighed, clearly disappointed. "I always wanted to ride on a Harley."

"Tomorrow," Arlen heard himself say. "I'll get you a helmet and give you a ride over to MTI to get your car. How does that sound?"

The shy smile returned to her face. "You really wouldn't mind?"

Yes, he would, some rational part of his mind pointed out. He would mind it a whole hell of a lot just as soon as Jessica was mounted on that bike behind him. Hell, he was minding it just thinking about how it would feel. "No trouble," he said firmly. "Maybe we'll even detour onto some country roads if the weather is nice enough."

Jessica clapped her hands together in frank delight. "Fantastic!"

Her eyes were positively shining as she looked up at him. Looking into them, Arlen could feel all his resolutions weakening. Maybe he should assign one of the other agents to this case. Maybe he should walk out that door right now and never look back. And maybe he should just give up and thank God that Jessie Kilmer had walked into his life. Because, painful though it was, he couldn't regret waking up from the numbness of the past few years. Conscience aside, job aside, *everything* aside, at this moment he was damn glad to be alive.

Jessica heard the hiss that always signaled the coffee maker had finished brewing. Embarrassed to suddenly realize she had been staring at Arlen, she took a quick sideways step and hurried across the kitchen.

"Coffee's ready," she said brightly. "Would you like some?"

"Yes. Please." Her back was turned toward him as she busied herself with the cups, and Arlen took a moment to collect himself. He should have come over here wearing a suit and driving the damn sedan, he told himself. Getting on the bike had been a big mistake, because it had made him feel young and hungry and a little sad, almost exactly the way he'd felt at seventeen. Restless and empty, as if he'd lost something important and couldn't quite remember what it was. Luce had quieted those feelings; that was the main reason he'd married her.

"Why don't we go sit in the living room?" Jessica suggested.

Arlen nodded agreeably and accepted the cup of coffee she offered him. Following her out of the kitchen, across the entry hall and into the living room, he listened to the clomp of his boots on her bare wood floors and wondered if he were suffering from some sort of midlife crisis. When Jessica perched on the couch he promptly took the armchair, setting a safe distance between them, a distance in which the coffee table served as a boundary.

"Okay," she said and set her cup on the table.

"Okay?" he repeated questioningly. "Okay *what?*"

"Okay, I'll do it."

The cup paused on its journey to his mouth, and his gray eyes narrowed. "Spell it out, Jess. You'll be a double agent for us if the opportunity arises? Is that what you mean?"

Twisting her fingers together, she nodded. "Yes. I will. If you're sure there's no real danger. I'm a coward, Arlen. I kid you not. If things get scary, I'll fall to pieces."

He leaned forward, placed his cup on the table and rested his elbows on his knees, hands dangling loosely between his thighs. "It'll be nerve-racking at times, Jessie. I won't kid you about that. But it's not dangerous. Never, ever, has anyone been hurt while acting as a double agent for us. In fact, I'll go even further than that. Foreign intelligence operatives have never, ever, harmed a U.S. citizen on U.S. soil."

"Never?"

"Never." His gaze was steady and unwavering. "These operatives aren't thugs who've been dug up out of the gutter, you know. They're the best their countries have to offer. They're highly educated, politically savvy, very decent, very dedicated people." He gave her his crooked smile. "In fact, the only difference between most of them and most of us is ideology."

"You talk like you know them."

"I know quite a few of them. In Washington we all attended the same parties, and we talked shop with one another."

Jessica kicked off her shoes and curled her legs beneath her. "So there's no danger at all?" she asked, feeling inexplicably disappointed. Good grief, she didn't *want* to be in any danger—did she?

"What do you want me to say, Jessie? Nobody can guarantee the future one hundred percent. There's always a possibility that things could be different just this once, but it's a slim one. The thing you really need to understand is that the opposition stands to lose more than it could ever gain if it hurt you. In order to get Americans to cooperate with them, they have to be able to make them feel perfectly safe. How can they do that if they act like thugs? Who would *ever* spy for them?"

She searched his face, more because she was hungry to look at him than because she thought she would discover some hint that he was being less than honest with her. He wasn't a conventionally handsome man, but she wouldn't have found him attractive if he had been. "Okay. It's not dangerous."

"You won't be doing this alone, Jessie," Arlen said, hearing an uncertain note in her voice. "The only time you'll be on your own will be the next time Leong approaches you—if he does. Once he's introduced an agent to you, they won't take you by surprise again. Each and every meeting will be arranged in advance and designed to gain your confidence."

"How can you know that?"

He couldn't hold still for another second. Conflicting impulses pulled at him, tugging him this way and that, and there wasn't a one of them he could heed—because, damn it, he was on a case, and he needed this woman to act as a double agent. He could neither reach out and haul her into his arms nor stride from the house and ride his Harley into emotional oblivion somewhere out on the interstate.

Arlen rose to his feet with a quickness that deprived the movement of any nonchalance. Watching him pace around the living room, Jessica was reminded of a caged lion. She had sensed his tension the instant he had walked through her door, and she had the distinct impression that he was growing less relaxed by the minute.

"I can be sure," Arlen said in answer to her question, "because once the agent is introduced to you, one of his primary tasks is going to be getting your complete trust. He's going to want you to feel as safe as a baby in a cradle around him, and he can't achieve that if you get surprised in any way. He'll know, though, that you aren't going to pass classified information to someone you don't trust."

Jessica folded her arms beneath her breasts and shook her head. "It's absurd to discuss trust and treason in the same breath."

His mouth framed one of his crooked smiles, but he never paused in his restless circumnavigation of her living room. "I doubt that'll be the last absurdity you encounter.'' He thrust his hands deep into his pockets and paused before the fireplace to study the framed miniatures on the mantelpiece. ''Are all these folks your family?'' They were all old pictures, many from around the turn of the century, but there was no other common thread to them.

''None of them are family. I picked them up in various antique shops.''

Why? He almost asked the question, then caught himself. An investigator's natural curiosity could too easily lead him to ask questions that shouldn't be asked. Which reminded him. Turning, he faced Jessica.

''There are two things I wanted to tell you,'' he said.

She watched him draw up in some inexplicable way. It was almost as if he somehow closed up on himself to become the clone again. Suddenly his rough motorcycle clothes looked like a costume, and Arlen Coulter looked every inch the FBI agent.

''First,'' he said, ''Vicki Grier called the Bureau this afternoon to report that Barron had been investigating your missing document just prior to his death. She reported it stolen.''

Jessica sat up straighter. ''She did? How did she know? She didn't come with Barron when he talked to me, and he was convinced it was just mislaid.''

''Evidently he had a few doubts about that, because he started writing a report that concealed none of the facts, and that included all your statements about being sure it had been there the night before. Grier came across the report this afternoon when she was looking through Barron's office for some other paperwork. She called us right away.''

''Did you tell her I have the report?''

Arlen shook his head. ''I don't want anyone to know you're involved with the Bureau except possibly on a personal level, remember? I didn't say a thing about it. You call her on Monday and tell her you found it. At this point, she's certainly not going to believe you mislaid it, so don't worry about it. And she'll keep quiet about the incident because I asked her to.''

Jessica was dismayed to realize her main reaction to all of this was jealousy. Vicki Grier was a lovely woman with hair the color of sun-drenched honey and a figure Jessica could have achieved only through major plastic surgery. She was also unattached and closer to Arlen's age. "You're sure she's trustworthy?" As soon as the question escaped her, she felt like a jealous vixen and was embarrassed by it.

Arlen noticed that Jessica's bright eyes seemed to dim a little, but that was none of his business, so he didn't ask. A professional distance. He would keep it if it killed him.

"On this, at least. Otherwise she wouldn't have called the Bureau. It would have been the easiest thing in the world for her to disclaim all knowledge of the missing document, since it's apparent that Barron hadn't told anyone about it before he died. Which is another odd circumstance."

"It sounds as if Barron may have been involved in this somehow," Jessica said.

"Well, that's what's odd about it," Arlen admitted. "On the one hand, he was writing a report that would seem to indicate he was on the up-and-up. On the other, he didn't mention the missing document to his assistant." He shrugged and shoved his hands into his pockets, reminding himself not to talk too freely. Details of any investigation were confidential.

"The other thing," he said, "is that we did a BI—background investigation—on you."

"Me?" Startled, Jessica stiffened. "What kind of background investigation?"

"Something like what you had to go through to get your Top Secret clearance, but we didn't go into as much detail, since your clearance record contained most of your past history. A credit check, Jess. That kind of thing."

"Did you find out anything interesting?" she asked.

His smile didn't quite edge past the corners of his mouth. "Depends on what you mean by interesting, Jessie. I learned that you invested a huge portion of your savings in this house, and that some people could conceivably think you might be strapped for cash."

Jessica gasped. "That's not true!"

"I didn't say it was. I said it could be construed that way. That may be one of the reasons you've been targeted—they think they might have a lever."

She was outraged. "You mean these...these *foreign agents* can find out about my finances? About things like that?"

"All they have to do is check with a credit bureau. Any car salesman can do that on the PC at his desk, Jess. What makes you think the KGB or any other intelligence group is going to be able to do any less?"

He spoke reasonably, but he understood her distress. Most people didn't think about things like this, even when they went to buy a car or a house. It never occurred to them that anyone could find out these kinds of intimate details, or that the information could be used for unsavory purposes.

She looked up at him, and there was something almost hurt in her expression. She had lost a little of her innocence. "Do you think that's why Greg Leong approached me? Do *you* think I'm strapped enough for cash to sell out my country?"

"God, no, Jess!" He shook his head. "Of *course* I don't. I'm just telling you what may be behind this recruitment attempt. That's all. *They* may think you might be interested in making a little money, that's all. They're always on the lookout for something like that."

He shoved his hands deeper into his pockets. "Want to hear an ironic story? At least, I've always thought it was ironic. Probably the most ironic case I've ever worked on, and I've worked on more than a few."

Distracted from her unhappy realization that there was no such thing as privacy, Jessica nodded. "Sure."

"A naval officer in the Washington area found himself seriously short of money. The details don't matter, but he needed twenty-five thousand, and he needed it fast. He happened to know a naval attaché at the Soviet embassy, so he arranged to meet the guy for lunch. And he asked the Soviet to set up a meeting for him with a KGB official."

Arlen shook his head. "Would you believe that the Soviet offered to lend the American the money? Would you believe he told the American, 'You really don't want to sell out your country for money.'" Arlen shook his head yet again. "It's small wonder the other side thinks Americans will do anything for a little money. They see us do it all the time."

He looked down at her sitting there all curled up, arms folded beneath deliciously full breasts, feet tucked up under her. His groin stirred, and some traitorous portion of his mind reminded him that this delectable morsel of a woman had welcomed his advances only a few hours ago. Upstairs there was a white satin comforter.... Hell! He still didn't know what she looked like with her hair down. He couldn't possibly be contemplating that degree of intimacy with a woman whom he'd never even seen with her hair down.

Oh, yes, he could, some undeluded corner of his mind acknowledged. The problem was that he was a gentleman, and a gentleman didn't take liberties like that with a lady. And Jessica was a lady.

Having succeeded in making himself feel guilty, he was able to pick up his jacket and pull it on.

"I'll come by in the morning," he said, moving toward the door. "Is nine too early?"

"No." Disturbed by his abrupt departure, she unfolded herself and rose to her feet. "Nine is fine. But I can call a cab, Arlen," she said, making the offer even though she didn't want to. "You don't have to go out of your way."

He managed a fleeting smile. "No problem, Jessie. It's my fault your car is at MTI. Besides, I promised you a ride on my bike. See you in the morning."

He was gone before she could say another word. Whatever had gotten into him? she wondered. The silent, empty house offered no answer.

Chapter 6

Jessica stared at her reflection in the full-length mirror and acknowledged glumly that no amount of wishing would make her look really good in jeans. There was simply too much of her to ever achieve that long, lean look for which jeans were meant. Still, she couldn't very well wear anything else on a motorcycle. She compromised by selecting an oversize blouse that would cover her below her hips. Sins that couldn't be banished could be hidden. Her hair, as usual, she pulled into the severe chignon she'd been wearing since she turned sixteen and discovered a need to be taken seriously.

The March day was turning into one of those spectacular days that were so common this time of year in central Texas. The sun was warm, steadily burning off the night's chill, and the temperature promised to hit a perfect seventy-five or eighty degrees.

A perfect day for a picnic, she thought. It had been years since she'd gone on a picnic. There was no point in going on one alone, and these days all her friends were married or getting married or living together. There was, she freely admitted, nothing as boring as somebody else's twosome, and nothing as boring to a pair as a single friend. But, oh, how nice it would be to go on a picnic.

Nice or not, however, she didn't have the nerve to suggest it. She'd used up every bit of her nerve and self-confidence last night when she had asked Arlen to give her a ride on his bike.

Arlen was resigned, after struggling with himself half the night, to the intimacy he was going to have to endure with Jessica today. He had, after all, promised by implication to take her out riding in the countryside today, and the weather obviously wasn't going to give him a convenient excuse.

Standing on her back porch, looking down into her smiling, eager face, he decided there could be far worse fates than spending a chaste day with Jessica. There was, for example, the fate of spending a gorgeous Saturday alone with himself.

"Why don't we go on a picnic?" he heard himself suggest out of the clear blue sky. Coulter, you're losing your mind, he told himself. But he watched the smile widen on her lovely face, and saw the color bloom in her cheeks, and some part of him decided he wasn't losing his mind, after all. Hell, maybe he was finally becoming sane. "A picnic would be nice, don't you think?"

"I'll need to stop at the store," she said in what she hoped was a cheerfully brisk tone. She absolutely didn't want him to guess how much that simple invitation meant to her.

"No problem," he said. "What do you like to take for a picnic, Jess?"

"Cheese and crackers?" she suggested tentatively. "I don't know. Whatever sounds good to you. They have a nice deli at Corbett's."

"Let's go look, then." Taking her elbow, he drew her down the steps to the Harley. She looked good, he thought in spite of himself. She fairly glowed with health and vitality, and her hair shone in the sunlight. He noted the over-size blouse and, with the wisdom of a man who'd been married for better than twenty years, he knew immediately why she was wearing it. The understanding tugged at him in an uncomfortable way. Damn it, he found himself thinking, this was the lady he'd twice lost his control over, something he hadn't done in better than a quarter century. This was the lady he'd all but made love to on his couch yesterday because she was so damn sexy. And she believed... Hell's bells, he couldn't even complete the thought, it made him so damn mad.

Grabbing up the helmet he had bought first thing this morning, he turned and settled it on Jessica's head. It was one of the souped-up helmets with a faceplate and chin guard, and he'd selected it because riding a motorcycle was dangerous even when driven by skilled hands. If anything happened, that helmet would be Jessie's only protection, and he wasn't going to risk her lovely face.

"Does it feel okay?" he asked her as he straightened it and reached to fasten the chin strap.

"I guess." She laughed, a small, breathless sound. "I've never worn a helmet before. I don't have any way to judge."

His mouth pulled into one of his crooked smiles. "It should feel snug, but it shouldn't hurt." He tugged on it a little.

"Snug," she said, "and it doesn't hurt. It's okay, I guess."

He showed her where to put her foot, warned her about the hot exhaust pipes and helped her onto the bike. Jessica sat on the broad saddle and reached behind her, trying to hang on to the metal backrest.

"Uh-uh, Jess," Arlen said. Reaching around, he tugged at one of her hands and guided it to his waist. "Hang on to me," he said. "I want to know exactly where you are. And when I lean, lean with me, even if your instincts say to go the other way."

"Okay." Excitement and a little fear had her heart fluttering wildly, and her mouth was getting as dry as a bone. She couldn't remember ever having done anything this daring before.

When Arlen had strapped his own helmet on, he kick-started the Harley, then settled back onto the saddle. "Hang on, Jess," he shouted over the bike's roar.

Obediently, she leaned forward and wrapped her arms around his waist. She tried to hold on loosely, but as soon as the bike started to roll forward she tightened her grip and pressed herself snugly up against Arlen's back.

Yep, he thought, it was going to be sheer hell. Jessica's thighs embraced his intimately. He tried not to think about which part of her anatomy was cradling his tush. How, he wondered, could a man of forty-two be so damn horny? He was sure he hadn't been this consistently hot since his early twenties.

The Corbett's Supermarket wasn't far, and it was with relief that Arlen pulled into a parking slot. How the hell was he going to handle this all day? Five minutes had just about turned him into a raving maniac. He would have to call off this outing.

But Jessica was smiling brightly when he helped her out of her helmet, and her eyes were glowing with excitement. He doubted he'd seen a happier face since first thing on Christmas morning when his kids had been little. Nope, he was just going to have to rely on good sense and self-control to get him through this one.

"That was fantastic!" she enthused as he reached out to steady her. Swinging her leg over the bike wasn't hard, but her foot slipped.

He caught her. It was either that or let her fall to the pavement. His hands snatched her right under her arms, and he hauled her up against his chest. Hard met soft, and the world spun away with dizzying speed.

"Jessie..." Her name slipped past his lips on a barely audible sigh. He looked down into her brown eyes, eyes that seemed to glow with their own inner light. He felt his body tightening, swelling, hardening, for her, even as something deep inside seemed to open wide to the warmth of her light. God, she was soft...so soft.

With a boldness that astonished her even as she did it, Jessica reached up and captured Arlen's head, slipping her hands into his soft hair, tugging his head down to her. Intuitively, she understood that he had to know that she wanted this, too, that he wasn't somehow taking advantage of her. "Please," she whispered.

A car's backfire jolted him back to reality. They were standing in a parking lot, for crying out loud, and he'd forgotten that simply because he was holding her. This lady was dangerous. Carefully he set her on her feet and stepped back.

He also realized he had given her the right to demand his kisses. He had given her the right yesterday on his living-room couch. And somehow he didn't want to take it back. Damn it, she was making him feel desirable. Desirable and alive.

"Later, bright eyes," he heard himself say. Reaching out, he cupped her cheek briefly, gently. "Let's go get our picnic."

Later. Jessica hugged the word, felt her heart leap at the promise. Then Arlen took her hand, and she was sure she was walking on air. What had happened to all his resistance? What had changed his mind? Glancing sideways and upward, she studied his profile as they entered the store, but there was nothing there to illuminate the change.

Arlen grabbed a hand basket from the stack just inside the door. "Crackers and cheese," he said. "What about some wine? Do you like wine? Any particular kind?"

Jessica, who'd had a glass of wine exactly twice in her sheltered life, both times in the company of her girl-friends, thought it sounded romantic, but she frankly didn't like wine. "Get whatever you like," she said.

Gray eyes settled thoughtfully on her face. "You don't like wine, do you? Be honest, Jess."

"Not really," she admitted. "But if you like it—"

His crooked smile reappeared, one corner of his mouth tugging upward, the other tugging down. "I'm driving, remember? I won't drink anything, anyway."

They were rounding the corner at the end of an aisle, headed toward the cheese counter, when Jessica nearly tripped over her own feet. "Arlen!" she whispered and quickly darted down another aisle, dragging him with her.

He was quick, mentally and physically. His work required it, of course, but he'd been blessed with more than average abilities in those departments. Most people would have immediately started demanding to know what was going on. He simply followed swiftly, allowing Jessica to take her evasive action without hindrance. Questions could wait.

Halfway down the aisle, she stopped. Pulling him with her over to the very edge of the aisle, she faced him.

"It was him," she said breathlessly. Her heart was hammering fit to burst, and she felt as if all the air had vanished. This was it, the moment she hadn't really believed in.

"Him? Leong?"

She nodded.

"No doubt?"

She shook her head. "It's him. I'm sure of it."

She was still clinging to his hand with a drowning man's grip, so Arlen wrapped his other arm around her shoulders and pulled her close. To hell with what people thought.

"Will you be all right, Jess?"

She nodded. "In a minute. Just a minute." She had expected to feel nervous if this moment came, but she hadn't expected to feel so frightened. Resting her cheek against Arlen's chest, listening to the creaking sound of his leather jacket as he moved his arm to rub her back soothingly, she felt the fear subside to a tolerable level.

"Nothing's going to happen, honey," he was saying. "This is a public place. What can he possibly do? Besides, he's just a student."

Besides, Jessica thought, *you're* here. That thought gave her more courage than anything. "I'm okay." She would have been happy to let him hold her like this forever, but it just wasn't possible. Taking a deep breath, she stepped back and met Arlen's eyes. "Let's go see if he says anything."

He touched a finger to her cheek. "Are you sure about this? You don't have to."

"I said I'd do it and I will." She squared her shoulders visibly.

He smiled faintly. "Gutsy lady. I'll hang back so I don't keep him from speaking to you. I'll only be a half dozen steps away, Jess."

"What's he going to do to me?" she said, managing a nonchalant shrug. "Public place, right? Plenty of people around, right? My own personal G-man nearby, right?"

Arlen chuckled. "Right."

He stationed himself at the head of the aisle, pretending a fascination for seven or eight different kinds of rice. From there he watched Jessica walk over to the cheese counter.

Greg Leong, instantly recognizable from a photo Arlen had managed to get his hands on, stood only a few steps farther away, at a table of baked goods. It was apparent to Arlen, who'd spent more time on stakeouts than he wanted to recall, that Leong was on a kind of stakeout himself. He looked bored and not at all interested in baked goods. He was no more going to buy an angel food cake than Arlen was going to buy rice. In fact, Leong was so obviously waiting for something or someone that Arlen dismissed any possibility that the man was an agent himself. Leong's actions were clearly those of an amateur.

Jessica was a lot more believable, possibly because she really *was* buying cheese. She was mulling over two brands of Edam when Greg turned away from the cakes and spied her. At once his face brightened and he wasted no time but approached her immediately.

"That rice you're holding doesn't taste as good as this brand, young man," said a gray-haired lady on Arlen's right.

He glanced at her, sensing that the quickest way to deal with her was to agree. "You're absolutely right," he said quickly and exchanged the package of rice he was holding for one of the brand the lady was pointing out to him. "Thanks."

Now he had to move or look suspicious. What was it about supermarkets? he wondered. Dressed as he was, no woman in the world would have ventured to speak to him except here in a supermarket. In the past four years he'd learned that it didn't matter how disreputable he might look. Let him linger over the produce counter or hesitate over the cleaning supplies, and some woman would immediately advise him.

Giving the helpful lady a smile, he moved around the end of the aisle and feigned an interest in angel food. Leong was saying something to Jessica, and she was smiling, nodding pleasantly.

Arlen picked up a cake and sauntered over to them. Now, he decided, was as good a time as any to establish his and Jessica's supposed relationship. That way, he could be with her whenever it seemed necessary without being out of place.

"Hi, Jessie," he said as he reached her side. She jumped visibly, startled by his approach. She hadn't expected him to take part in this. Covering, Arlen quickly slipped his arm around her. "Is something wrong? Is this guy bothering you?"

"Bothering me?" she repeated blankly.

Clearly, Arlen thought, joining these two had not been one of his brighter ideas. Hell, he should have guessed he would rattle Jessie. But she surprised him then, looking first at him and then back at Leong. He could almost see her brain slip back into gear.

"No, he's not bothering me," she said swiftly. "Greg is one of Professor Kostermeyer's students. You remember Kostermeyer, Arlen?"

"Yeah, sure," he agreed, and started to smile. The smile evidently reassured Leong, who had started to back away. The younger man returned the smile. Arlen offered his hand. "Arlen Coulter."

"Greg Leong," said the student in crisply British English.

Arlen looked down at Jessica. "You about ready, Jess?"

"In just a minute." Darn, the palms of her hands were damp, her mouth was as dry as cotton balls and at the moment she didn't know who was making her more nervous, Arlen or Leong. "Greg and I were talking about getting together for lunch next week."

"Oh?" Arlen looked at Leong.

Leong nodded quickly. "Yes. I wished to ask Ms. Kilmer for some more details on the paper she published last year regarding external heap sorts. A brilliant algorithm, but there are a few details I wish to clarify, if she will be so kind."

All of which was out of Arlen's bailiwick. "She's the person to ask, all right," he said easily. "I'll get that cheese,

Jessie." Giving Leong a nod, he turned and moved a little farther down the counter.

Looking down at the cheeses, Arlen listened as Jessica and Leong arranged a lunch date. Deciding he couldn't decide, either, he snatched up a piece of cheese at random and stuffed it into the basket with the rice and the cake he didn't want. Weird picnic stuff. He looked back just in time to see Leong walking away. Jessica turned to him.

"I did it," she said, and expelled a long, relieved breath.

"Let's talk about it later, Jess," Arlen said. There was always a possibility that Leong hadn't come here alone. Someone else might have accompanied him solely for the purpose of "making" Jessica—in other words, having Leong point her out to him. That was often the case when an approach was made this way. Even though the contact was completed now, that person might still be watching.

Jessica was willing to follow his direction unquestioningly for the moment. After all, he was an experienced agent and she was a software engineer.

Instead she asked, "Why in the world did you get a bag of rice?"

Arlen shrugged. "There was this lady—never mind. You'll never believe it."

"And a cake. Do you like angel food?"

"I can't stand it."

"Then why...?" Looking up at him, she let her words trail off. There was a very definite sparkle of humor in his gray eyes. "Never mind," she said.

"It's too damn sweet, to be honest about it," he said cordially. "I'll take a devil's food cake any day. But I picked it up, so I'm buying it, just like I'm buying the rice. Do you want any kind of cheese besides Edam?"

Between them, they chose two more cheeses, and then they had a friendly wrangle over what kind of bread they should buy. Arlen contended that no Texan knew the true meaning of French or Italian bread, and that he wanted no part of either. It would have to be rye bread or nothing. Then he spied the fried chicken, and she watched in silent dismay as he bought some. Her mind was totting up calories so fast that she felt she ought to run before it was too late. Cheese was sinful enough. How had she gotten into this?

"So tell me, Arlen," she said as they walked back out to the parking lot. "Where do we put this stuff?" She couldn't imagine how she would hang on to him and two plastic grocery bags at the same time.

"Voilà!" With a key and a flourish, he opened a compartment beneath the seat and amazed her by being able to fit everything into it with ease—except the cake, which he ruthlessly flattened.

"Okay, Jessie," he said, once again putting her helmet on her head and fastening it. "Let's go tear up the roads."

It might have been years since Arlen had roared down an open country road feeling wild and free, but those years rolled back that morning as if they'd never been. For nearly three hours he drove them along a maze of ranch roads and farm-to-market roads that led them deeper and deeper into the hill country.

It was after noon when he slowed the Harley down and pulled over beneath a shady live oak tree beyond which a creek could be seen bubbling along. Past the creek there was a barbed-wire fence, and beyond that were a few dozen placid-looking cows.

Arlen looked more relaxed than Jessica had ever seen him. A big, flat table of limestone rose from the creek bank, carved out by many years of spring floods. He discarded his jacket and stretched out on the rock in a puddle of sunshine.

Pillowing his head on his hands, he closed his eyes and sighed deeply. "Heaven," he said. And it was. Years and tensions, griefs and angers, all the baggage he'd been carrying for so long seemed to have blown away. It was just simply, absolutely wonderful to be alive on such a perfect day in such a perfect place, doing exactly what he wanted to, no more and no less.

It *was* heaven, Jessica thought. Free for the first time in their brief acquaintance to feast her eyes on him, she sat cross-legged beside him and did just that.

Powerful biceps stretched the short sleeves of his black T-shirt, and his strong, bronzed forearms bore a fretwork of powerful veins. Where his T-shirt met his jeans, his stomach and abdomen were entirely flat. He was no body builder, but he obviously took care of himself.

Sighing, she rested her chin on a raised knee and tried not to look any lower. Her eyes were in no mood to behave, however. They continued their journey, studying the powerful thighs that were cased in snug denim and brazenly noting the bulge that lay between them. Remembered feelings from yesterday began to tingle through her body.

Arlen's voice startled her, causing her cheeks to flame and her gaze to dart guiltily to his face. Thank goodness his eyes were still closed.

"You're meeting Leong on Monday?" he asked lazily.

"Mmm-hmm. We're having lunch at the Corner Pub."

"I'll make sure one of my agents is there, Jessie. If Leong introduces you to someone, we'll want to get a make on him so we can ID him. Maybe we can track the whole thing down before you get much more deeply involved."

"That'd be nice." She suppressed an urge to reach out and touch him. "You know, you really knocked me for a loop back there when you came up to join us. I wasn't prepared for that."

"Yeah." His voice was deep and lazy. "A miscalculation on my part." He opened one eye and regarded her with evident amusement. "I'm so used to working with pros, I forget you amateurs are easy to rattle."

"Why, you—"

Laughing, he reached up and covered her mouth with his hand. "Uh-uh, Jess. You don't want to say things like that to your personal G-man." Idly, his fingertips stroked slowly across her lips. He felt her catch her breath, and something inside him caught, too. "You were great, Jessie. Honest to God, you were great. I'm sorry I rattled you, but you handled it like a pro." He dropped his hand and closed his eyes again, feeling he'd handled about all he could for the moment. Too much more and he would be making love to her right here on this damn rock.

"Why did you come over, anyway?" she asked him.

"Because it occurred to me that it might make sense to establish our relationship." He shrugged one shoulder without opening his eyes. "It may never be useful, but then again, maybe it will be. It just seemed like an opportunity I shouldn't pass up."

But Leong seemed a long way away right now, and the questions that had been bouncing around in her head when they had first left the supermarket were starting to take definite second place to the feelings Arlen was evoking in her just by being here. She turned a little and stretched out on the rock beside him. Her breathing grew noticeably deeper as she closed her eyes.

"You getting hungry, Jessica?" His voice had grown even deeper, lazier, almost drowsy.

"No. You go ahead if you want. Leong was waiting for me, wasn't he?"

"Mmm-hmm. People are pretty dependable. I'd be willing to bet that you go to the supermarket every Saturday morning."

Jessica turned her head enough to see Arlen's profile from the corner of her eye. "Are you saying I'm predictable?"

"Hell, Jess, we all are. Habit is the cornerstone of human existence. When I'm working on an investigation, the first thing I do is learn my subject's habits. That fills in about ninety percent of his time, and I'll always know where to look for him."

Something icy prickled along Jessica's spine. "You're saying someone has been watching me. Learning my habits."

"Looks that way," he drawled.

All the lazy restfulness she'd begun to feel vanished. Someone had been watching her, watching her closely enough to learn her habits. "Arlen?" Her voice sounded thin. "I don't like the sound of that."

"Nobody would, Jessie." After a reluctant moment, he turned his head in her direction and opened one eye. Finding her stretched out beside him, her breasts in enticing silhouette, was exactly what he'd hoped to avoid. Deep in his center, a slow, steady throbbing began.

He tried to be reassuring. "I'm sure they didn't watch you all that closely. They were primarily interested in finding out when you went regularly to some public place where Leong could pretend to bump into you. I'm sure they didn't look any closer than that. They really didn't need to."

"Except for my finances. You said they'd probably looked into those, too." She kept her eyes closed, refusing to look at him for fear she would throw herself into his arms. None of this was fair, she found herself thinking. Here he was, right beside her, and she couldn't take advantage of his strength. She didn't have the right to turn to him for comfort, and she didn't have the courage to turn to him for anything else.

"Probably. Look, here's the likeliest scenario. Somebody at MTI is already working with them. He passed some kind of information to them that got them interested in your project. They did a financial check on the members of your team and found, lo and behold, that you'd just dumped the major part of your savings into an old Victorian house that probably needs megabucks worth of repairs. They figured there was a possibility you might be interested in quick, easy money. Making things even easier, they found that you'd already met one of the students they keep tabs on, so they had an easy introduction. Hell, maybe they even arranged for Leong to be introduced to you by Kostermeyer. It wouldn't be difficult."

Jessica nodded, not at all sure how much of this she really believed. It was all so far removed from reality—her reality.

"So," Arlen continued, "they sent somebody to park across the street from your house on weekends and figure out your routine well enough that they could arrange for Leong to bump into you casually in a public place." He closed his eyes again and tried to ignore a certain demanding throb.

"You've done things like that, haven't you?" she asked.

"Sure," he drawled drowsily. "Any teenage girl with a crush can tell you how easy it is to meet someone if you really want to."

"I never had a crush."

"I know, Jessie," he said softly. "You're as fresh as spring daisies."

She didn't quite know how to take that remark. Opening her eyes a little more, she turned her head for a better look at him. His eyes were wide open and silvery as he looked straight at her. "Arlen?"

The uncertainty in her voice was his undoing. He was a sucker for this woman's vulnerability, for her absolute need to be wanted and needed. How could he refuse, when he could make her feel good, make her feel desirable and attractive? How could he deny her anything it was in his power to give her so easily? How could he decline to give what he so badly wanted to give?

He rolled onto his side and propped his head on his hand. "Do you want to sleep or eat? Or do you want that kiss I promised you?"

Her breath caught in her throat, and her lips parted in unconscious invitation. In her neck, a pulse began to beat visibly.

"Jessie?" But he didn't wait for her answer; he didn't need to. He cupped her cheek with his hand and rubbed his thumb gently along her lower lip. "Lady," he said quietly, "you are so damn sexy." And that was the understatement of the year.

The cynical, sensible, FBI-trained portion of his brain told him that he would regret this. It warned him that he was letting his hormones rule him, that just as soon as he was satisfied he was going to feel like a seducer of virgins, like the world's greatest sleaze. And then that cynical, sensible portion of himself shut down, washed away in a rising tidal wave of long-unsatisfied hungers. Damn it, Coulter, be honest about it. You want this woman like you've never wanted anything before.

She looked up at him with a sweet trust that both tore at him and warmed him. She lifted a hand, tentatively, shyly, and cradled his cheek. All the liking he'd begun to feel for her rose in a rush and added a new dimension to his desire.

He did not think of himself as desirable, as attractive to women. He had attracted only one woman in his life that he knew of. If there had been others, he had certainly never noticed it. From the moment he met Lucy, other women had ceased to exist. Until now. Until Jessica.

And Jessica was touching his cheek as if she longed to touch him in other ways but didn't quite dare, looking at him as if she needed him, sighing as if she were being transported by the simple touch of his thumb to her lip.

Bowing his head, he found her mouth with his. She welcomed him immediately, lips and teeth parting readily for his invasion. Sweet. She tasted so sweet, so warm, so *alive!* And she kissed him back, thrilling him with her response, her eagerness.

Little sounds escaped her as he took her head in his hands, cradling it to protect it from the hard surface beneath as he deepened his kiss. He let her catch a quick breath, and then he dived again, needing the heat, the welcome, the shy enticements of her tongue.

Somehow her hands found their way under his shirt, and she caressed the bare skin of his lower back. They both froze at the exquisite sensation, gray eyes boring deep into brown ones, two people caught between one breath and the next.

How long had it been, Arlen wondered, since last a woman had touched him in need? How long had it been since he'd felt a woman's hands on his skin? How long since he had taken the time to satisfy a need of his own? Years. It had been too many years.

"Jessie." He whispered her name raggedly. "I'm being selfish."

Swollen pink lips smiled at him. "Mmm. Me, too." Daringly, she ran her hands up his back as high as the shirt would allow her. "You have such warm, smooth skin," she murmured. She wished her palms could soak up the feeling and permanently imprint it on her brain. Why had she never imagined how exquisite it felt to touch another person's skin?

Arlen shuddered and shifted, drawing her head onto his forearm, inadvertently pulling her hands around to his front. "Jess, don't," he mumbled as she explored the hard, flat plane of his stomach.

"Don't you like it?" she asked shyly, her hand pausing.

"I love it," he growled, then cursed his own truthfulness as she took him at his word. "Honey...not here. Anybody could come along the road...."

Jessica heard him, and some part of her even acknowledged the justice of his warning. She was, however, caught up in the awe-inspiring magic of her woman's ability to arouse a man. She'd never dreamed that she, Jessica Kilner, could make a man tremble, could cause a man to groan and shudder as if from an internal earthquake. Nor had she ever suspected how good it could make her feel to bring pleasure.

"Jessie..."

"We'll hear if someone comes," she murmured, shifting still closer to him. Her own hungers were steadily building, growing from tingles to throbs, from craving to an ache. Whatever good sense she might have was rapidly drowning in all those wildly new sensations.

"Oh, damn," he groaned and rolled onto his back, carrying her with him so that she lay sprawled across his chest, her tempting, tormenting hands caught between them. He couldn't let this go any farther because it could end up being the most awful experience of her life. She had no notion of how she would feel if someone did come upon them, but he could guess. And more, she deserved a better, safer setting, a calmer lover and plenty of time. He had to be strong for them both.

"Jessie," he muttered. "Jessie, honey. Later. Later. Okay?"

"No." Her voice was muffled against his shoulder, and he felt her stiffen against him. "No."

His sigh was nearly a groan as he battled for restraint, control and sense. "Why not?" he asked. "What's wrong with later?" He sounded impatient, which wasn't bad, considering.

"You'll change your mind," she mumbled.

A smile caught at the corners of his mouth and tugged them upwards. Suddenly he didn't feel anywhere near so impatient or frustrated. "We'll see about that," he said.

*   *   *

After lunch Arlen felt drowsy, surely the fault of a nearly sleepless night spent wrestling with himself. When he caught Jessica smothering a yawn, he lay back on the rock and patted his shoulder.

"Use me for a pillow, Jessie. It looks like we could both use a short nap."

He was touched by the way she didn't even hesitate but immediately curled up beside him, her head on his shoulder, her hand on his chest.

God, he'd missed this! How could he have forgotten what a comfort it was just to be able to hold another human being? Maybe he'd forgotten because during that last year he had held Lucy to comfort *her*, and in return had felt only a deepening of his anguish and sorrow. And, finally, there had been the last time he'd held her. The night she died, he'd held her, talked comfortingly to her, making sure she didn't die alone.

Until Jessica Kilmer, Arlen Coulter hadn't touched another soul except in the most casual ways—a handshake, a kiss to his daughter's cheek, a pat to his son's shoulder. He'd cut himself off completely and probably would have stayed that way, safe in a desert of isolation, if not for Jessie. Somehow, he acknowledged with a kind of rueful dread, she'd managed to make a place for herself right inside his walls.

Well, she wouldn't stay for long. He wasn't sure why she was attracted to him, but he suspected it had more to do with his job and his experience than with anything about him personally. At some point she was bound to decide he was too old, too scarred and too much trouble. At some point she was bound to realize that she wanted all the normal things, things he couldn't give her. Off she would go, and she would find a man nearer her own age. Which was just as it should be.

Closing his eyes against the brilliance of the midday sun, Arlen dozed off, vaguely aware that he hadn't felt so content in one hell of a long time.

* * *

When they awoke, the afternoon was nearly gone and the northern horizon bore the blue imprint of an approaching cold front.

"We'd better get back," Jessica said as she studied it. A lifetime in Texas told her that a blue norther would hit in the next couple of hours, bringing with it a significant temperature drop. Her thin cotton blouse would offer scant protection.

Arlen stood on the rock, hands on his hips, and studied the blue wall. "It's amazing," he said. "I swear this must be the only place on earth where you can *see* a cold front."

"Naw," Jessica said with a gentle laugh. "They see northers in Oklahoma, too. Maybe the only reason you don't see them back east is because you have so many trees."

"I have to admit," Arlen said as he turned, "that's one of the things I miss about the East. Lots of big trees. Especially in autumn."

"What else do you miss?"

"Real Italian sausage." He jumped down from the rock and reached up to help her. "Bagels fresh from a bakery at six in the morning. Those bagels they sell downtown almost make it, though. Almost." He closed his hands around her waist and lifted her down. "Hot pretzels. Snow."

Still holding her by the waist, he bent and kissed her lightly on the lips. "Yeah," he said huskily. "Snow. Mostly snow at Christmas. Snow falling like fairy dust in the dark, muffling the world in silence while you curl up in front of a fire and make love with your lady...."

He had given up the fight, he admitted. Further argument with himself would be self-deluding. He wanted this woman, he wasn't going to be able to resist her forever, and since she wanted him, too, there was no point in fighting it any longer.

So he wrapped both his arms around her, drawing her full length snugly against him as he cupped her bottom. Bending, he brushed her lips with his and watched as her eyelids fluttered downward. "Think that norther will get cold enough for a fire?'' His voice was a husky growl, and he felt her shiver in response.

"Who cares?" she asked breathlessly, feeling as if she were already *on* fire. "I'll turn on the air conditioning to make it cold enough, if I have to."

Arlen chuckled and hugged her tight before releasing her. "Only a Texan would think of something like that," he teased.

After he helped her into her helmet—as if she were precious, Jessica thought—he insisted she wear his bomber jacket. "If that storm hits before we get back to town, you'll need it, Jessie."

The jacket smelled of Arlen, of man and soap and leather. Sitting on the back of the bike, arms wrapped snugly around his waist, she felt as if she were surrounded by him. Sheltered by him. Protected by him.

She felt as if she were riding another motorcycle, too, an emotional one. Something had happened to Arlen's resistance; something had caused a marked shift in his attitude toward a relationship between them. Where before he had made her feel like something he wanted but hated himself for wanting, now he just made her feel desirable. And that gave her the same headlong rush that riding this bike did, the same sense of excitement and adventure and happiness.

It was also scary. Yesterday, just yesterday, she had gotten her first taste of the power of passion. She had discovered how it could override common sense and inhibitions and make a mockery of normal restraints. It was overriding her common sense even now, drawing her headlong toward an unknown destination. And there was no reason to believe that Arlen was being any more sensible than she was about this. That meant there might be regrets for both of them.

And she really didn't know how she would handle that. As they leaned into a curve, she felt her throat tighten as if in premonition. She wanted this, but she could very well wind up regretting it. She could wind up hurting, badly.

Even knowing that, she knew she would still plunge ahead. She wanted this man with an ache so deep the only thing that could possibly hurt any worse was never having him at all.

She was about to take the biggest risk she had ever taken in her entire life.

Two hours later the Harley growled to a stop beside Jessica's car in the MTI parking lot. The wind had begun to gust before the approaching storm, and the temperature felt as if it had begun to drop.

Arlen helped Jessica off his bike and saw her safely buckled into her car.

"I won't follow you directly," he said. He held her car door, preparatory to closing it for her. "There are a couple of things I need to do before I come over."

Her heart and her stomach both plunged, and her hands took the steering wheel in a death grip. "Okay," she managed to say. He was having second thoughts. Next would come the apologetic phone call. He would say something had come up at work.

Something of her feelings must have shown on her face, because he suddenly squatted beside her. Catching her chin in his hand, he turned her face toward him.

"I may go to hell for this, Jessie," he said, "but I'm not changing my mind. I really *have* to check in. I've already been out of touch too long. I'll see you in a little while." Leaning toward her, he placed a soft, warm kiss on her lips.

She felt better, but only briefly. As she pulled out of the parking lot, she saw Arlen in her rearview mirror. He straddled his bike and watched her go, and there was something about that sight that made her feel achingly sad.

The phone call came an hour later. He was sorry, he said, and sounded as if he really meant it. There had been some developments in a case that required his presence. He didn't know when he would be free.

"Jessie?" The question rumbled over the line, fleshed out by his tone though the words remained unspoken.

"I understand, Arlen," she said through stiff lips. Please, God, just let me get off the phone before my voice cracks. She couldn't bear for him to know how much this mattered, how much it hurt. It was foolish, after such a short time, to care so much. A few days ago she hadn't even known he existed, so how could his absence take on the proportions of a disaster? Pride kept her voice calm and her eyes dry, while a soul-deep disappointment pierced her.

"Do you, Jessie? Do you really understand?"

"Of course I do," she said sharply. "You're an FBI agent. Your work is important, and it isn't confined to usual business hours."

"As long as that's really what you understand, and you're not imagining something else. I'll call you when I'm done."

"Sure. Good night, Arlen."

That was when Jessica cried. She felt foolish for crying, but she couldn't help it. A deep, hollow ache filled her, and it hurt too much to ignore. Curled up in a corner of the couch, she cried until exhaustion dried her eyes and carried her off to sleep.

She'd had so little human warmth in her life, she thought as she drifted away. Was it wrong to want it so badly?

Chapter 7

Hours after Jessica fell tearfully asleep on her couch, Phil Harrigan stuck his head into Arlen's office. "You ready to go, Arlen?"

Arlen looked up from the notes he was making and shook his head. "I'll be an hour or more yet, Phil," he told the other agent. "Say, are you tied up Monday around noon?"

"Not that I know of." Phil leaned against the door frame. "Ed's going to take the videotape we made tonight up to the U. S. Attorney's office, but he doesn't need me for that. You got something coming down?"

"Looks that way."

"So count me in. I mean, catching a federal judge accepting a bribe from a local cop is a big deal and all, but it'll wear off by Monday. You know me. I gotta have my adrenaline jolt."

Chuckling, Arlen leaned back in his deep leather chair. Like Harrigan, he wore jeans and a black windbreaker with the initials FBI plastered on the front, back and sleeves in bright white letters. Arlen was very much in favor of those windbreakers. It sometimes amused him to recall that he'd been shot at only once in his entire career, by a drunken hunter. He had been placing a surveillance camera in the Maryland woods to videotape an expected drop of classified documents by a suspected mole. Along had come a pickup full of hunters who, for some reason, had taken exception to Arlen's activities.

Knowing there were two possible sets of headlines that could come out of the encounter, Arlen had decided the director would definitely prefer FBI Agent Shot By Local Hunter to FBI Shoots Local Hunter. Consequently, he'd dived behind a log and waited for the hunters to tire of their game. A few years later, when the windbreakers made their appearance, he was foursquare in favor of them, because sometimes a simple thing could avert tragedy. To this day he felt those hunters would never have shot if they had known he was with law enforcement.

Besides, in the heat of a crisis, when bullets were flying in every direction, blazing identification was essential. Not that he'd ever been in that situation. Not that he ever wanted to be. But he'd been in plenty of situations with that kind of potential.

"On Monday," he told Phil, "I want you to go to the Corner Pub on North Lamar, say about eleven-thirty. At noon a lady named Jessica Kilmer will arrive to meet a student named Greg Leong." Reaching into his desk, he pulled out two photos, one of Jessica and one of Greg Leong. They'd been taken by surveillance cameras, so neither was really crisp, but they were good enough to make an identification from.

"The lady," Arlen continued, "has agreed to work with us as a double agent. I believe that Leong has been pressured to introduce a KGB agent to Ms. Kilmer. I expect the introduction will take place Monday at the Pub. I want you to get a good make on the person Leong introduces to her. Get a photo, if you can."

"Will she be wired?" Phil asked.

Arlen shook his head. "I don't see the point in it. Whatever introduction is made will be casual, and nothing of any real importance will be said."

Phil nodded. "What about a tail? You want me to tail the guy?"

"Not this time. Later, if we need to, but I don't want to risk rocking this boat in any way right now, Phil. Something fishy is going on over at MTI, and I suspect this may be part of it. If it is, there's more at stake than whether we can pick up one guy for asking Jessie Kilmer to pass classified." Glancing at his watch, Arlen almost groaned aloud. It was nearly midnight, and by now Jessie was sure to think he'd turned tail. He returned his attention to Phil. "We'll talk more about this Monday morning. Do you have any objection to partnering with Lisa on this one?"

"No. Should I?"

Arlen shook his head. "No, you shouldn't, but you might, and this is one case where I don't want any chafing personalities. It's apt to go on for a long, long time."

Phil turned as if to leave, then asked, "This Kilmer woman. Does she live around here?"

"She lives over on West Chestnut." Arlen frowned faintly. "Why the interest, Phil? Is something bugging you?"

Phil shook his head. "Nope. Just thought the name rang a bell. I suppose you'll be wanting me to keep an eye on her?"

"We'll see."

Alone again, Arlen considered calling Jessie, then decided it was too late. Forty-five minutes later, he couldn't stand it. He picked up the phone and dialed her number. It might be late, but waking her was better than letting her believe for another minute that he'd deliberately stood her up. Instead of ringing, however, he got a busy signal.

Well, he thought, it was Saturday night, and for a Saturday night it wasn't *that* late. He replaced the receiver and returned to his notes.

Forty-five minutes later, uneasiness had destroyed all possibility of finishing up his notes on the night's operation. Jessica's line was still busy, and his uneasiness wouldn't let him dismiss it. She could be talking to a friend. She could have taken the phone off the hook for some reason—like maybe she was really ticked off at him. He sure couldn't blame her for that. She didn't seem like the vindictive type, but then, how well did he really know her?

With a curse he stood up and reached for his gun, snapping the holster to his belt. There was only one way he was going to be able to relax. He would have to go over there and assure himself that she was all right.

After he'd left Jessica in the MTI parking lot, he'd driven home to shower, shave, change and check in. The checking in was what had gotten him tangled up in this business. Hell, he'd meant to go by the drugstore, and he hadn't even done that.

He pulled his sedan to a stop in front of Jessica's house a bare fifteen minutes later. The night had turned cold and windy, and there was a taste of rain in the air as he studied the front of Jessie's house, seeking any indication that something was amiss. Seeing nothing untoward, not even a car parked along the street, he crept around the side of the house to the back door, silent in the jogging shoes he'd exchanged for his boots for. Since he was no longer on official business, he'd left his FBI windbreaker behind in favor of his own nylon jacket, but as he worked his way around the house he began to wonder if that wasn't a mistake. If some neighbor noticed him and called the cops, he could well live to regret it.

At the back of the house everything appeared normal, too. Jessie's car was parked at the back door, and all the lights in the house were out. She'd probably gone to bed. She'd probably taken the phone off the hook simply because she didn't want to be awakened.

But he wouldn't rest until he saw with his own two eyes that she was okay. Well, he could beat on her door, a good, solid police-style hammering that would wake the dead, not to mention half her neighbors.

He chose instead to let himself in to the house and check things out. If someone was in there with her, he didn't want to startle them. People got hurt that way.

A credit card unlocked her back door for him. Arlen made a mental note to see that she got a dead bolt on that door. Feeling stupid, sure that he was overreacting, yet unable to talk himself out of it, he crept through the house and up the stairway. He would find Jessica curled up safely in her bed. Then he could get the hell out of here and never admit to a soul that he, a veteran agent of sixteen years' experience, had gone off the deep end because a woman he hardly knew had taken her phone off the hook.

Right.

He might not have known her long, but she was important anyway. She was important at a gut level that was dragging him through a dark house at two o'clock in the morning to make sure she was okay. And if that wasn't the stupidest part of this whole thing...

At the top of the stairs he paused, listening intently. Not a sound disturbed the silence. A step brought him to the door of her bedroom. It was open, which he guessed wasn't surprising, since she lived here alone. Somebody ought to tell her, though, that it was safer to sleep behind a closed door, because thieves were reluctant to enter closed rooms, unsure of what they might find. And then, of course, there was the fire protection factor provided by a closed door....

He could see the shimmer of her white satin spread in the dark, and he crept toward it, hesitating only when a board creaked beneath his foot. She wasn't in the bed.

She wasn't in the bed!

Alarms went off in his head, and his hand dived under the jacket for his gun. The last thing he felt now was stupidity. Something was definitely wrong. Without wasting another moment, moving with a silent stealth learned in the dangerous jungles of Southeast Asia, Arlen began to check every nook and cranny of the upstairs.

Finding nothing, he headed downstairs, stepping at the outside of each riser so it wouldn't creak. The adrenaline shot he'd gotten when he looked into Jessica's bed had his heart hammering rapidly. The increased demand for oxygen forced him to breathe through his mouth in great, silent gulps.

When he reached the foot of the stairs he held his breath and listened. The pounding of his heart was so loud that he wasn't sure he would be able to hear anything quieter than the roar of a freight train, but he listened, anyway.

There was something, a sound more felt than heard, so faint beside the pounding in his ears that he couldn't be really certain he heard it. Crouching, he inched toward the living room and then through the arched doorway.

Again a sound, like a soft, muffled moan. It came from the couch. Straightening, holding his gun at the ready in both hands, Arlen stepped around the end table and looked down at the couch.

It was Jessica. His eyes were dark-adapted enough to make out her features in the faint light that filtered through the crack between the curtains of one tall window.

Leaning over, he found the switch on the table lamp and turned it. Fifty watts of golden light poured over her, revealing every detail.

"God," Arlen breathed prayerfully.

She was all right. She was sleeping. Tearstains marked her soft face, but otherwise she was all right. Relief left him feeling shaky. He shoved his gun back into the holster and looked down at Jessie, taking in every detail. She was wrapped in a silky robe, something old-fashioned looking, with large pink flowers on a beige-and-cream background, something edged in beige lace that fell gently around her throat, across her breasts, around her wrists. She looked softly, sweetly feminine. She looked like something a man ought to grab and hold on to. Someone he ought to gather close and protect and shelter and love.

"Jessie." He murmured her name, bending closer, smelling the fragrance that was especially hers, a light, fresh scent like a rainwashed spring day. "Jessie."

She stirred a little, and her eyelids fluttered. "Arlen?" Her voice was husky with sleep. She licked her dry lips and tried to pry her eyes open to see him. "I thought you weren't coming."

"I'm here," he said as a deep, inexplicable ache bloomed in him. "I'm here, Jessie. I'll carry you up to bed."

"No," she mumbled as he slipped his arms beneath her. "You'll hurt yourself."

"Hush, honey. Just hush." In one easy movement he lifted her high against his chest. One of his arms cradled her shoulders; the other supported her knees. Instinctively she turned toward him, wrapping an arm around his shoulders as she buried her face in the warm curve between his neck and shoulder.

"I'm glad you came." She sighed sleepily as he began the climb up the stairs. It was all a dream, she thought hazily, this dark trip up the stairs in strong arms. Just a wonderful dream that would make her smile come morning. "You'll stay, won't you?"

"I'll stay." He didn't know how he was going to handle it, though. Missing the drugstore earlier tonight was rapidly becoming a serious mistake. He suspected, however, that the tearstains on her cheeks were his fault, and he couldn't do that to her again. No way. Not if every bit of common sense in him argued that he ought to get the hell out of here.

Without turning on a light, he carried her across her bedroom and lowered her gently to her feet beside the bed.

"Let me pull back the comforter, Jessie."

Stifling a yawn, she leaned against him. "I need to take my hair down," she said drowsily. He felt so good, so hard and strong. And he smelled so good, she thought. "I can't sleep with all these bobby pins." What a funny thing to worry about in a dream.

Her hair. Arlen was suddenly distracted from his single line of thought: to get her into bed and covered quickly before his traitorous mind and body could come up with other activities.

Her hair. From the moment he first set eyes on her he'd been wanting to get her hair down. "I'll help you," he said.

Jessica found herself sitting on the bench before her dressing table, staring at her reflection in the mirror. Arlen had turned on the small bedside lamp, the one that gave her just enough light to see her way to the bathroom when she needed it. The dim glow highlighted her face from the side, giving her a light-dark look of mystery. The beat of her heart had become a heavy throbbing. This was no dream. This was real, and she was at last waking to the reality of it.

In the mirror she watched Arlen remove his jacket. Then he unsnapped the holster from his belt and placed it on the bedside table. He was really here, she thought, excitement pounding in her blood. He was really here, and the simple acts of removing his jacket and gun suddenly seemed incredibly intimate. Incredibly wonderful. He filled the virginal room, dominated it, a dark, virile presence amid all the soft white fluff of her childish dreams.

This was it. She clenched her hands in her lap and waited for whatever was to come. For the first time in her life she truly understood what it meant to tremble before the unknown. No book, no movie, could prepare a person for the reality of this moment. Nor would she ever have believed that it was possible to want and fear the same thing.

Suddenly Arlen was behind her, his hands resting gently on her shoulders. "I made you cry," he said softly.

She wanted to deny it, but as she met his eyes in the mirror she knew she couldn't. Mute with embarrassment at what she felt had been childishness, she simply looked back at him.

Lifting one hand, he stroked her soft cheek with a fingertip. Jessica caught her breath and watched, mesmerized.

Arlen spoke quietly. "I made the mistake of calling in to work to see if anything earth-shattering had happened while I was out of touch."

"And something had."

"Something was about to," he corrected. "I'm sorry, Jessie. Really sorry."

Slipping his fingers into her hair, he began to remove the pins one by one, tossing them on the table as he found them. Jessie shivered delightfully as she felt the gentle touch of his fingers against her scalp. Never in a million years would she have guessed that *that* could be erotic.

"You don't have to apologize," she said, a catch in her suddenly breathy voice.

"Yes, I do. Another time maybe I wouldn't but this time, all things considered, I really do have to apologize for how I made you feel."

The last lock of her hair fell free, and Arlen stared in pleasure at long, shiny locks that fell all the way to the bench on which she was sitting. "Your hair is beautiful, Jessie. I've never seen such beautiful hair."

"Thank you." Pleasure flushed her cheeks, made her heart skip a beat.

"I've been wanting to see it down since the moment I laid eyes on you," he confessed. Leaning forward, he took the brush from the dressing table. Then, slowly, gently, he began to brush the heavy, shiny veil. "And while I'm making all these apologies and confessions, there's another one I'd better make straight out."

Jessica was already sinking into the luxury of having her hair brushed, but now she stiffened slightly. "Is something wrong?"

"Hell, yes," he said wryly. "I never made it to the drugstore."

"The... Oh!"

"Right. *Oh.*" He smiled at the way she clapped her hands to her hot cheeks, but then she laughed, startling him. "Jessie, don't you understand? I didn't get any—"

"That's okay," she said swiftly, her voice dropping an octave with embarrassment. "That's okay."

"How can it be okay?" He felt a little irritated. It was late, he was tired, he was horny as hell and there wasn't a condom in sight. "Damn it, Jessie, it can't be okay. I know perfectly well you're a... you're not real experienced. You can't possibly be protected, and I'm not taking any chances with you. It's like wearing a helmet on a Harley. Only a fool rides without protection."

"I, uh..." She squeezed her eyes shut and clenched her hands. "Damn it," she said tautly, "I *bought* the darn things without any trouble. Why can't I just *say* it?"

"Say what?" Arlen's hands paused in her hair. "Bought what, honey?" He had an idea, though, and it was soothing his irritation.

"I went to the drugstore myself," she said in a rush. "The bedside table."

He crossed to the table and pulled the drawer out enough to see the familiar box. "Jessie, I'm impressed. How'd you ever whip up the nerve?"

She still couldn't look at him. She cleared her throat. "I, uh, I'm liberated enough to think a woman is responsible for her own, uh, protection. Besides," she said almost petulantly, "buying them was *easy*. Telling *you* is something else!"

Arlen laughed. He couldn't help it. "Jessie, Jessie," he said warmly as he came up behind her. His hands settled on her shoulders again, and he bent, bringing his mouth to her ear. "God, woman, I've been wanting you!"

His roughly whispered words caused a sharp thrill to pierce her very center. The unexpected pressure of his teeth on her earlobe did even more. She arched back toward him, and his hands tightened on her shoulders.

"That's it, Jess," he said softly and knelt behind her. "Lean back against me."

He parted her hair so that he could kiss the nape of her neck, and Jessie sank immediately into a warm languor. Her limbs felt weighted, and her eyelids grew too heavy to keep open as Arlen's lips did incredibly arousing things to her neck. Another erogenous zone she'd never dreamed of, she thought hazily, and then just about stopped thinking as his arms wrapped around her and his hands each captured one full breast. She felt her nipples pucker immediately, straining eagerly for more of the delicious treatment he'd given them yesterday.

Arlen watched them both in the mirror, watched the way Jessie's eyelids drooped closed, the way her head sagged back against his shoulder in complete surrender. He watched his hands shape her breasts through the flowered silk, watched his thumbs brush her beading nipples. He heard her quickened breaths, the soundless sighs, felt the slight, restless stirring of her body as he stroked her. The knot of need that had been with him virtually every moment since he met her hardened even more. He felt his own breath speed up, felt his control slip a notch, and then another notch.

Fantasies were filling his mind. A fantasy of slowly disrobing Jessie here before the mirror, of touching her with intimacy while they both watched. A fantasy of her lying on her white satin spread with nothing but her yards of dark hair to clothe her. Oh, yes, he had fantasies such as he hadn't had in years, but not for tonight. Tonight was for

Jessie and Jessie only. A first time should be special, and he was determined that hers would be.

"Mmm," Jessie moaned softly and arched her breasts hard against Arlen's hands. "Arlen . . ." His name was a sigh that trailed away into another moan.

If he didn't move them now, he doubted he was going to be able to move them at all. Rising, he scooped Jessie up from the vanity bench and carried her to the bed. Holding her by her shoulders, he let her feet trail to the floor. She steadied herself as he bent to tug the satin comforter back.

Jessica saw the invitingly pulled-back covers, and without any coaxing at all she climbed right in and threw herself on her back. The smile she gave Arlen was nearly beatific. "Hurry," she said, her voice a low purr.

The urge to laugh rose in Arlen. It was a happy urge, a joyous urge, something so long forgotten that it startled him. He didn't laugh, but his crooked smile spread across his face in answer to hers. Standing right beside the bed, he began to undress.

Breathlessly she watched. In college she'd seen a magazine with pictures of nude men in it, but she'd never seen a real, live man without any clothes. Arlen would be beautiful, she was sure, but natural curiosity and natural shyness were warring within her.

First he pulled his black T-shirt over his head and tossed it onto the vanity bench. Jessica drew an audible breath at the sight of his broad, hard chest. She had known that he was sheathed in flat muscle—she had felt it when he held her, when he carried her—but she'd had no way to know whether he was hairy. He was not. He was smooth and firm and golden in the lamp's dim glow. How she wanted to touch him!

A click drew her eyes downward, and she stared in fascination as Arlen unbuckled his belt. Here there was hair, she saw, dark hair arrowing downward from his navel to the waistband of his jeans. Unconsciously she licked her lips. A nervous, edgy fluttering filled her, an uneasy uncertainty.

Arlen saw the nervousness, but that was exactly why he was standing beside her bed undressing like a two-bit stripper in a bad floor show. If virginal nerves were going to scare her off, he wanted them both to know it before things went too far. Before he lost the last bit of the self-control she'd been chipping away at so steadily. Before he lost the ability to behave like a gentleman.

He certainly wasn't doing this because he thought he was pinup material. His own mouth was dry with nervousness. Damn it, maybe he needed to see a shrink. He'd made love to only one woman in his entire life, and that was hardly a measure by which to judge his skills. Yet here he was, getting ready to climb into a virgin's bed and telling himself he was going to make it good for her. Just how was he proposing to do that?

But his hands kept moving, anyway, unclasping the belt, popping the buttons, yanking the zipper. Damn, he wanted this woman. He couldn't remember *ever* having wanted like this. How had she done it? How had she gotten inside to pluck at his feelings and draw out his responses? How had she made him so hungry when he had been sure he would never be hungry again?

He shoved down his jeans but left his briefs in place. He heard Jessie's faint gasp, and he looked quickly at her. Her gaze seemed to be stuck on the bulge in the front of his briefs, the rather obvious evidence of his arousal.

"Jessie?" He spoke gently. "Want me to stop?" The unsure part of him half hoped she would.

"No...no," she answered unsteadily, astonishing him. "Arlen, please...I ache..."

That did it. The plea, the sound of her breathless voice, the yearning in her bright brown eyes, all combined to untangle the twisted skein of his feelings. In an instant he became a man with a purpose. He might not be a Lothario, but he could be caring and gentle and patient, and, by heaven, he would.

He lay beside her at last, still wearing his briefs, and wrapped her in the strength of his arms, tugging her close to his heart. She sighed with apparent pleasure and turned her head so that her cheek rested against his breast. Her hands were caught between them, small and soft, and her fingertips touched him in gentle, kneading strokes that reminded him of his daughter's cat.

"It feels so good to hold you," he murmured, rubbing her back from shoulder to hip with his hands. He knew instinctively that she needed every bit of praise he could shower on her. He thought himself uncertain, but she was even more so, lacking any experience to counter her mistaken self-image. He had seen enough to know that she felt plain and unattractive. None of it was true, in his opinion, but he was honest enough to admit others might have given her reason to feel that way. She was not conventionally pretty, but in his eyes she was something much more. She had the soft warmth that made puppies and kittens so appealing. In her plain little face he saw loveliness that wouldn't wear away, and in her eyes he saw the shining of her soul. But perhaps the most amazing thing he needed her to understand tonight was that both his mind and his body found her to be absolutely the sexiest woman he'd ever seen.

"You're so soft," he murmured against her temple. As one hand swept downward, he pulled her hips closer, pressing her abdomen to his arousal. He heard her soft gasp, and with a smile he rocked himself against her. Just once, just enough to remind her. "You make me hot," he said frankly, and soaked up the warmth of her unexpected smile.

"You make me hot, too," she confided, her brown eyes sparkling up at him.

He brought his hand up to cup her cheek, to slide into her yards of silky hair. "When I came up here the other night with those boxes—remember?"

She nodded, watching him with heavy-lidded eyes.

"I took one look at this bed, and I got hit right between the eyes with an image of you lying here covered by nothing but your hair. I've been wild ever since."

Color stained her cheeks, visible to him even in the dim light. "I don't know if I'm quite ready for that," she admitted.

"Of course you're not." He kissed her forehead, ran his fingers from her ear to her chin. "I'm saving that up for later, anyway."

"Later?" The word caught on her breath as his hand, quite deliberately and quite boldly, slipped into the front of her dressing gown, found its way past the thin strap of the teddy she wore and grasped her breast in a warm, firm hold.

"Ahh," Arlen sighed, closing his own eyes as he felt her satin skin, the hard button of her straining nipple. "Your breasts are so beautiful, Jessie. They feel so good...."

Jessica nearly groaned when he pulled his hand from her breast, but a new excitement clenched her deep inside as he tugged at the tie of her robe.

"I want to see you, Jess," he said huskily, pulling the tie loose and parting the robe. "I want to touch you everywhere." He smoothed the robe from her shoulders, and in growing eagerness she helped him free her from it.

Pink skin and white satin. She was wearing a white satin teddy that draped her curves loosely, tentatively, temptingly.

"Damn it, Jess," Arlen said. "You know just how to drive me out of my mind!"

The smile she gave him was shyly pleased. "You like it?"

"I like it," he replied. "I like the way you look in it even better."

She turned toward him, holding out her arms, but he stopped her gently, pressing her back onto the mattress. "Uh-uh," he said, brushing a kiss on the tip of her nose. "I'm not through going crazy over how you look." He also needed a moment to slip a leash on his escaping control. After a while he lifted smiling gray eyes to hers. "Now," he said quietly, "I'm going to touch."

And touch he did. Jessica caught her breath and then stopped breathing altogether. His hands wove a web of magic on her skin, through the thin satin that slipped erotically against her most sensitive parts. When her sighs turned to soft moans, he took her mouth in a deep, searing kiss that echoed the primal rhythms he was evoking in her.

"Arlen...Arlen..." Her own hands couldn't remain still as powerful needs took her, shook her, turned her inside out so that she felt like a mass of hungry, throbbing nerves. She found his broad shoulders and clung, trying to draw him closer, but he resisted. Instead he opened the snaps of her teddy and skimmed it off her.

Her eyelids fluttered as she felt it go, and she arched toward him. She'd never felt anything like this before, but she knew what she wanted.

"Arlen...I need...I want to feel you...."

"Touch me, Jessie." His voice was a husky growl. "Touch me, baby. Go on."

Her eyes opened sleepily. "Show me," she whispered. "Show me how."

That request fanned his inner firestorm. There were ways he'd needed to be touched all his life long, ways he'd never been touched. As Jessie spoke, something inside Arlen exploded in a conflagration long denied. Only as she spoke did he realize what he'd missed.

"Show me," she murmured again, turning toward him, heedless of her nakedness, unaware of how beautiful she looked to him. She wanted, needed, to make him feel some of the pleasure he gave to her. She wanted, needed, to feel his skin and his shudders, to hear his moans and sighs, to weave the same magic web around him.

He was shaking as he took her hand. His needs took a momentary back seat to the wonder of this woman's request, but not for long. He pressed her palm to his chest and rolled onto his back.

"Like this," he whispered, drawing her hand downward. As he guided her, he hung suspended in a kind of hell, wondering if she would pull away in shock. "Like this," he whispered again, closing her fingers around him through the cotton of his briefs. He was grateful for the briefs, suddenly, grateful that the shock to her could be minimized by that thin, soft barrier.

But Jessie's shock was both instant and fleeting. She drew a deep, shuddery breath and stroked him with instinctive need, encouraged and inflamed by his evident pleasure. She had imagined, but imagination didn't hold a candle to reality. He was harder, bigger.... She stroked him again, marveling, melting.

Arlen jerked and moaned. "Again, Jess," he ground out. "Again. So...damn...good!"

Her insides clenched almost painfully in response to his sounds of pleasure, and she wrapped herself around him, a leg over his legs, her hand on his hips, and her mouth—ah, with her mouth she learned a dozen ways to make him groan, to make his arm tighten around her shoulders. It was she who tugged his briefs from him finally. She knelt over him in awe and touched him in wonder.

And destroyed his patience and self-control.

"That's it, Jessie," he growled. Catching her by the shoulders, he flipped her gently onto her back and leaned over her. He kissed her swollen lips with an aching gentleness and brushed her silky hair back from her face. A fierce tenderness, a purely protective instinct, gripped him. "Are you sure, Jessie?" he asked hoarsely. "Are you really sure?"

She lifted trembling arms and looped them around his neck. "I'm sure," she said on an uneven breath. "Absolutely." Why was he hesitating? Every nerve in her body throbbed in a plea for completion. She was almost completely past the ability to think.

He swept his hand downward to the apex of her thighs and combed his fingers through soft hair. "It'll hurt, sweetheart. I don't think there's anything I can do to prevent that." He slipped a finger into her, causing her to gasp and arch. She was warm, tight and wet. So wet and ready. So damn virginal. He wished he could skip this part somehow. He remembered another time, and he might have frozen right there, except that Jessie's hips undulated against his hand as if she enjoyed the sensation of penetration, and she turned her head toward him, finding his nipple with her tongue.

"Mmm," she panted. "I know. I don't care." She tugged on his shoulders.

But he hesitated a little longer, trying to prepare the way, to ready her as much as possible. There was the awful minute when he had to turn to the bedside table, but he returned swiftly, again stroking her deeply with his fingers until she was writhing, one hand clutching desperately at him, the other clutching at the sheet. She was as ready as she could ever be, he thought, and he was damned if he could wait any longer.

As soon as he moved between her legs, she stilled.

"Jess?" Doubt assailed him again, one last flicker of clear thought in a mind gone red and hazy with driving, pulsing need. Damn, she was soft. So soft, so warm, so wild. "Jess?"

"Do it," she whispered. "Oh, please, Arlen. Now!"

He wanted to move slowly, but as soon as he started to enter her, something inside both of them snapped and their hips lunged together. The barrier was gone almost before he was aware of it, and he was fully sheathed in her tight, hot depths. Smothering a groan of incredible satisfaction, he raised his head and looked down into Jessie's suddenly pale face. He cupped her head, stroked her hair back, restrained his hunger as he waited for her reaction.

"Jessie?" He spoke in a husky whisper.

"I...just need a second," she whispered back. "Just give me a minute. I'll be okay."

He filled the time by kissing her softly everywhere he could reach. When he lifted his head again, she smiled and her eyes opened, looking straight into his.

"Are you okay?" he asked.

"Mmm." She sighed, then reached up to stroke his shoulders with her hands. "It wasn't that bad. And you feel so good inside me."

Her truthfulness delighted him. "Tell me," he coaxed, and moved a little, just a little, within her. "Tell me how it feels."

She whispered in his ear, broken phrases, trying to tell him how he completed her, how he filled an aching emptiness, how right, how good, this seemed. And as she whispered he deepened his movements little by little until her whispers turned to moans and her stroking hands began to clutch.

He had tested his self-control beyond what he'd imagined possible, but now it was failing him completely. He slipped a hand beneath her hips, guiding her untutored movements, straining to bring her the same pleasure she was giving him, knowing that he couldn't hold on much longer.

And then she convulsed with a groan that seemed to rise from her toes.

"Jessie!" With a guttural cry he followed her over the peak.

Chapter 8

Clad only in unbuttoned, unzipped jeans, Arlen stood at the window near the head of Jessie's bed and stared out through white lace at wet gloom. Rain dripped steadily from the eaves, and the day beyond the window was gray and faintly misty. As yesterday had been the best of Texas springtime, today appeared to be the worst.

It was early yet, only a little past seven, meaning he had enjoyed maybe three hours of sleep. He was used to short sleep, though, and as he got older, late nights followed by early mornings troubled him less and less.

Jessie's neighborhood was one of the older ones in town, and it was both quiet and graced with tall old live oaks that must be near a century in age. It reminded him very much of the small upstate New York town where he'd grown up— although he hadn't lived in a neighborhood as nice as this one. No, this type of neighborhood in his hometown was where the doctors, lawyers and merchants lived.

Ever since he had moved to central Texas, however, he frequently had been taken by surprise at the way some view of the hilly countryside or a city street would suddenly remind him forcibly of the Northeast. The sensation was particularly apparent here on Jessie's street.

He glanced over at her to make sure she was still asleep. This was one morning of her life when she shouldn't awake alone. It would be easy, he feared, for her to feel used. Hell, in the cool light of morning he was wondering what the devil was wrong with *him*. He'd let his judgment become seriously clouded by needs that shouldn't be running a man's life much past the age of twenty. Still, whatever penance he deserved for his selfishness and foolhardiness in climbing into her bed, he wasn't going to make her pay it. She had given him a priceless gift, and he was decent enough to value it. He would stick around until she got sick of him, which probably wouldn't take too long. Until then, he owed her whatever she wanted from him simply because he'd taken advantage of her.

He scanned the street again. It was quiet, as it should be so early on a Sunday morning. The only other soul stirring was that man down there leaning against a light post and smoking a cigarette while he waited for a dog to finish sniffing out all the bushes. Probably somebody else with a guilty conscience for the way he had spent his Saturday night, Arlen thought wryly.

A sigh from behind made him turn and look at Jessica. She stirred slightly, like the whisper of a dawn breeze. The top sheet was tangled around her legs and had slipped off one breast, a full, rounded breast with a large pink areola. A beautiful breast, he thought, on a beautiful, generously endowed woman. Her hips were meant to cradle a man, had cradled him perfectly. The memory of how she felt beneath him was enough to bring him surging to full arousal like a young buck of eighteen. He forced his attention back to the window and grimaced down at the solitary smoker below.

Part of what was troubling him this morning was the oddly uncomfortable perspective that last night had given him on his marriage. He didn't really want to think about it. His marriage had been a good one by just about any measure—except sex. He had loved Lucy and would still love her today if she were alive. There had been good times and there had been bad times, but never, ever, had he once even *thought* of ending their marriage, or wished it had never happened. They had been companions and friends and allies. Not once had he been able to envision anyone replacing Lucy.

But suddenly, on a stark, gray March morning, he couldn't escape the knowledge that he and Lucy had never been lovers. Not truly. He'd ignored that simple fact for twenty-five years now. Nothing he had tried, not all the love and caring between them, had been able to heal whatever was broken in her, or whatever she was missing. And he *had* tried. Forcing himself to face a truth he'd been turning a blind eye to for so long, he made himself look at his efforts, and made himself accept that it wasn't his fault. Lucy had been the way she had been. That was the sum of it. And he had loved her enough to ignore the problem as if it didn't matter to him, either.

His hands clenched into fists now as a deep fissure in him started, finally, to heal. Jess had started that healing, he realized. A woman scarcely older than his daughter, a woman utterly without experience, had given him the inestimable gift of knowing at long last that there was nothing wrong with him, that he was not a failure as a man.

"Arlen?"

The sleepy murmur brought him to the bedside. "I'm here, Jessie." He felt himself smile as he looked down into her sleepy, hardly awake face. She didn't know, he was sure, that her last movement had bared her to the waist. Not wanting her to discover it awkwardly—hell, wanting even more to feel her satin skin on his, he knelt over her on the bed and sought her mouth with his.

"Mmm..." She welcomed his kiss languorously, opening her mouth readily, waking to voluptuous sensation even before she awoke to the day.

When her hands rose to his shoulders, and began to knead lazily, Arlen lowered himself to his elbows and slowly began to rub his chest against her breasts. The relaxed openness of her movements told him exactly how good she was feeling as she woke from the pleasure of sleep to the pleasure of lovemaking.

"Good morning," he said softly as he lifted his head.

A slow smile spread across her face, but she didn't open her eyes. Instead she stretched beneath him like a contented cat. Arlen felt again that joyous urge to laugh.

"Beautiful lady," he said huskily, "you keep moving like that and I'll forget you must be sore."

Now her eyes did open, to sleepy slits. "I'm *not* sore," she murmured. "In fact, I'm wondering if I imagined everything."

Now Arlen did laugh, deeply and happily. "Are you being provocative?"

"I hope so." Her eyes opened a little wider, and with her increasing wakefulness came shyness. He was sorry to see it. He almost felt he was reading her mind. She didn't think she was sexy enough to entice him.

"You're provocative with every breath you take," he told her. Rolling away from her a little, he grabbed the sheet and pulled it from her, baring her from head to toe.

Jessica gasped and froze, while a blush burned her face and throat. Last night, carried away by passion in the dim light, her nudity hadn't seemed to matter. This morning was different somehow, as if the gray light put a sharper edge on reality. Deep inside, her body pulsed with longing for his caresses and lovemaking, but her mind was apparently hung up in a slightly different place.

"There," Arlen said with satisfaction, and smiled into her eyes. "I wondered where that blush started. Now I know it doesn't start anywhere. It just happens everywhere."

"Arlen..."

"Shh." He brushed a light kiss on her lips and then held her eyes with his as he trailed his hand to her breast and from there to the silky curls farther down. "I don't want you to be shy with me, Jessie. You stopped being shy last night, and we had a wonderful time, didn't we?"

She nodded, her eyes clinging to his, her teeth worrying her lower lip. As he boldly slipped a finger into her, her eyelids drooped and her breath caught, but then her legs relaxed, separating more for him.

"Tender?" he asked huskily, leaning nearer.

"N-no."

"Sure?"

Even if she had wanted to, she couldn't have prevented her hips from lifting toward his hand, and she didn't want to. His touch was swiftly sweeping her from modesty to a very basic human state. He pressed the heel of his hand against her, drawing a groan from her as he stroked that most sensitive part of her.

"Don't close your eyes, Jessie," he said. "Look at me. Let me see your eyes."

And somehow, looking into his gray eyes as his hands did wickedly wonderful, terribly intimate things to her, she felt her shyness dying. How could she fail to believe he found her beautiful when he looked at her like that while pleasuring her? And when his eyes left hers and traveled elsewhere, she heard the catching of his breath and felt the tensing of his muscles, and she felt proud of her body for the first time in her life. For the moment, at any rate, that was enough. She completely forgot everything in her rising passion for this man. When he was at last sheathed in her, she had one last moment to think how lucky, how very lucky, she was that Arlen had come into her life.

Arlen was tugging on his jeans for the second time that morning when he peered out the window and saw that his cigarette-smoking, dog-walking friend was still down there, propped against the lamp post. And that was when his neck started prickling. That man had been out there for more than an hour and a half. Not even the dumbest dog would have found those bushes that interesting.

Jessie came into the room, and he glanced at her to find her flushed from her shower, hair wrapped in a towel, robe wrapped snugly around her.

"What does your neighbor across the street look like?" Arlen asked her in what he hoped was a casual tone.

"Ordinary," she answered absently. Coming over to the window beside Arlen, she followed his gaze down to the man across the street. "Oh, him? He's not one of my neighbors. I don't know who he is, but he walks his dog here from time to time. Probably visiting someone."

She turned away and made it two steps before she paused and looked back at him, her eyes suddenly huge. "You said someone had probably been watching me...."

He wanted to kick himself for allowing her to make that connection. He'd been hoping she would think the question pointless and casual. Now it was too late to back-pedal. Jessica Kilmer was no fool.

He hauled her into his arms. "Jess, the reason I came over last night is that I was a little...worried, so I came over to check things out. I only planned to be here a short time because, well, frankly, I figured you'd be so mad at me you'd throw me out."

She tilted her head back and looked up at him with a faint frown. "I see." Oh, God, she *did* see, and what she was seeing clamped a painful vise around her heart. He had come only because it was his job. He had expected her to throw him out, not to welcome him as she had. He hadn't come for her. "Why..." She had to clear her throat to find her voice, and then she started again. "Why did you think I would throw you out?"

"Well, hell," he said impatiently, and ran his fingers through his tousled hair. Jessie might have smiled if she hadn't been hurting so badly. "I stood you up, right? And you took your damn phone off the hook, which is what got me worried in the first place. I mean, I realized you had every right not to want to talk to me, but I couldn't quite convince myself you would do something like that." He gave a short laugh.

"Anyhow," he continued, "I got uptight, and I came over here to make sure you were okay. And, like a damn idiot, I left my car parked out front."

"So?" She looked up at him in perplexity, swallowing against her disappointment and hurt.

"So if that guy is keeping an eye on you for some reason, I just threw a monkey wrench in the works."

"Oh." She should, she realized dimly, be upset by this development. She should be frightened that somebody had been watching her, and might now watch her even more closely because of Arlen's presence. Emotionally, however, she could cope with only one thing at a time, and right now she was barely coping with the knowledge that Arlen hadn't come last night to be with her.

She forced herself to turn away and pulled the towel from her head. Long, damp ropes of dark hair fell all the way to her hips.

"You get along pretty well without your glasses, don't you?" he remarked as she sat at her dressing table.

"My eyes aren't that bad." She picked up a brush and started working at the ends of her long hair. "Everything's kind of fuzzy right now, sort of like that cheesecloth blur they use on older actresses in the movies." Every beat of her heart hurt. She couldn't see him clearly, thank God, but she could feel him behind her, could sense the way he was focused on her. Why couldn't he just go take a shower or something and give her a few minutes to cope with the death of a barely born dream?

"Why *did* you take your phone off the hook, Jessie?" From the way she had welcomed him, he didn't think she had been angry enough at him to do that.

"I didn't." She compressed her lips, and her fingers tightened around the brush handle until her knuckles turned white. "I must have hung it up wrong. I was a little...upset."

Abruptly she slammed the brush down on her dressing table. "Sorry," she said bitterly. "Next time I'll make sure to hang it up right. If I weren't such a damn fool, you never would have come to check up on me."

"Jessie?" He stepped closer, startled and confused by her anger and her words. "Jessie, what's wrong?"

"Wrong? Why should anything be wrong?" Her voice rose, and her lower lip started to quiver. "I spent the night with a man who just told me he didn't want to spend the night with me."

"What?" Stunned, Arlen simply stared at her reflection in the mirror.

"Forget it, Arlen. You gave yourself away. You only came over here because it's your job." Fighting valiantly against the tears, she bit her lower lip until it hurt. Pressure grew in her chest, so heavy and tight that she had to battle for breath.

Seconds ticked away in utter silence before Arlen at last spoke. When he did, his voice was a low, hard growl, unlike any tone she had ever heard from him.

"Damn you, Jessie," he said harshly. "I just spent the night engaged in the most unprofessional conduct of my entire career. How dare you suggest I was doing my job!"

Her breath wedged in her throat, and her heart slammed forcefully. Before a sound could escape her, Arlen turned away.

"Where are your glasses?" he said curtly. "I'll get them for you."

"Downstairs on the coffee table." Her voice came out thin, squeezed past the lump in her throat. God, what had she done?

He would undoubtedly leave very soon. Up until yesterday afternoon he had shown a great deal of resistance to the whole idea of any kind of relationship, and he was still wearing his wedding ring—which ought to make her feel a little like the Other Woman, but somehow didn't. She just wished she could understand why he had stayed the night with her. If it wasn't his job, then what was it? What had broken down his resistance and banished his objections?

Her hand paused in brushing, and she stared at her slightly blurry reflection. It suddenly occurred to her that she'd given up quite a few romantic dreams last night. She'd always cherished visions of romantic dates, of—

Suddenly angry at herself, she yanked the brush through a tangle and winced. Ridiculous. Experiences like last night and this morning didn't grow on trees. She wasn't naive enough to think that just *any* man could have made her feel the things Arlen had made her feel. Nor did she think his kind of patience and gentleness were found on every corner. Arlen's lovemaking was worth a thousand romantic dinner dates.

Grow up, Jessie, she thought angrily. Stop thinking like a romantic child. This is real life, and real life is never perfect. Whatever his reason, no matter why he had come to her last night, Arlen had given her an experience that was precious beyond words. And if he had used her, he had given back exactly what he had taken, unlike Chuck so many years ago.

Closing her eyes, she drew several deep, steadying breaths. She prided herself on her practicality, on her realistic approach to life. Realistically speaking, she was going to hurt whether this relationship ended now or ended later. Like it or not, her emotions were involved with this difficult man. So, knowing that, why end it sooner? Why not seize the moment, seize the joys and pleasures he offered? Why not worry about tomorrow tomorrow? Just this once in her life, why not reach out with both hands for the day?

"Jessie?" Arlen came into the room behind her and handed her glasses to her. "Do you have any phones besides the one downstairs?"

She slipped her glasses on and enjoyed her first clear sight of him since yesterday afternoon. That chest was even more impressive than she'd thought. She had to draw yet another steadying breath, but this one eased the tightness in her throat and allowed her to take pleasure in looking at him.

"Jess?" Arlen broke into her thoughts.

She lifted her eyes to his, color flaming in her cheeks. "If you want me to pay attention, you'd better put a shirt on and button your jeans."

From puzzlement, his expression turned slowly into a smile that was laced with more than a little relief. He had been tempted to storm out a little while ago, angrier than he had been in a long time because of her accusation. During his few minutes downstairs, however, he had calmed down enough to remember just what it was he had done last night. He had made love to a vulnerable, inexperienced young woman. He owed her. He also owed it to her to make allowances for the fact that this morning she was apt to be hypersensitive and unusually emotional, and that she had plenty of justification for it—both his actions and the unknown watcher's.

Arlen bent over her from behind, cupping her breasts through her robe and kissing the curve between her neck and shoulder. "You're quite a distraction yourself," he murmured. "Jess, I hate to be a pain, but do you have any phones besides the one downstairs on the phone table?"

His hands slipped from her breasts to her waist as he spoke, and Jessica felt that it was once again possible to breathe.

"I have two other phones." Her bright eyes questioned him. She might not have known him long, but she'd quickly realized he didn't ask idle questions. "Why?"

He straightened. "Maybe nothing. Where are they?"

"There's one in my study across the hall, and the other one is in the kitchen, in the corner between the pantry and the refrigerator. I can't imagine why anyone would put a phone in there, but somebody did."

"Okay. I'll be right back." He spoke casually, but he could see she wasn't buying it. That was the problem when you dealt with somebody as intelligent as Jessie. They weren't easily misled or diverted. In his business he didn't deal with too many summa cum laude graduates, but it occurred to him that the FBI might be wise to devise special methods for them. *Casual* obviously wasn't making it.

Jessica tried to restrain her curiosity, telling herself that Arlen was the agent, he should be left to do what he felt necessary without her interference, that he would certainly tell her anything that affected her. . . .

She set her brush down and followed him to the study. She just plain didn't feel that trusting this morning.

It didn't soothe her at all to find him kneeling beside her desk, staring at the telephone receiver as if it were a snake. Did he have any idea just how low his jeans were riding on his buns? Did he have any idea just how gorgeous his buns were?

"What is it?" she asked.

"Just a minute, Jess," he said. "Let me figure out the parameters of the mess before I shoot off my mouth."

She smiled faintly at that. "Mess, huh? Big or little?"

"I'm hoping like hell it's little, but the back of my neck is telling me it's bigger than—" He broke off for lack of a nonobscene expression to use.

"What does the back of your neck have to do with anything?"

Realizing he had said something he hadn't meant to, Arlen cursed under his breath. "You didn't come up here last night after I called you?"

"No." Jessica stepped closer, and now the back of *her* neck was prickling. "Arlen, what's going on?" But she had already guessed. Heck, she *knew*. She'd known at some level below conscious thought ever since he'd asked if she had any other phones. She just hadn't *wanted* to know. Now she wanted him to look up and laugh and say her phones were out of order, but she knew he wasn't going to.

"This phone is hooked up to your modem, right?"

"Yes."

"Show me the setup."

She showed him how the modem was plugged in to the phone connection in the wall, and how the phone was plugged in to the modem.

"Simple," he muttered. "When you use the modem, is the phone disconnected in any way? Does the modem shut it down?"

"No. In fact, you can pick up the receiver and listen to the modem if you want to. Once I left the modem on by accident when I called a friend. As soon as my friend picked up her phone, the modem sent out its carrier signal, but I was able to talk to her right over it through the phone receiver."

Arlen straightened and pulled a Swiss army knife out of his front pocket. While Jessica peered over his shoulder, he pried at the handset of her phone.

"What are you doing?" she asked.

"I want to look inside."

With a soft pop the handset fell apart, and Jessie looked at a maze of wires and a few small metallic things that looked like thick buttons, or disks.

Arlen lifted one of the round metallic cases. "What do you use your modem for, Jessie?"

The question sounded casual, but she wasn't buying it. "Mostly I have fun. Bulletin boards, that kind of thing. I have a few friends I communicate with. Sometimes I access the national forums for information of some kind."

"You don't do any of your work on it, though?"

"Absolutely not!" Jessica was appalled. "Arlen, the work I do is classified. I'd be breaking every regulation and—"

"Okay. I had to ask." He glanced up at her with a smile that failed to make it past the corners of his mouth. Then he put her phone back together. "Got any coffee?"

"Sure." She frowned at him, not liking the way he was trying to change tacks, but willing for the moment to let him. Arlen usually had a reason for what he did. "What would you like for breakfast? I'd better warn you, I'm short on really good stuff, like eggs and bacon."

"I haven't eaten an egg in nearly ten years," he said as he stood. "How about oatmeal?"

There was oatmeal in her cupboard, and he insisted on making it himself in the microwave, while she toasted her usual English muffin.

They ate at her small kitchen table. Jessica managed to restrain her impatience until he settled back in his chair with his second cup of coffee.

"Okay," she said. "What's going on? Come on, Arlen, I'm going to scream. Do you think I don't know you found out I was being bugged? For crying out loud, tell me. What tipped you off?"

He frowned faintly and hesitated, but only briefly. "Well," he said slowly, "I came down here to hang up the phone I thought was off the hook. Only it wasn't off the hook. I reseated it a couple of times and still got an empty, dead line. It could have been something wrong with just that phone, or it could have been that one of your other phones was off the hook."

"But they couldn't have been," Jessica objected. "I didn't touch either of them after you called, and you couldn't have gotten through to me if one of them had been off the hook."

"Precisely."

Jessica didn't think she'd ever seen him look so grim. "Arlen, let me be perfectly frank here. I am not dumb. I am, however, running into some kind of mental stone wall on this. I *don't* want to believe what my mind is telling me is going on here. So please, just tell me in so many words."

Maybe, just maybe, if he said it out loud her mind would stop trying to reject it, and then maybe she could get down to...what? Coping? How the hell did somebody cope with something like this?

He shook his head. "The phone upstairs in your computer room was off the hook, as if somebody hadn't reseated it in the cradle exactly the right way. Once I hung it up, the line reopened."

"Then . . ." Jessica's voice trailed off as she realized that the obvious thing wasn't possible. "Arlen?"

"It appears," he said flatly, "that someone was in this house last night between the time I called you to tell you I wasn't coming and the time I called and found the line busy."

He had said exactly what she had feared, and he had made it real. Cold fingers of dread gripped her spine, and she wrapped her arms around herself. She wanted desperately to deny it, to argue with him, but not even in desperation could she believe for half a second that Arlen was the kind of person who could tell her something like that if he wasn't absolutely convinced of its truth. "Why?" The word was a bare whisper.

Arlen scooted his chair around the table and sat right beside Jessica, wrapping his arm around her shoulders. "Just to put a bug in your upstairs telephone. He bugged the one in the hall, too, but he missed the one by the fridge."

"You're sure they're bugs?" The words emerged as a jerky whisper. A stupid, dumb question. What else could they possibly be?

"The Bureau uses the same kind."

Her eyes lifted to his, and he saw how hard she was trying to contain her fright. He touched her cheek, tucked a strand of hair behind her ear. "Jessie, honey, he didn't want to hurt you. That's obvious. You were completely vulnerable, and he didn't even wake you. You don't have to be afraid of that." Damn, if only he could make all this go away for her.

"No," she whispered. "I just have to live with the idea that some perfect stranger came into my house while I was sleeping...that he could come again, any time he wants. That maybe next time..." She buried her face against his shoulder, and her hands clenched into fists. "I don't think I can stand it," she said tautly. "I don't think I can stand it."

"You won't be alone," he promised rashly. "Jessie, I swear you won't be alone."

She tugged back from him and laughed almost harshly. "Right. When the thing you most want is to get out of here before things get messy. You told me there was no danger in being a double agent, Arlen. This doesn't qualify as danger?"

The thing you most want is to get out of here before things get messy. It was a hell of an indictment, and there was more than an ounce of truth in it. Reaching out with both hands, he caught Jessie's face between them and pulled her mouth to his. He kissed her hard, with passion and some of the emotional uneasiness he felt. "It's already messy, sweetheart," he said roughly. "It'll probably get downright filthy, but I'm in for the count. You'll have to throw me out. I told you, the Bureau will protect you."

An eternity passed during the moments while Jessica stared unblinkingly at him. Well, you couldn't get much clearer than that. The Bureau would protect her. Arlen would protect her because it was his job. Something inside her felt as if it were dying, but she didn't know if it was Arlen's choice of words that was killing it or the knowledge that her life had just slipped out of her control. Somebody was watching her; somebody had bugged her telephones. Somebody was deadly serious.

At long last something inside her let go a little, and her lower lip quivered. Drawing a deep breath, she closed her eyes for a moment and gathered her resources, such as they were. When she felt reasonably calm she sat back in her chair.

"And what about the intruder?" she asked in a fairly level voice. "What do you think that's all about?"

Arlen lifted one of her hands and studied her delicate fingers. Clever fingers, as he'd discovered. "Jessie, let's put that subject on the back burner for a bit. We'll talk about it later." Looking at her, he smiled ruefully. "Right now I'd just be shooting off my mouth, the kind of wild speculation that never gets anybody anywhere. I need to just let it simmer a while, okay?"

She nodded, keeping her eyes on his face.

"In the meantime, there are a couple of things I want to do. First, I want us to go together to my place. I need to change into some fresh clothes, and I want to pack a suitcase to bring back here." He saw the surprise in her eyes. "I told you, you won't be alone. I meant it. I'm here for the duration."

An unhappy smile curved her lips. Just doing his job again, of course.

"Then I want to go to the hardware store and get dead bolts for your doors. You have no idea how easily I got in here last night."

She tried to repress a shudder. "I'm beginning to get a notion."

"I plan to take care of that," he assured her. "Okay?"

Jessica nodded. Something inside her had frozen up, as if she had used up all her reactions for the time being. After Arlen squeezed her hand and let it go, she moved it back onto her lap and turned her head to look out the window at the backyard. Rain still fell in a steady drizzle, and the sky promised no improvement.

"Jessie?"

She looked at Arlen and saw he was frowning at her. "You know, I thought I'd finally made it."

"Made it how?" He never took his eyes from her. Somehow there was more going on here than her very justifiable distress about what had happened. She'd been struck in some other way, and he hoped for a clue so he could help her with it.

Jessica shrugged. "It doesn't really matter." Again she looked away.

"Jessie, talk to me."

"Why bother?" she said harshly. "Aren't things already messy enough? Anyway, I told you I was a coward."

But he didn't believe it was cowardice that put that ineffably sad look on her face. Damn, she looked like someone who'd just seen the death of all her dreams.

The cigarette smoker across the street had vanished by the time Arlen and Jessica left her house, but Arlen was sure the surveillance was continuing from some other direction. They would want to know about him, about why he'd shown up sometime during the night right after they placed their bugs. He reassured them by draping his arm around Jessica's shoulders as they hurried down the wet walk.

Jessica didn't want to go to Arlen's apartment, but he offered no other option. She was in no mood now to face the specters of his past. She had gone from the heights to the depths in an amazingly short time.

She had awakened this morning feeling positively exuberant about the night just past. She'd never dreamed that lovemaking could be so incredibly magical. Just as astonishing, though, was the amazing sense of freedom it had given her. She had lain with a man, naked skin to naked skin. They had engaged in an act of shattering intimacy, demolishing barriers she hadn't been aware of until they were gone.

Little champagne bubbles of joy had seemed to rise in her, tickling every nerve ending. She had actually made love with this man! She had been wrapped in his arms and he in hers. This highly controlled, *experienced* man had shuddered and groaned at her naive touches, had actually *begged* her to touch him again. When she remembered his encouraging whispers, the way he had gently guided her, everything inside her clenched in painfully exquisite longing.

But now she felt horrifically fragile. Reality had shattered all her wonder and joy. Arlen was an agent on a case, and she was part of that case. She had only herself to blame for losing sight of that very significant fact. There was no excuse for her shock this morning when the order of his priorities had been made clear to her. Whatever he might feel for her, and she did him the justice of thinking he felt *something,* he was first and foremost an agent. First and foremost a man who didn't want any entanglements. Hadn't he told her so, more than once?

When they arrived at his apartment, Jessica wanted to stay in the car. She didn't want to face those ghosts again. Not on top of everything else.

"Absolutely not," Arlen said flatly.

His refusal to let her wait in the car inadvertently revealed that he was worried about her safety. She felt her tension hike another notch. Was she actually supposed to endure this?

"You told me I'd be in no danger," she reminded him as she stood in the middle of the living room and watched him lock the door behind him. *That* made her edgier.

He was smiling lopsidedly as he faced her. "You sore?" he asked.

Puzzled, Jessica shook her head. Actually, she *was* a little sore, but not enough to complain about.

"Good," Arlen said. As he walked toward her, he tugged his shirt off.

Jessica swallowed and filled her eyes with the sight of smooth skin and lean muscles. She swallowed even harder when he stopped right in front of her and unbuckled his belt. Somehow, when she looked at him, it didn't seem to matter that she was just a job to him.

"You're in danger, all right," he said gruffly as he popped the snap and tugged down the zipper of his jeans. "From me."

Jessica's eyes snapped up to his face and found nothing but sincerity. He leaned forward and dropped a kiss on the tip of her nose.

"However," he said as he straightened, "I don't think you're ready for what I have in mind, so I'll just go take my shower alone."

Jessica watched him disappear down a short hallway. Her heart was beating heavily, and her blood felt as thick as molasses with desire. She wanted to lie down with him again. She wanted to run her palms over his warm, smooth skin, to feel the roughness of his legs against hers, to...

Instead he'd left her here with all his cherished re-
minders of why he didn't want to get involved. Muttering
a very unladylike word, she plopped onto his couch and
looked away from the photo of Lucy Coulter.

Damn it, Jessica thought. Damn, damn, damn. All he
had to do was kiss her or look at her in that certain sugges-
tive way and she forgot everything but her hunger for him.
Damn, it was unreal!

And she had no one to blame for this but herself. He'd
warned her. How many warnings did she need, anyway?
He'd been up front about his ring, and he sure as hell
hadn't been subtle about it when he brought her here on
Friday and showed her his shrine. He'd even come right out
and said it in so many words: he wasn't in it for the long
haul anymore. He'd said that right to her face.

Stretched out on her back, head propped on the arm of
the sofa, Jessica found herself looking at the picture of his
daughter, Melanie. She and Melanie were definitely con-
temporaries, and she could see that that might be a big
stumbling block for Arlen.

As for his wife... Deliberately Jessica turned her head
and looked at the photo of Lucy Coulter that sat on the table by the easy chair. It was stupid to envy the dead, but
Jessica admitted to envying Lucy Coulter. Arlen's wife had
had twenty years of steadfast love of the kind Jessica could
only imagine. In fact, she was feeling a whole bunch of
unpleasant, immature feelings she had never felt before,
everything from jealousy to possessiveness to anger.

"Damn." She sighed and turned her attention to the
ceiling. Maybe he hadn't brought her here because he was
concerned about her safety. Maybe he'd brought her to remind her.

That idea hurt. It hurt so badly that she felt the prickle
of tears. Squeezing her eyes shut, she turned her face to the
back of the couch and confronted her own folly. In spite of
repeated warnings, she'd given this man everything. And
now, now when she ought to heed her common sense, she
was unable to turn her back and walk away. She *needed*
him! And that was the worst folly of all.

Was it really too much to wish he was moving in with her because he wanted to be with her, not because he felt honor bound to protect her? Was it too much to wish that his motive was clear rather than so muddied?

"Jessie."

The husky murmur preceded the gentle touch of fingertips on her cheek. She felt the couch dip as Arlen perched beside her and turned her face toward him. Struggling against a tangle of emotions, she kept her eyes closed.

"Aw, Jessie," he said gruffly, and the next thing she knew she was sitting up within the tight circle of his arms, held snugly against his hard chest. He smelled like soap, and his T-shirt smelled a little like bleach, and his touch was somehow so reassuring and comforting that the tears came anyway.

"I know," he murmured, rocking her gently, stroking her hair, rubbing her back soothingly. "I know, honey. It's all too damn much at once." And he *did* know. What twenty-one years of marriage hadn't taught him, twenty-three years of raising a daughter had. A woman who'd just given her virginity ought to be able to snuggle up to the man who'd taken it and worry about nothing at all. She ought to be able to savor her changes and try out her new powers, and by God somebody ought to be pouring champagne and telling her she'd made him feel like a king, like a conqueror, like Tarzan.

Instead she'd learned that her phones were tapped, that her house had been invaded by strangers while she slept and that she was being watched.

And then he had brought her here. Looking at Lucy's photo, Arlen tightened his arms around Jessica. Eventually, he thought, you had to let some things go. Eventually he would have to let Lucy go. He wasn't quite ready, he admitted, to take that portrait and put it away, but that didn't give him the right to hurt the woman who was in his arms. He was being unfaithful not to Lucy, who was gone, but to Jessica, who was here.

Jessica spoke on a broken sob. "I feel so dumb...."

"Shh. You're not dumb, Jessie. Not dumb at all." He tilted her face up and kissed away her tears, acknowledging how much he had missed being needed. How much he needed to once again bring a smile to a woman's face, how much he wanted to kiss away tears . . . and how damn tired he was of being alone. "It's been a rough morning," he said, and wiped away the last tear with a fingertip.

"Yeah." She sniffled. So rough she couldn't even decide which part was roughest.

"I told you once before that the whole Bureau would be looking out for you if you agreed to help us. I meant it, Jessie. After what I found this morning, you can count on never being alone for a minute."

The damn job again. She was getting sick of hearing about the Bureau. It was, however, an inescapable fact of her life at the moment, and she would be foolish to ignore reality just because she was emotionally tender. She leaned back a little to better see Arlen's face, but he didn't loosen his hold on her. When she spoke, she sounded incredibly weary. "Then there *is* danger."

"I don't know," he said honestly. "All I know is that those bugs and the fact that somebody entered your house just don't fit the usual recruitment scenario. Something else is going on, and it makes me uneasy as hell."

"That's why you didn't want me to stay there alone?"

He shook his head. "Not entirely. The fact is, I don't know how many bugs there may be in the place, but it's safest to assume the ones in the phones aren't the whole thing."

"Can't you find out?" The idea of her whole house being bugged struck at her in deep, painful ways. She felt so *victimized*.

"Honey, I could look, but I couldn't be sure I found everything. And, unlike in the movies, an electronic sweep isn't something that can be done in a couple of hours. It takes *days* to sweep a single room. And even that's no guarantee, because it's possible for somebody to sit across the street with a microphone that can pick up the vibrations of the windowpanes and hear every word you say. And that's why I wanted you to come with me. Part of the reason. We need to talk about this, and for the time being I don't think we ought to do it there."

He stroked her cheek with his fingers, hating the horror and pain he saw in her eyes. "Jessie, honestly, I really don't think anybody's going to be listening. I truthfully think the phone bugs are the sum of it."

"Why?"

"Because you live there alone. Nobody would be interested in anything you might say to yourself. I just want us to be cautious, that's all."

That made sense, and a hard knot inside her eased a hair. "But now they know about you."

"I took some precautions. Relax. Nobody will get in there without me knowing about it now."

"Relax? Arlen, I don't want people I don't know listening to *anything* I say!"

"I know, Jessie. I know."

"You *don't* know, Arlen. You *can't* know. You can't possibly understand how this makes me feel."

"Then tell me, Jessie. Tell me." He cradled her head against his shoulder, feeling the tension in her.

"The only home I ever had until now was when I was little," she said after a moment, wondering how she could possibly make anyone understand. "My daddy was a roughneck in the West Texas oilfields. We lived in Midland, and Daddy would come in from the fields on weekends. I can still remember the way he used to come through the door. He was a big man, really big, with huge hands, and he used to pick me right up and swing me in circles over his head until my sides ached from laughing. Then he'd set me down and pick Mamma up and kiss her till she turned all pink."

Feeling shy again, she stole an upward look at Arlen and found him listening intently. Reassured, she plunged on.

"Anyhow, Daddy was killed in a well blowout when I was seven. Mamma and I went to live with Daddy's mother. She really didn't want us there, and she was forever saying so, but I don't think Mamma ever heard her, or ever cared. Mamma just started drinking, and she pretty much kept to her room and stayed drunk."

Arlen's arms tightened around her, as if he could shelter her from remembered pain.

"Basically," Jessica said, "it wasn't a home. It was a place where I slept and did chores to earn my keep. And when I got older, my grandmother started to get suspicious. I don't know if I actually did something to start her off, or if she just got a little crazy, but she started rifling my belongings nearly every day, and she listened in on every one of my phone calls. I can't tell you how hard I worked to graduate early and get a scholarship so I could go away to college. Arlen, I can't stand the thought of anybody doing that to me again."

He smoothed her hair back from her face and then looked down into her brown eyes with an intensity that left no doubt about his sincerity. "I can't stop them from listening, Jessie, but I promise I'll get them. I'll see that they pay for it."

His words touched her so deeply that she once again had to blink back tears. "I won't hold you to that. I know how hard it is to get criminals for anything these days." Closing her eyes, she leaned into the comfort of his warmth and strength and tried to let go of her anger and fear. "I don't suppose I can just move into an apartment somewhere?"

"No." The single word conveyed Arlen's regret and determination. "Don't you see, Jessie? Right now you're our *only* link with this person or persons. Somebody is obviously very interested in you, but if we let him know we're on to him, he's apt to vanish back into the woodwork and turn his attention elsewhere. Right now you're the only lead we've got."

"So I'm bait." She shivered.

"I'll take care of you."

And then, because he couldn't stand the tension between them another minute, because he felt responsible for wounding her, because he wanted her to smile for him, he scooped her up from the couch and carried her into his bedroom. It was all he had to give her, but he would give her the absolute best that was in him. He would make her forget everything else.

When Arlen laid her down on his bed, Jessie was almost afraid to open her eyes, sure that she would see a picture of Lucy Coulter on the bedside table. Her heart had risen to her throat and hammered nervously as she listened to him move around. He closed the curtains against the gray day; the sound was unmistakable. Then he sat on the edge of the bed beside her.

"Jessie," he said gently.

Her bright brown eyes opened and met his, and in them he saw her fears and her questions. He waited as she darted nervous glances around, taking in the sterility, the lack of color. The lack of photographs. When her gaze returned to his, he cupped her cheek with his palm and gave her the only reassurance he could.

"I've never shared this bed with anyone, Jess."

Jessica squeezed her eyes shut again. It was silly, she told herself, to worry about such things. The man had loved Lucy, after all. That was a *fact,* and nothing was changed by whether this had been her bed. But it mattered anyway, and she wished there was some way to thank him for understanding that. Here, at least, there were no ghosts.

Then Arlen began to undress her. He supposed there were seductive tricks to undressing a woman, but he had never learned them, and he wasn't in the mood for that, anyway. He wanted no seduction, no tricks, no skills and practiced gestures. He wanted to get at something more elemental, more honest. Something real.

At last she lay naked before him, with her eyes still tightly shut. Her hands betrayed her, however. They made restless little movements against the gray bedspread, movements that told him how difficult it was for her to pretend passivity. He started to reach for her, but then snatched his hands back. There was something they had to deal with first, something that had wounded them both.

"Damn you, Jessie," he said gruffly for the second time that day. "What kind of man do you take me for? I'm so damn mad at you I can hardly stand it."

Her eyes snapped open. "Then why are you doing this?" she demanded hoarsely. "Is this a punishment?" The possibility tore at her, and she thought the pain would kill her.

"Hell!" he swore fiercely. "Damn it, woman, I want you to admit you know better than that. I want you to admit that I *want* you. I want you to stop putting us both down by believing that I could, that I *would* make love to you for any other reason!''

Standing, he yanked at his own clothes and then stood before her magnificently naked and fully aroused. ''I *don't* prostitute myself, Jess.''

She gasped, and the color drained from her face. ''I didn't think...I never meant...'' Oh, God, was that what she had made him think? Was that what her fear sounded like?

Arlen sat down on the bed beside her, facing her, but still refusing to touch her.

''It may be all I have to give a woman, Jessie, but at least it's *honest*. It's truthful. I want you. Now, damn it, I want to hear you admit it! Admit that I want you!''

She scrambled onto her knees and flung her arms around him, everything forgotten in the horror of the wound she had given this man. She hadn't meant it the way it sounded. Such a thought had never occurred to her. And somewhere, dimly, she heard her voice saying exactly that.

Arlen's fingers tunneled into her hair and clutched her close to his shoulder. ''Say it,'' he said hoarsely. ''Flat out. Just say it, Jess.''

''You want me,'' she said.

''Say it again.''

''You want me.''

''Why did I spend the night in your bed, Jessie?''

''Because you want me.''

He sighed, a heavy sigh, then lowered them both to the bed. ''Whatever else is going on here, Jessie—and I don't pretend to have all the answers—that's one thing you can damn well be sure of. I want you.''

She thought she could live with that surety as his hands began to ignite marvelous fires all over her aching body. His job might be the reason he was moving in with her. In fact, it certainly was, since he wasn't interested in any entanglements. His job might be the reason he spent so much time with her, and the reason he looked after her and watched over her. But at least when he climbed into her bed she would believe he was there because he wanted to be. And when the job was over and he at last went away, she would still have that surety to comfort her. He wanted her.

Chapter 9

The first thing Arlen did on reaching his office Monday morning was tip his chair back and look out at the sky. An errant patch of blue winked at him through chasing clouds, hinting at the possibility of a sunny day.

Not that he cared. This morning he felt anything but normal. His mind seemed to have gone off to never-never land. Beneath the top level of his thoughts, whispers from the day before made a background symphony. Jessica had the smoothest, softest skin, the...

"Hell," he muttered, and swiveled his chair so that he faced his desk. So what if he had figured he would never know a weekend like that as long as he lived? So what if he had believed himself too old, too staid and too rational to experience anything like that? The fact was, he *had* experienced it, but that was no excuse for acting like a moon-struck calf.

Maybe he ought to send some roses to Jessie....

"Arlen?" Donna walked into the office carrying a large brown envelope. "This came by messenger from the medical examiner."

Thoughts of Jessica took a back seat to the realization that the M.E. had found something he considered too important to trust to the telephone. Arlen tore impatiently at the flap and pulled out a manila folder with a typed note paper-clipped to the front of it. Five minutes later he buzzed Donna and told her to ask Lisa and Phil to come to his office.

"The facility security officer at MTI didn't commit suicide," he told the two agents as soon as they were seated across the desk from him. "The M.E. says it's definitely murder disguised to look like suicide. He included a bunch of photos I'm going to transmit to the National Crime Lab for verification, but that's pro forma. I don't expect them to find any differently."

He tossed half of the stack of photos to Phil and half to Lisa. "Take a look. The key is the ligature mark around the left wrist. Whoever did it tried to avoid leaving a mark by using a broad binding, but Dumberton found the traces anyhow. Dave Barron's hands were tied behind him when he died."

Phil muttered an oath. "Then there's no powder on his hands, either?"

"Actually, there is. Our bad guy is no typical dummy. He must have wrapped Barron's hand around the weapon and fired the second shot, the slug we found in the wall just behind Barron's chair, the one that looked like Barron might have missed on his first try. There's definitely powder penetration. But it doesn't negate the fact that Barron died with his hands tied behind him."

Lisa finished thumbing through the photos and reached for a diagram of the bullet's path through Barron's skull. "Any other tip-off?"

"Dumberton thinks the angle of the bullet penetration is an unlikely one to result from Barron shooting himself. It's *possible,* but doubtful, because he would have had to get into a strained and somewhat unnatural position. There are a dozen easier angles from which he could have shot himself."

"But that's not conclusive," Lisa observed.

"No," Arlen agreed, "but the ligature marks settle that. Dumberton says the blood pooled in the hands behind the restriction in a way that indicates the binding was removed *after* the heart stopped.''

"*That*'s conclusive," Phil said. He tossed his stack of photos back onto the desk. "And this ties in to the business with the Kilmer woman?"

"I'm afraid it might." Arlen was surprised that Phil had drawn the connection so immediately, but then, Phil was nobody's fool. *The Kilmer woman.* That was how he ought to think of her while he was working on the case, but he couldn't manage it. An image of her long, silky hair on the pillow this morning flashed before his mind's eye, and he felt himself stir in response. Not now!

"Her phones are bugged, and I'm pretty sure her house was being watched yesterday morning." He saw Lisa and Phil exchange glances and figured they had speculated on his relationship with Jessie. "I don't need to tell you this isn't a typical recruitment scenario. It occurred to me that perhaps Leong's approach to Jessica triggered this other stuff somehow, although I can't imagine why. It just seems too damn coincidental, though, that we could have a recruitment attempt on one hand and this other hanky-panky on the other, and not have any link between them. Top that off with the M.E.'s report, and this is beginning to look like a hell of a mess."

Leaning forward, he retrieved the photos and slipped them into the envelope. "It also occurs to me," he said slowly, "that somebody is scared to death. Maybe Barron did something, or threatened to do something, that scared somebody badly enough to kill him. That could be a lot of things, of course, but the thing that leaps forcibly to mind is that Barron was preparing a written report detailing the theft of a classified document, and that he was planning to submit that report to us. His death prevented that. A little too neatly, to my way of thinking."

He looked from Lisa to Phil, then back again. They were both listening intently, reserving judgement, so he plunged ahead. "The next coincidence is that the document theft Barron was planning to report happened to involve Jessica Kilmer. What's more, she refused to accept Barron's supposition that it was mislaid, and she made a lot of noise about it."

Phil gave a low whistle. "You're right. It's too much co-incidence, especially when she's being watched."

"So we can assume somebody's running scared," Arlen remarked. He lowered his chin to his chest and stared at his hands. "Damned if I see how Leong might fit in, though. Talk about left field."

Leong was till somewhere out in left field twenty minutes later when Lisa and Phil left Arlen's office. It was easy enough to build a scenario of a spy scared enough to murder Barron to prevent him from calling the FBI. It was easy to suppose Jessica's phones had been bugged and that her house was being watched for the same reason, to see if she turned to the FBI. Of course, there were little discrepancies, and there were more than a few questions. Like why had Barron been murdered, while a wait-and-see approach had been taken with Jessie? Would Jessie be in danger if the watchers discovered that Arlen was a federal agent?

The thought disturbed him more than he wanted to admit. He almost wished he hadn't thought of fear as a motive. A man after money was fairly predictable as to how he would handle events. A terrified man was a loose cannon capable of unpredictable devastation.

Standing, he looked out the window at the street far below. He wouldn't, he realized, feel comfortable again until he had Jessie close, within sight and within reach. Where he could protect her and be certain of her safety. In his arms, her satin thighs against his...

A short, muffled laugh escaped him. Damn, he thought, there he went again. And just what the hell did that say about him?

Jessica arrived for her lunch date with Greg Leong feeling a more than ordinary amount of edginess. It wasn't so much that she feared this meeting—Arlen had been insistent that absolutely nothing would happen except a possible introduction to someone else—but it had been a bad morning from the outset, and she had no hope that lunch would go any more smoothly.

Lisa Gonzales and Phil Harrigan were already in the Pub, seated at a central table and facing one another in a way that Jessica imagined gave them a full view of everything in the restaurant. Arlen had shown her file photos of them last night so she would recognize them, and she supposed they had seen photos of her, too. She wondered what photos the FBI had of her and shifted a little uneasily as she wondered how they had come by them. MTI had a photo in her personnel file, of course. Maybe that was it.

A glance at her watch told her that Leong was ten minutes late; her lunch hour was dwindling away. Deciding not to wait any longer, she ordered the house salad and iced tea, and tried not to look at Phil and Lisa again. Somebody else might be watching her, too; Arlen had warned her of that earlier as they stood in the chilly morning air beside her car. He'd looked so businesslike, so reserved and controlled in his gray suit. Every inch the federal agent. Every seam and button and hair in place. Unapproachable. Unreachable.

And then he'd robbed her of her breath by bending from his great height, wrapping his arms around her and cupping her bottom in his large hands. His own breath had had a ragged, tattered sound as he pulled her slowly, snugly, deliciously against him for a long moment.

"Hold that thought, Jessie," he'd whispered into her ear, sending a delectable shiver of anticipation shooting right to her core.

She was holding that thought now as she stared down at a limp-looking house salad and felt everything inside her go into a tailspin of longing.

"Miss Kilmer?"

Greg Leong's British-accented voice reached through her pleasurable haze and jolted her unpleasantly. Her stomach gave an anxious lurch. Somehow she managed to invite him to sit and brushed aside his apology for his tardiness.

"Dr. Kostermeyer asked me to say hello for him," Leong said after he'd placed his own order. "He wants to know if you might be able to come by the university next week sometime. He has that reference on nonlinear response you asked about."

"I'll give him a call," Jessica promised. "I'm surprised he found it. I sure didn't give him much to go on."

The conversation continued in a desultory fashion. With half an ear Jessica listened to Leong's description of his graduate research. It wasn't long before she developed the conviction that he had no more interest in this meeting than she had. He, too, was marking time until he could do whatever it was he'd been sent to do. That realization made her even edgier, because it confirmed that Arlen hadn't been mistaken in his impression that this was a recruitment approach.

And, frankly, she didn't know if she could handle that right now. It had been scary enough when she thought it was the only thing going on, but added to the fact that her phones were bugged and someone had been watching her house—well, it was just too much. She struggled with an overwhelming urge to throw down her napkin and tell Leong to get lost. She had promised Arlen she would do this, but she wasn't at all sure she could make it through this one lunch.

And just when she was sure her nerves would force her to take some kind of action, a large, dark hand clapped down on Leong's shoulder.

"Greg! How have you been?"

Jessica was never sure afterward what she had expected, but it certainly hadn't been a government clone type with an Eastern European accent.

That evening, over dinner at a quiet restaurant, Arlen laughed as she described her reaction. "You expected a short, squat, ugly Neanderthal," he told her. "Something out of a B movie."

"I guess," she admitted. "I was surprised that he seemed so normal. Fashionable. Even his haircut was the latest style."

"These guys are simply foreign editions of your average government agent, Jessie. Like I told you, no difference between them and us except ideology. The last thing they want is to stand out like a sore thumb."

"Well, he would have passed for a banker or a life insurance salesman."

Arlen's laughter faded, and he reached across the table to cover her hand with his. Dinner out had been as much a necessity as a romantic invitation. As a precautionary measure, they couldn't discuss any of this once they returned to her house. "Phil and Lisa got a picture of him. Who did he say he was?"

"Jan Dobrocek. He said he's from Czechoslovakia, and that he's studying mechanical engineering at the university. He certainly knows enough about engineering school to substantiate that."

"That wouldn't surprise me." He'd ordered a white wine, and now he paused to refill Jessica's glass. He knew she didn't really care for it, but she was wound up as tight as a top, and she was drinking it without even realizing it. For all that her meeting had been boring, she had invested a lot of what Arlen called *adrenaline time* into it. It was hard to come down from that kind of high. "A surprising number of Eastern bloc students also have intelligence missions. And some students are also members of intelligence organizations like the KGB and GRU."

"GRU?"

"Russian army intelligence."

Jessica gave him a faint, embarrassed smile. "I don't mean to be naive, Arlen, but with all the easing of tensions lately, and with things happening like the Berlin Wall coming down, all this cloak-and-dagger stuff sounds even harder to believe."

"Since *perestroika* and *glasnost,* Russian intelligence activities in this country have increased tenfold. Spying isn't a matter of hostility, it's a matter of common sense. No nation wants to deal from a position of blindness or weakness. Plus, we've got a lot of technology, both military and otherwise, that makes spying a worthwhile activity no matter how friendly we get. In fact, some of our best friends spy on us all the time. Want me to name a few?"

Jessica felt her smile broadening, softening. She liked it when Arlen got wound up on his hobbyhorse like this. She wondered if he even knew it was his hobbyhorse, or that all his earnestness made something inside her feel warm. It was nice to know that some people didn't become cynical and uncaring, that some people still believed in the old-fashioned ideals. She caught herself trying to store up every nuance of his expression, as if she were taking a mental snapshot for posterity. But then, posterity was all she would have. Deliberately, she took another mental snapshot.

Gray eyes suddenly twinkled at her. "Are you even listening, Jessie? Spying is supposed to be fun and exciting."

She wrinkled her nose. "If lunch was a taste of it, it's going to be the most boring thing I've ever done."

"I hope it stays that way." Honest to God, he did. But he was afraid, with neck-prickling certainty, that this time the game was following no known rules. Foreign intelligence operatives weren't above homicide, but they invariably reserved it for their own people who strayed or defected. Arlen honestly couldn't think of a single instance where an American on American soil had been injured by a foreign intelligence operative.

Until Dave Barron. He was inclined to believe Barron had been killed by a fellow traitor, but regardless, something truly unusual was going on. For the moment, however, he didn't want Jessica worrying about such things. He just wanted her to be cautious. Extraordinarily cautious. So how did he casually persuade a brainy lady to act as if her life was in danger without admitting to her that it actually might be?

"Arlen?"

Jessie's soft voice roused him from his preoccupation, and he looked across the table at her perplexed face.

"You're lovely, Jessie," he said abruptly, from the heart. Her hair was caught up in that ridiculous knot he had wanted to take down almost from the minute he laid eyes on it, but suddenly he didn't mind that. In fact, it was just fine with him if nobody but him ever saw that shiny, thick, brown glory tumbling down around her hips. He liked knowing it was there, knowing he could reach out and pull the pins free any time he chose. He liked the pink flush on her silken cheeks and the small dent in her upper lip, her tiny nose and her long, thick eyelashes. He liked the fact that she wasn't pretty and she wasn't beautiful. She was lovely, and that was infinitely more precious.

Her blush in response to his compliment made him smile, and he was tempted to let the whole damn case go to hell while he spent a little more time telling her things that would deepen her blush. That, however, would be foolhardy. Besotted he might be, but foolhardy he had never been, and he wasn't about to start.

"Jess..."

There was a sober note in his voice that she couldn't ignore. The FBI agent was back, serious and grave and very businesslike.

"Give it to me straight," she said. "I can take it."

One corner of his mouth lifted, but the smile didn't reach his eyes. "I want you to be very careful for a while."

The unease that hadn't once left her since the bugs in her phones had been discovered now clenched her stomach in a death grip. "How careful?" she managed to ask steadily.

He'd been right, Arlen thought. She wasn't going to be easily led...or misled. "Very careful," he repeated. "I'm sure I'm being overly cautious, but...some things just aren't adding up right. That makes me nervous, so I get...overly cautious."

Jessica's brown eyes never wavered behind her glasses. "Cut to the chase. *How* cautious? Am I supposed to act as if there might be a contract out on me? You want me to make sure there isn't a car within half a mile when I cross the street? Or just something more reasonable, such as never going anywhere alone? Come on, Arlen. Lay it out for me."

Admiration stirred in him, and he reached across the table, capturing both her hands in his. "You're really something else, Jessie Kilmer."

She licked her lips nervously. "What I am is scared, and you're scaring me more by not answering my question."

Her gaze was almost beseeching, and he yearned to erase the fears that were plaguing her, but there was no way he could. Not now.

"Look," she said. "I've known since you found the bugs in my phones yesterday that this is no longer something I'm volunteering for. Like it or not, I'm in it up to my neck, and there's no way out. Whatever is going on, I'll do what you tell me, because that's the smartest thing I can do now. Just tell me and get it over with. And while we're on the subject, maybe you can let me in on what's really going on. I don't like being in the dark."

"I can't tell you what's really going on, Jessie. Partly because I don't know much, and partly because what I do know is official information. Need to know only." That was something Lucy had never understood about his work. She had always resented the secrecy it forced on him. Now he found himself tensing in anticipation of a similar reaction from Jessica.

It never came. She looked disappointed, and for an instant her lips parted, as if she wanted to ask a question, but then she nodded her acceptance. "I guess I can understand that. What is it you want me to do?"

He squeezed her hands one last time and then released them so the waiter could serve their dinners. When they were alone again, he plunged in.

"You pretty much got it right when you asked if you ought to behave as if someone has a contract out on you."

Jessica, who had just lifted her fork, immediately set it down. "I don't suppose you're exaggerating?" she asked hopefully.

He smiled wryly. "Slightly. I want you to be cautious, honey. I want you to avoid being alone, and I want you to avoid going anywhere with only one other person, myself being the only exception to that rule. To be perfectly frank, I don't have any concrete reason to believe you stand in any physical danger, but some things have happened that make me feel it would be wise to *act* as if you might be."

"An ounce of prevention."

"That's one way of looking at it. Honestly, I don't want to alarm you unduly, but I'll feel a whole lot easier if I know you're being careful. On the other hand, I don't think you're in so much danger that I need to get you a bodyguard. Okay?"

He hated to do this to her. There was something unspeakably hurtful about depriving someone of the basic sense of personal safety that ought to be a human birthright. Unfortunately, Arlen could see no way around it.

Without knowing why Barron had been killed, it was impossible to evaluate the risk that Jessica faced. Nor could he protect her without her full cooperation. It wouldn't matter how many agents he surrounded her with if she wouldn't exercise her own common sense for her own protection.

"Okay." Her expression never faltered, but there was a small catch in her voice as she answered.

He watched her pick up her fork again, and he ached for her, but there wasn't a damn thing he could do about it. He was stunned by the burst of savage possessiveness he suddenly felt for her, and he battled an urge to simply sweep her up from the table and carry her away. He wasn't used to feeling such caveman impulses—could not, in fact, remember the last time he had had such an urge. Unsettled, he stared at his food as if it had grown mildew.

Arlen looked tired, Jessica thought. Every hair on his head was still neatly in place, his tie was still carefully knotted, even the front of his white shirt was still crisp and fresh looking, but there was something about him that nonetheless said it had been a long, hard day. Now here it was dinnertime, and he was still working.

"Is that it?" she asked.

He looked at her, arching a single dark eyebrow. "Isn't that enough?"

"Absolutely." She summoned a bright smile. "So now the workday is over and we can relax?"

For an instant he looked startled, as if he didn't know what to make of her reaction to all this, but then, gradually, his expression gentled, and the tension seeped almost visibly out of him. "Sure," he said. "Now we can relax. It's been a hell of a day."

"I thought so," Jessica said gravely. "I suppose you're used to working all the time, but I'm not. My evenings are sacred for relaxation, and I mean to keep them that way. Maybe you ought to try it."

He gave a short laugh. "Sure, next time I have time."

"You have time right now."

Again his expression gentled. "You're right. I do."

After dinner, instead of going directly to her house as she expected, he drove them out of town to a secluded hilltop overlooking the lake. Moonlight turned the water to molten silver, and silvery clouds raced across the star-studded sky. A study in chiaroscuro, the night was breathtaking.

"'Deep in the heart of Texas.'" Arlen murmured. Turning, he studied Jessica's profile. "When was the last time you made out in a car, Jessie?"

"Never." She turned her head to look at him. "My education has been deficient in some respects. I'm sure you noticed."

"Nothing I'd call a deficiency." His voice was soft, husky, as he reached out and pulled a single pin from her hair. A heavy lock tumbled down her shoulder and across her breast.

Her heart began a slow, heavy beating, and she was suddenly aware that she was breathing through her mouth, as if she could no longer get enough air. He looked so serious in the shadows, so intent as he reached out yet again and loosened another lock of hair to tumble downward. She took another mental snapshot and tried to block out all her fears and worries. Each moment with Arlen was precious, because they were numbered. Because there was an inevitable end, she didn't want to miss a single instant.

"Arlen?" She spoke his name on an indrawn breath, a soft, hesitant sound.

"Shh," he answered quietly, and slid toward her. "Shh . . ."

He captured her head gently between his hands, sifting his fingers into her hair, turning her mouth up to his. His lips caressed hers, brushing lightly back and forth in a movement so gentle and enticing that she felt her own mouth open in silent demand.

"Shh . . ." he murmured again, as if she had said something, and with his tongue he traced her lips, moistening them, teasing them.

"Arlen . . ." She sighed his name and turned her body toward him, raising her arms to lay her palms on his chest, to stroke them upward to his broad shoulders. Just to feel his strength, his warmth, his hardness, his *reality*. Never had she dreamed how important, how reassuring, how comforting, such things as a person's scent could be. The way he smelled, the way he felt beneath her hands, these things had become familiar already, familiar and incredibly *good*. Being close to him like this filled her with purely emotional warmth and well-being that had nothing to do with desire.

"Sweet Jessie," he whispered just before his tongue plunged into her mouth. It could have been a demanding kiss, but somehow it wasn't. It was warm, enticing, arousing and tender, an invitation to play rather than a seduction. When his mouth left hers to trail toward her ear, Jessica snuggled closer and reciprocated, nipping at his earlobe.

A low, husky laugh rumbled up from his chest. Releasing her head, he wrapped his arms around her and hugged her close. "Nope," he said. "No deficiency at all."

He settled himself more comfortably against the seat and tucked Jessica's head onto his shoulder. "There was a time when I would have taken things a lot farther, but, frankly, I'm too damn old now to get that turned on in a car. I guess that's one gap I'll have to leave in your education, Jessie."

Jessica found a shirt button with her fingers and, taking care not to let him know what she was doing, eased it from the buttonhole. "You've got a real self-image problem," she scolded him. "You talk like you're ninety." Her fingers found another button.

"I guess I've been feeling old," he admitted. "Damn it, Jess, I'm going to be a grandfather."

"So?" She eased the second button free. "Does that mean you automatically graduate to a walker and a cane?"

Again that laugh rumbled up from his chest. "Are you trying to make me feel dumb?"

"No. I'm just trying to point out that by today's standards you're still a young man. Younger than most grandfathers, I'll bet, and very likely to be around to be a great-grandfather." She slipped her hand inside his shirt, resting her palm against warm, smooth skin. "I like your skin," she whispered, suddenly breathless. Her heart slipped into high gear, partly at her temerity in touching him like this, and partly from excitement at his nearness.

"Sneaky lady," he murmured, his voice deepening. "What are you up to?"

"I like to touch you," she admitted on a whisper.

"I like you to touch me." His lips found her forehead, and she didn't know which stirred her more, the sound of his kiss or the warm feel of it on her skin. "Go ahead, Jessie. Whatever you like."

"I thought you were too old to get turned on in a car?" she teased ruthlessly as her hand slid farther into his shirt, approaching but not quite touching the nub of a very sensitive nipple.

"So I was drowning in self-pity," he muttered, turning a little toward her. "Lying, even. Right now I feel like eighteen."

"Good," she said with a sigh, drawing the word out. "Good...."

Such warm, smooth skin, Jessica thought as she ran her palm over his ribs and chest. She knew what he wanted—one of the nice things about him was that he made no secret of his likes and dislikes—but, for the moment she withheld it.

"Vixen," he muttered on a truncated laugh. Catching her chin, he tilted her face up and bent to plunder her mouth. They were both still dressed for the office, but a few extra layers proved to be scant impediment. When Jessica next caught her breath, her beige blouse lay open, revealing the beige teddy beneath.

Arlen smoothed his palm over her satin-covered breast and felt her nipple bead in response. "Ah, Jessie," he said unsteadily, "you commit all your sins in lingerie shops."

"Not anymore."

He laughed again, a rough, low, intimate sound that sent dancing tingles along her spine. "Not anymore," he agreed, then planted a soft, hot kiss at the base of her throat. "It feels so damn good to hold you and touch you and taste you...."

She knew exactly what he meant. She was curling into him, melting into him, yearning for closer, deeper touches.

The confinement of the car annoyed her; the seat was suddenly uncomfortable. She wanted him on her, in her, with a fierceness that beggared simple passion. She needed the *emotion* of being his woman, even if only for a short time. She needed to feel possessed and claimed. And she needed to give him all the comfort and all the pleasure she might be capable of giving. She felt expansive, all woman, all womanly.

"Damn!" Arlen muttered the word explosively and caught her tight against his chest, stilling her. "Let's go home," he said thickly.

A small, muffled sound of disappointment escaped her.

"I know," he murmured. "But we could get arrested for this, never mind what I'm *thinking* about doing." It was easy to imagine the headline: FBI Agent Arrested For Public Lewdness. "The director wouldn't like the publicity."

"I guess not." Jessica released her tension in a long, shaky sigh, then relaxed against him. "I guess I wouldn't much like it myself."

He kissed her temple and fumbled at the buttons of her blouse, fastening them. "You're dynamite, lady," he told her gruffly.

"So are you."

He gave her a quick, hard kiss, then started the car and headed back toward town. A few minutes later he reached over and took her hand, bringing her palm to rest on his thigh.

It was hard now for her to believe that only a couple of short days ago she had sat in this same car and wondered what it would be like to be able to rest her head on his shoulder as she was doing now. Nor had her imaginings even begun to approach the reality.

Of course, a couple of days ago she hadn't been in love.

The realization settled over her gently, like dandelion puffs or goose down. And, like a goose-down comforter, it felt warm and cuddly. Right. Inevitable. Predestined.

It was going to hurt eventually, and eventually she would feel like a fool, but right now she wrapped herself in the glow and settled down to enjoy it. She had always believed that feelings were something that happened, that they couldn't be controlled or changed by argument. If she loved Arlen, she loved him, and there was nothing she could do about it except accept it. And be careful not to let him know.

The house looked very dark and very empty when Arlen pulled into the driveway and parked in the rear beside her car. He turned off the ignition, and the silence was almost deafening, punctuated only by the ticking of the cooling engine.

Suddenly she didn't want to go in there. She still wanted to be with Arlen, still wanted to curl up in a private, dark place with him, but her house suddenly wasn't it. In there lurked threats of an amorphous kind. In there, people listened. In there, she was watched.

"I'm suddenly feeling very paranoid," she told him.

"I can imagine." That was the other thing that should be a human birthright, but, unfortunately, too often wasn't: the inviolability of privacy, the sanctity of the home. He, too, stared up at her house and understood that her dream had been destroyed.

"We could go to my place, Jessie," he suggested, even though he didn't think it would be wise to break her routine. Startling a nervous opposition could be dangerous. He was only human, however, and he hated what he was doing to Jessica.

"No," she answered flatly. His place was worse. Hers might be bugged, but his was haunted.

He bit back promises that he suddenly longed to make, promises about solving this case, promises about how things would feel normal again, about how the memory of the violation would fade. They were promises he didn't have the power to keep or enforce, so he silenced them, and in the silence he ached.

Arlen Coulter's soul had been meant for a knight-errant. He had once cherished dreams of fighting for truth and justice, of righting wrongs and defending the defenseless. Life had shown him the vanity of such aspirations and taught him the dimensions of his own limitations. It had not, however, reshaped his soul to fit reality. Once again he came up hard against his inability to live up to his own standards. Once again he faced his human inadequacies. He could not protect Jessica in the ways she most needed to be protected.

She sighed and reached for the door latch. "No point in sitting out here in the dark," she said firmly.

Arlen followed her into the dark kitchen, catching her hand before she could flip on the light.

"No," he murmured, and carried her hand to his lips. No lights, no harsh, glaring reality. There was more than enough of that to go around. Unable to change reality for her, he would banish it for a while.

There was just enough light seeping through the fan window above the front door to light their way up the stairs. In Jessica's room the shades hadn't been drawn, and moonlight poured through the sheers to puddle on the floor. Arlen lighted the scented candle she kept on her dressing table and then drew the blinds, sealing them into a dimly lit cocoon. Yesterday he had brought a large portable tape player from his apartment and set it on the bedside table. Tonight he chose Mozart to drown out any listeners.

"Now," he murmured in her ear, drawing her into the pool of light and turning her to face the mirror. "Now we're going to try something."

Jessica's breath caught, and she thought she would never breathe again as she realized what he was doing. "Arlen..."

"Shh," he whispered soothingly. "Shh..."

With a gentle sweep of his hands he slipped the suit jacket from her shoulders and tossed it onto a chair in the corner. Her glasses were on, and he knew she could see clearly. He wanted her to see clearly. He somehow felt that if she could see how he enjoyed touching her, how much he enjoyed looking at her, perhaps she would come to believe in her own beauty.

Her blouse slipped away like a wisp of gossamer, and her skirt followed just as easily, gone almost before she noticed. He had swept her hair all to one side, to fall over her shoulder, and he pressed soft, wet kisses on the nape of her neck. In the mirror, in the candlelight, she could see how absorbed he was in each touch, each gesture. He was weaving a fantasy around them, she realized with a blossoming ache of longing. He was, with his hands and lips, wresting perfection out of jagged reality. And with each touch of his hands and lips she sank deeper into the silky web of beauty he wove around her, into the feelings that drove away thought.

He paused, stepping away just enough that she could see him in the mirror, too, and he removed his own clothes, all the layers that made him a government agent, that shielded him from the world. When he returned to her he was naked and hungry and as vulnerable as she was. Then, with incredibly gentle hands, he took away her last disguise. The satin teddy vanished, the panty hose disappeared and she stood before him unadorned.

And then his hands began to make a wicked, enticing journey over her hills and hollows.

"No, no," he chided gently when her eyelids fluttered closed. "Watch."

Helplessly she watched, finding it incredibly erotic to see what she was feeling as his hands shaped her breasts, as his fingers tugged gently at beading, aching nipples. His skin was darker than hers, and the darkness defined his every movement against the canvas of her pale skin. He murmured words of praise in her ear as he stroked her and petted her, his whispers twining with magical Mozart.

Then he turned them both sideways, face-to-face, so that she could see how she looked in his arms. And when she was trembling so hard she was sure her knees couldn't hold her, he lifted her as if she weighed nothing at all and carried her toward the bed.

"You shouldn't carry me," she gasped, clinging to his neck. "Arlen, I'm too heavy!"

"I can't imagine why I spend so much time working out if I can't carry a neat armful like you to bed," he said, his voice at once heavy with passion and full with teasing. He was smiling as he sat on the bed and then slowly eased her back onto the mattress. "And you're not nearly as heavy as you seem to think you are."

A groan escaped her as his mouth found and closed on an aching nipple and sucked so strongly that she felt it all the way to her center.

Macho, she thought hazily. No matter how gentle and sensitive and secure a man was, he still had a streak of macho in him. He carried her to bed like a conquest....

With a shiver of longing she surrendered, reaching for him, grasping him and caressing him. He needed to be needed, he wanted to be wanted, and he hungered for her hunger. How she knew these things she had no idea, but she sensed in him a fierce, deep need, and she answered it by tugging at him, by telling him with her sighs and cries, with the undulations of her body, that only he could give her what she needed, and that she needed all he was capable of giving.

Mozart reached a fantastic crescendo with them, a crescendo that drowned every other sound. Only later in the silence did the foreshadowing of loss pierce Jessica's heart and her joy. Only later. Too late.

Chapter 10

Two weeks later, on a rainy Sunday afternoon, Jessica sat in the window seat on the stair landing and stared down into her backyard. Water dripped steadily from everything. It had been a wet spring, but on the heels of several years of drought, no one was complaining too much.

Downstairs in her kitchen sat an FBI agent from San Antonio. He had come to the house yesterday morning shortly after Arlen had left, had come driving Arlen's sedan and wearing a duplicate set of clothes. Even his hair was a close match. From a distance he would pass for Arlen, as he had been intended to. His name was Wade Gentry, and he was here because Arlen refused to let her be alone.

That refusal disturbed Jessica more than anything that had yet happened. Two weeks ago Arlen had asked her to be careful because matters were following an unpredictable course. Since then nothing—at least, nothing *she* was aware of—had occurred.

Now, once again, she was faced anew with Arlen's concern for her safety. She was also reminded that probably one of the main reasons he was still staying with her was concern for her safety, not . . . other things. And she was reminded of his family and his determination not to become involved again, because this weekend he was visiting his daughter in Waco.

It was probably silly on her part, but she felt a little hurt that he hadn't suggested she join him. Of course, a man didn't want to introduce his daughter to his mistress, and of course he didn't want to show up at Melanie's with a strange woman on his arm. More importantly, he probably didn't want to expose Melanie to the danger he appeared certain was swirling around Jessica's head like a dark cloud of doom.

All of this she could understand, but it hurt, anyway.

And the most ridiculous thing of all, she told herself sternly, was to feel so sharply the very pangs that she had known were bound to come from loving Arlen. He had made his position clear, but she had persisted in pursuing him, anyway. There had been ample opportunity for her to bail out before things went too far, but she had plunged ahead regardless and thrown her heart over the moon.

Sighing, she leaned her shoulder against the cool glass and stared down at the wilderness her backyard seemed to have become almost overnight. The grass needed cutting desperately, and if it didn't stop raining soon it would probably be more than her small mower could handle.

This relationship, she admitted with a heavy sigh, was harder than she had expected. Two weeks ago, high on the newness of being in love, she'd believed it would be enough to love Arlen, that she would be happy with whatever crumbs he chose to give her. Such foolishness, she thought now. Such naïveté.

With each passing day she became increasingly aware of all Arlen withheld from her. The distance between them could be measured in years—not the years separating their ages, but the years he felt he could not give. She still wanted his crumbs, but she knew they were crumbs from what could have been a banquet.

She drew up her legs and clasped her arms around them, resting her chin on her knees. In fact, she thought, because Arlen was so consistently courteous, kind and gentle, she'd begun to feel as if she were some kind of penance he was performing. Except for that one time, he never even lowered his guard enough to grow irritated with her, and heaven knew she had given him cause from time to time.

No, he was the government clone from dawn to dark, and it was beginning to drive her crazy. Only when they made love did she feel she came close to the real man, and even then she felt his restraint. Some portion of himself was always kept tightly under lock and key.

She couldn't help wondering if he'd guarded himself this way with his wife, or if this was something he'd devised to protect himself since Lucy's death.

And she was beginning to understand how it was that a woman could want to provoke a man. She had managed to provoke him into her bed, but now she needed to provoke him out from behind his emotional walls. She needed to drive him into feeling something. Anything. Just so long as it was strong enough to break down the barriers.

And that might be really dangerous, because he might not return her feelings. In fact, when she thought about that she couldn't see any reason why he *should* return her feelings.

All of which was an indicator of the confused state of her heart and mind, she thought ruefully. She wanted things from him, yet she was afraid of the consequences if she got them. A classic case of the dithers.

A footstep on the stairs alerted her, and she turned to watch Agent Gentry come up to her. For better than twenty-four hours they had shared the same house yet had hardly shared a word. On the few occasions where they'd had to exchange important information, they had done so in whispers. Otherwise, they'd kept pretty much to themselves.

Now he squatted beside her on the landing and spoke in a voice that was little more than a barely audible whisper.

"I'm leaving now, Ms. Kilmer. Agent Coulter radioed to tell me he's on his way and should be here shortly."

Jessica nodded. "Thank you."

From the rear he really *did* look like Arlen, Jessica thought as she watched him descend the stairs. Especially from the rear. No casual observer was likely to note the differences that Jessica noticed—differences that would have made her blush if she'd had to describe them to someone else. His buns, for example. Or the exact shape of a denim-covered thigh. Or the angle of his head when he paused to look around. Little things that only someone who knew him really well would notice. The little things that made him so unique that Jessica could have picked him out of a crowd of look-alikes.

With another deep sigh Jessica dropped her chin to her knees once again. Agent Gentry's footsteps faded from the house, and she heard the kitchen door close with finality.

She still wasn't alone, though. Arlen had assured her that the house was being watched by the Bureau, though he wouldn't say from where. He wanted her to feel safer, knowing the FBI was protecting her. Jessica wasn't sure it made any difference. Emotionally she hated knowing that someone was either watching or listening all the time. It hardly mattered anymore whether it was the FBI or the unknown listeners. Either way, she didn't have a shred of privacy. Not even in her bedroom. There she bit back cries and sighs, and pillow talk was nearly nonexistent. Sure, they played music loudly enough to drown out anything short of utter mayhem, but she held back anyway, because she couldn't quite forget. Arlen couldn't know, of course, just how she was holding herself back, but *she* knew. And when he whispered sweet things in her ear, she whispered nothing back. It was even worse at other times, when the music wasn't playing. They had nothing approaching a normal conversation unless they were out of the house.

God, what a mess!

Nor would it end until they got whoever was behind the bugs in her telephones. She was beginning to think that if she could conceive of any way at all to force matters, she would. Somewhere along the line she had lost her fears. Maybe a person just couldn't stay afraid forever. Whatever the reason, she wasn't afraid, but she *was* tired and angry, and very, very frustrated.

And not just about having her privacy shot to hell. Here she was, in love for the first time in her life, having the big affair of her life, and she might as well have her grandmother looking over her shoulder every minute. She wasn't saying things that should be said, and she was withholding intimacies and confidences because she wasn't alone with Arlen.

Which was probably a relief for him, she thought sourly. After all, *he* didn't want to get involved. She, however, was very much involved and hated the way this spy business warped everything. Even if it *was* all one-sided, she ought to be able to throw herself wholeheartedly into what was undoubtedly going to be the best relationship of her life.

Very likely it would be the *only* relationship of her life, she amended glumly. She cherished no illusions about her ability to attract the opposite sex. Arlen told her she was sexy, he whispered that she was lovely, and sometimes, in the lamplit bedroom as he hovered over her, he told her huskily that she was beautiful. Jessica, however, prided herself on an unwinking, unblinking approach to life. She was not delusional, and she would not allow herself to be deluded.

Arlen, she told herself, found her sexy because he was horny and she was handy. Handy? Heck, she'd practically hurled herself at him. Maybe, she allowed, maybe long hair turned him on. She did not, however, believe her plump, mousy self to be lovely, let alone beautiful. Nope, those were words spoken in the heat of passion, and men were notorious for, well, *exaggerating* at such times. And besides, Arlen was a nice, kind man. He probably wanted her to feel good about herself. She didn't think his compliments were calculated or conniving—he wasn't the type. No, they were well-intentioned, which made them equally meaningless.

So here she was, experiencing something she would probably never experience again, and she couldn't even fully savor it.

"That was a heavy-duty sigh."

Arlen stood at the foot of the stairs. Clad in a black turtleneck pullover and snug, well-worn jeans, he looked so good to her that tears sprang to her eyes, blurring her vision. She didn't even bother to blink them back. And to hell with listeners.

"I missed you," she whispered through a tight, aching throat.

For a moment he didn't move. He simply stood looking up at her, studying her almost solemnly. And then, one riser at a time, he climbed toward her.

"How's Melanie?" she asked quietly, hating the way her voice thickened with her unshed tears.

"Happily married, happily employed and happily pregnant. If she weren't my daughter, I could almost resent all that happiness."

He was only a few stairs away now, and she managed a watery, wavery smile. "Some people *do* seem to live charmed lives," she said with false brightness. "It's enough to make you believe in fairy godmothers."

Arlen knelt beside the window seat so that his head was on a level with hers. "Everybody has troubles and grief. Sometimes they're just not visible from the outside."

"I know." A shaky sigh escaped her as he covered her clasped hands with one of his.

"You're all curled up on yourself, Jessie," he said, gently tugging her hands apart. "You look like you want to roll up into a tight ball and hide."

She guessed she did, but she tried to joke about it. "Like a pill bug?"

He shook his head. "Like you're hurting. Am I hurting you, Jessie?" In his heart he believed he was, and he steeled himself for her answer.

"No," she whispered. "Oh, no. Don't even think it. I'm just—just—"

Blindly she reached for him, and then just as quickly tried to stop herself. She felt free to reach for him out of desire, but she did *not* feel she had the right to reach out with her emotional needs. This was supposed to be a light, uninvolved relationship, after all. He had made that clear from the outset.

But as soon as she hesitated, Arlen moved. He gathered her swiftly to his chest, and the next thing she knew she was sitting on the edge of the window seat, tangled all around him. Her face was buried against his neck, her arms embraced his shoulders and her thighs cradled his narrow hips.

She felt his kiss on her temple, felt his big hand stroking her back with so much gentleness, so much kindness.

"I'm sorry, Jessie," he said, as if everything were his fault.

"Don't be. None of it's your fault. I guess I'm just tired of feeling like a bug under a microscope." Even now she whispered, hoping to evade the unseen listeners.

"It's a strain, all right." He thought of taking her to a hotel, but was afraid any watchers would be unnerved by such an inexplicable move. Impatience was eating at him— nothing at all had happened for two solid weeks—but not for anything would he take the risk of increasing Jessica's danger.

She was so warm and soft against him, and though he felt like a traitor for even thinking it, he could not remember ever having found it so satisfying to hold Lucy. Jessica seemed to soothe longings he hadn't even been aware of until she touched him.

But right now he felt her tension and frustration, and knew he had to do something to help. Unfortunately, he couldn't think of a damn thing that would really help matters. A rainy afternoon drive in the country, a trip to the movies, anything at all, would only give her temporary surcease.

His pager chose that moment to chirp, and the word he muttered under his breath, right into Jessica's ear, shocked a laugh out of her.

"Sorry," he said, reluctantly releasing her. "Come on, Jessie, let's take a little drive."

To a pay phone. Since he had just driven back from Waco, Jessica doubted that he wanted to go one step farther than that. She was getting used to these interruptions, though. There was seldom an evening when Arlen didn't have to call in about something, and she had gathered from things he had let slip that she was far from being the only case he and his agents were handling right now. In fact, from what she was able to discern, he was making quite an effort to manage things so that he could spend as much time with her as he did.

The trip to the pay phone, as usual, took longer than the five minutes the direct route required. Only when he was certain that they weren't being followed by anyone did Arlen at last pull into the parking lot of a convenience store, nosing the sedan right up to the row of pay phones.

As far as he knew, no one had attempted to follow either him or Jessica at any time, and he was beginning to think the cigarette smoker who had stood across the street that long-ago morning had simply been innocently walking a dog after all. It was as if, once the bugs had been planted, the perpetrators had gone up in smoke. The notion frustrated him even further, because unless they got a break of some kind they were never going to get to the bottom of this case. The thought of subjecting Jessica to much more of this made him angry in a way he had seldom experienced.

Phil Harrigan was the agent on call this weekend, and he answered his phone on the third ring.

"Phil? Arlen. What have you got?"

"You said you wanted to know immediately if there were any developments in the MTI case."

"So tell me." He shifted from his right foot to his left and tried to restrain his impatience. Turning his back to the phone, he looked at Jessica. She sat in the car, watching him through the windshield, and, damn it, she looked too pale to please him.

Phil spoke. "Maddy Kazin called to tell me she might have screwed up. Royally. You told her to look into Barron's personal acquaintances as well as his financial situation."

"Right." Arlen nearly sighed. What had happened to all his patience?

"Anyhow, she came across a real close buddy of Barron's. The two practically lived in each other's pockets, I guess. If they weren't fishing together, they were hunting on a deer lease they own together down south. Kazin says she let it go because it turned out that this guy, a fellow named Carl Stratton, was Barron's brother-in-law. Martha Barron, the widow, is Stratton's sister."

"Okay." But it was not okay. After the Walker spy ring, how could any serious agent or investigator fail to realize hat people could make a family practice out of spying? Kazin was right, she really might have screwed up. "What changed her mind?"

"Well, it seems you asked her to investigate the Czech student that Greg Leong introduced Jessica Kilmer to at lunch that day."

"Right, I did. That's what Kazin does best, investigate." The woman was something to behold with a telephone and a computer terminal. Nobody's secrets could withstand Maddy Kazin's interest. Hoover would have loved her. "So spell out the connection, Phil." At times Phil could be unbearably ponderous. Patience, Coulter.

"So the connection is that Jan Dobrocek, the Czech guy, is also a fishing buddy of Carl Stratton."

Every hair on Arlen's neck stood up. "How good a fishing buddy?"

"Last year the two of them went to Mexico on a deep-sea fishing trip out of Mazatlan. Hear they caught some good-sized sailfish."

"Kazin's sure about that?"

"As sure as credit card charges and customs records can make her. It seems our friends had the sailfish stuffed and mounted and shipped back. Dobrocek's credit card was used to pay for Stratton's fish and for a room registered in Stratton's name."

Arlen muttered an oath and closed his eyes. "How often does Dobrocek go to Mexico?" Mexico was the best place to go if you wanted to pass information to the Soviets. The embassy in Mexico City was watched by U.S. agents, but there was no way it could be watched as well as the Soviet embassy in Washington, D.C. More than one American had sold out his country on a little jaunt south of the border.

"Oh, every month or so, according to his credit records. He flies Aero Azteca, and he usually goes to one of the resort cities, like Mazatlan, Cozumel, even Acapulco. And while he's there he always makes at least a one-day trip into Mexico City."

"So when the hell does he do his graduate work?" Arlen demanded irritably. He needed to be angry at someone.

"He's working on his thesis, according to the department. Independent research that's being funded by the Czech government. Or was. The funding got a little hazy during all the freedom uprising in Eastern Europe."

"I imagine." Arlen's tone grew dry.

"Anyhow, he doesn't have to be on campus all the time, so he's free to come and go as he likes. He evidently doesn't make any secret about his traveling. Kazin says he's been known to take a coed with him from time to time."

"More recruitment." Arlen sighed. "I guess he must be good. How long has he been operating right under our noses?"

"Do you really want to know?"

"Stupid question, Phil. The point is, I don't have a choice. How long?"

"Five years."

Arlen could have groaned. "Five years," he repeated woodenly.

"Well, that's how long he's been at the university, and that's how long it's been since he entered the country for the first time. It's possible—"

Arlen cut him off. "Spare me. Start getting together the stuff the U. S. Attorney is going to need from us to get a court order for wiretaps on Dobrocek and Stratton."

"Kazin says she's already compiling it. It'll be on your desk first thing tomorrow. In the meantime, do you want me to start surveillance?"

Arlen thought about it for a moment. "I don't know that there's any immediate rush, Phil. Unless he's scheduled to go to Mexico, that is."

"Not that Kazin knows of at the moment. I'll have her keep an eye on the airline bookings, though."

"Okay, let's leave it there until tomorrow, unless something else comes up. I want to think about this some more before I make any decisions." He looked at Jessica again. "Phil?"

"Yeah?"

"Try not to need me in the next four or five hours. If you really, really have to, page me, but I'd be grateful—"

"Sure," Phil interrupted. "No problem. National emergencies only."

Arlen gave a short laugh. "Yeah. I'll check in later."

Standing in the rain, Arlen pondered for a couple of minutes. He would have bet his last dollar just then that Dobrocek and Stratton were mixed up in Barron's death. Maybe Barron had been involved in the espionage, or maybe he'd stumbled onto something. Either way, he was dead, and either way his brother-in-law was probably involved. Arlen remembered all too clearly the grief stamped on Martha Barron's face when he had interviewed her two weeks ago. Familiar himself with the toll of such a loss, he would have recognized it instantly if she had been faking it. She had not been. A man who could inflict that kind of suffering on his own sister was a man to be wary of.

And Jessica knew Barron. Jessica had met Dobrocek. A cold shiver passed down Arlen's spine, the kind that supposedly meant someone was walking on your grave. In that moment he would have given ten years of his life for a way to pull Jessie from this mess. The best he could hope for, however, was to keep her from getting in any deeper. How the devil was he supposed to accomplish that?

Sliding into the car beside her, he turned and studied her with that same solemnity that had made him pause at the foot of the stairs earlier. Jessica Kilmer thought herself a knowledgeable, sophisticated adult. Arlen Coulter knew differently. There was an innocence to her that he felt whenever he was with her, an innocence that came from the lack of the kind of experience that caused emotional calluses. She was incredibly open, incredibly warm, incredibly vulnerable. Her readiness to accept him exactly as he was took his breath away.

Lord knew she had more than enough cause to complain. He'd stolen her virginity without so much as a promise, and now he was conducting their relationship under watchful eyes. Hell, he hadn't even taken her out on a real date. Their dinners out together were as much business as anything, arranged to give them time to talk away from bugs. Small wonder she was looking frayed and pale. She deserved better than this by far, and she certainly deserved to discover her sensuality in privacy.

He knew she was holding back when they made love simply because she had not held back the first few times before he had found the bugs. Even in her restrained, uptight state she was a much more active lover than his wife had ever been, and far more passionate, but Arlen was well aware Jessie had more than that in her. And she deserved to enjoy it, deserved not to have to bottle it up because of unseen listeners. Damn it, if nothing else he could at least set her free for a few hours!

So he drove downtown to the Regency Hotel overlooking the lake. Jessica watched with huge eyes but never questioned him as he took his suitcase out of the trunk where he'd left it, intending to go for it after dark, and took her arm to lead her inside. This was a good hotel, one of the best, and a person couldn't check in without luggage.

She said nothing as he passed his credit card to the clerk and checked them in for the night. She even remained silent throughout the trip in the glass elevator, though he could tell she felt miserably out of place in her jeans and faded sweatshirt. In a couple of minutes, though, that wasn't going to matter any longer.

Their room overlooked the lake, not that he cared. He tipped the bellhop, closed the door and faced Jessica.

"Arlen?" Her tone was uncertain. "What happened?" His grimness was frightening, his quiet intensity unnerving. That phone call must have been disturbing.

"What happened is that you and I need time away from all of that crap. We need to be truly alone. We're alone now, Jessie." He took a step toward her. "Absolutely and utterly alone. And, by God, I'm going to make love to you the way I *feel* it, without worrying about being overheard."

Pink color blossomed in her cheeks and he heard her breath catch. "You felt that way, too?"

He opened his arms to her. "I felt each and every sigh you swallowed, and every time you bit back a sound, I hurt."

Darn it, her eyes were swimming in tears again. He had noticed, which was mortifying, and he had cared, which was incredibly touching.

Arlen folded her into his arms and pressed a kiss on the top of her head. She smelled like spring rain, fresh and sweet, and holding her made him feel warm in places that had been cold for a long, long time. For a long moment he simply hugged her, savoring her closeness. And for the first time he admitted to himself that he wasn't going to walk away unscathed from this. She was bound to tire of him, though, tire of the multitude of sins that went with his work and the way it made him live. She would tire of him just as soon as she didn't need him around to make her feel safe. It was as inevitable as the rising of the sun, but only now did he realize that it was going to hurt. Just a little, he assured himself. Just a little.

"I'm going to call room service," he said, rocking her gently and stroking her hair and back. "I'm starved, and I don't want to bother with them later."

He caught her chin with a gentle hand and tilted her face up to him. Her brown eyes were suspiciously bright behind her glasses, and there was the faintest tremor to her lips. Bending, he kissed those lips and felt them quiver and cling to his. "What you need," he murmured huskily, "is a long, warm soak in the tub. I happen to have a pajama top that'll make a perfect bathrobe for you."

"You? A pajama top?" A fugitive smile tugged at the corners of her mouth. The Arlen she knew slept flagrantly nude; in fact, he hardly ever stayed under the blankets.

He flashed his crooked smile. "Yep. Believe me, I do *not* sleep in the raw on my daughter's couch."

She lifted on tiptoes. "Then," she whispered, "you wore it last night?"

The heaviness was growing in him, the weight of the need she evoked in him. "Yes," he murmured, sliding his hands downward to rub them against her soft bottom.

"Then it'll smell like you."

Her husky whisper sent a thrill racing from his ear straight to his groin. His teeth clenched as he rubbed himself against her welcoming hips. "Yep," he bit out.

"Good." She wiggled up closer to him and tugged his head down to her. "I wish I were taller," she muttered as she tried to find his mouth.

He kissed her. Her mouth was already open, begging for his possession, and he accepted the invitation with a sweeping, plunging stroke of his tongue that spoke of greater intimacies.

"Kiss me back, Jessie," he gasped a little later. "Come on, baby... Like that. Yeah."

Somehow his pullover was riding up under his arms and she was biting—biting!—at one of his nipples in a way he never would have imagined anyone doing, nor would he have dreamed it could feel so good that his knees were threatening to buckle....

"I'm just the right height for that," she whispered as she felt a tremor rip through him. "You like that, don't you?"

"Yeah.... Damn it, Jessie... Baby, don't..."

But she did, and he went nuts. For one of the very few times in his life, Arlen Coulter lost his self-control, every last damn vestige of it. Afterward he retained only the vaguest memory of tearing at her clothes, at his clothes, of tumbling onto the bed with her. He *did* remember putting his mouth on her in places he'd never put his mouth before, places he'd fantasized about kissing her, but had been afraid to for fear of shocking her or upsetting her.

He remembered, too, that while she might have been a little bit shocked at first, she hadn't been at all upset. No, Jessie had sobbed and writhed and dug her nails into him and driven him to take even greater intimacies.

"Harder," she gasped. "More," she groaned, and her fever fueled his. And later, "Like this?" as she took similar liberties with him.

He remembered the hard, driving ache that propelled his hips against hers, the helpless, wrenching, rocking need that made him plunge over and over and over.

And he remembered the sheer beauty of her shrill cry as she crested the pinnacle with him.

He'd never made a woman plead before, or cry out. He'd never known the wonder of sharing a moment so intense it was etched in pure crystal. Now he knew. Humbled, he held her tightly to him and gave silent thanks.

Arlen would have provided candlelight, but that would have meant going out and finding some place to buy a candle, and Jessie wouldn't hear of it. Besides, there was a night-light in the bathroom that served almost as well.

Sitting in the deep, steaming tub, she sipped champagne and soaked up the relaxing heat. Arlen sat on the floor beside the tub, on the fluffy mat, and watched her with a half-formed smile that seemed to soften his every edge. He made her feel beautiful and cherished, and her throat ached every time she looked at him.

Time was slipping away so fast. Too fast. She tried to seize the moments, but they slipped through her fingers like water. Much as she wanted to escape from under the threat that clouded her days, she knew that the end of the investigation would be the end of this, too. Because Arlen would move out of her house as soon as he didn't need to protect her, and then he would move out of her life to avoid the entanglements he didn't want. Smothering a sigh, she forcibly turned her attention away from such thoughts. There was no sense in wasting these precious moments worrying about what had happened yet.

"You know everything about me," she remarked lazily. "And I still don't know very much about you."

Reaching out, he touched her warm, damp cheek with a gentle forefinger. "What do you want to know?"

"Have you ever been shot at?"

"As an agent, you mean? Because I sure as hell got shot at in Nam."

"Well?"

"Once."

"Just once?" That surprised her.

"Just once, by some drunken hunters who never would have done it if they hadn't been full of good old Kentucky bourbon. They didn't even come close, but it was a little tense."

"Did you shoot back?"

"I wasn't even armed. We're not like local police. We don't carry weapons all the time, and on that case, I wasn't authorized to carry a gun. In fact, most of the time this job is about as tame as they come."

Jessica handed him her glass. "No more for me, thanks." Sighing, she closed her eyes and let her head rest against the pillowing towel. "Tame. I find that hard to believe."

"Well, it's usually not dangerous, and a lot of what we do is legwork and paperwork. Investigatory stuff. Sometimes we go undercover, but that's about the only time things get hairy. Surveillance is a boring pastime, and I've done my share of it. Things usually don't begin to get exciting until a case starts to break."

The finger that had caressed her cheek now ran along the curve of her soft, smooth shoulder.

"I enjoy my job," he said after a moment. "I like solving puzzles, and I meet a lot of interesting people. And it's important work." His gray eyes lifted to her face, and he smiled his crooked smile. "Disappointed?"

"Relieved," she said frankly. "I'm not a good worrier."

"Well, you don't need to worry about me," he said firmly. Usually that was true, so he didn't feel as if he were lying. He didn't tell her how fast that could change, how fast he had *seen* it change. Or that he was working on a couple of cases that could get nasty if something went wrong. She didn't need to know such things.

Opening her eyes just a little, she looked at him from beneath her lashes, soaking up the way he looked. Wearing only his jeans, he sat with one knee raised and an arm resting on it. Lithe, lean, all male. She blushed a little when she saw the mark she'd left on his chest, just above the coppery disk of one nipple. She'd never imagined she could get so carried away.

To Arlen, it looked as if she were about to fall asleep in the tub. "Is that *all* you wanted to know?" he asked, amusement evident in his voice. "Whether I'd ever been shot at?"

Jessica opened one eye wider. "It's an important question. And I already know the really essential things about you."

"What kind of essential things?" The crooked smile was still on his mouth, his posture was still casual, but she sensed a tension in him.

She answered, her voice soft. "I know how kind you are, how gentle and generous, how honest and caring. I know you're a good man, Arlen Coulter. The rest is just frosting to make you even more appealing."

Even more appealing. Arlen heard the words, but, more importantly, he felt them in his gut, a sinking sensation that told him he was in trouble. *Even more appealing.* Well, what did he expect? She was hardly older than Melanie. She could hardly have the first great affair of her life without getting emotionally involved.

For that matter, the sinking sensation told him that he wasn't as indifferent as he would have liked to be, either. It mattered that she found him appealing. It mattered that he could make her feel good or bad. All of it mattered too damn much, and he didn't know what the hell to do about it. Wait for it to wear off? It had to wear off. No woman like Jessica, with so much to give and so much life ahead of her, could possibly stay infatuated for long with a man who had so little to offer in the way of a future. Sooner or later she was bound to come to her senses. In the meantime, he would just have to take care that he built her some good memories, that he made this a good experience for her.

"Appealing, huh?" he said gruffly. "It makes me more appealing to have been shot at?"

Jessica couldn't hold back her laugh. "No, it makes you more appealing that you don't get shot at with alarming regularity. Actually, I'm sorry you ever had to be shot at."

Again he was touched. She touched him easily, frequently.

"Well," she said after a moment, unnerved by the unblinking way he was looking at her, "I'm glad to know your job is tame. Not like TV and the movies."

It could get to be like the movies or TV, and had, but she didn't need to know that. "Yeah. Tame. Not dull. It's not a dull job, Jessie. And I usually feel really good about what I accomplish. That makes me a lucky man."

"What made you decide you wanted to be an FBI agent?"

He smiled, that wonderful crooked smile that sent rivers of warmth rushing to her toes. "Eliot Ness and the Untouchables," he said. "I wanted to be Robert Stack."

She felt her own smile widen, and her heart squeezed with emotion. "You must have been such a neat little kid. I can imagine what you must have been like. Serious, right? A solemn, serious little boy."

"Maybe, when I was little. When I got older I was something of a hell-raiser." He stroked her soft cheek with a fingertip. "I managed to avoid any real trouble, though. I always wanted to be one of the good guys."

When she decided it was time to get out of the tub, he insisted on toweling her dry himself, and he took unabashed pleasure in the task, lingering in ways that made her feel desirable and prized. The pajama top he gave her to wear was simple blue cotton, but it was soft with many washings, and it smelled like him. By the time he settled her on the bed and tucked the covers around her legs, she was feeling totally pampered.

Propped against pillows, she smiled up at him. "You sure know how to take care of a lady."

He perched on the bed beside her and leaned toward her to give her a warm, caressing kiss on the lips. "I'm glad you think so."

She reached up and cupped his face in her hands, reveling in the scratchy sensation of his beard. "What brought all this on, Arlen? Did something happen?"

The habit of secrecy was deeply ingrained in him from his better than sixteen years with the Bureau. The FBI released information from current investigations only when there was some advantage in doing so. As Special Agent in Charge, he had for years been making the decision about what could be usefully revealed, and he was usually inclined to reveal nothing. Even now, looking into Jessie's worried brown eyes, he leaned toward silence. He didn't see how it could possibly help the Bureau or her for her to know about Carl Stratton, or the connection between Dobrocek and Barron. Or that Barron had been murdered. Not even when he needed to persuade her to be careful of her safety had he told her that a murder had been committed.

Jessica's gaze skipped over his features, taking in every nuance of his expression. "You don't have to tell me anything," she said quietly. "I realize you can't talk about your cases. I shouldn't have asked."

But the questions were there in her eyes, and he could read them clearly. He sighed when she leaned forward and touched a light kiss to his rough chin.

"I need a shave," he said. He could see the redness his beard had left on her cheeks and neck. "I need a shower."

She smiled. "Go ahead. I'll bet there's plenty of hot water."

He started to smile as she settled back against the pillow. She's a treasure, he thought. An honest-to-God treasure. And then his smile faded completely.

"Jessie," he said. "Jessie, I know it's hard to sustain a high level of caution for a long period. I know that it's been wearing you to a nub and that you're getting past the point of fear. I can see it."

Her bright brown eyes regarded him steadily, but he saw the leap of the pulse in her throat, a sign he was scaring her. Damn it, he *had* to keep her scared to keep her safe. "Jessie, don't trust anyone. Please. This case has gone beyond the usual limits. There's a very real danger."

Her own expression grew serious as she waited for him to explain. When he didn't speak, she felt a certainty settle like lead in her stomach. It was something she had suspected all along.

"Dave Barron didn't kill himself, did he?"

His silence would have been answer enough, but he was never one to take the easy way. Nor would he lie. "No, he didn't kill himself."

Jessica drew a sharp, shaky breath. "I wondered. I couldn't really believe that he had."

He took her hand and held it between both of his own. Rubbing it gently while his mind raced, he tried yet again to find a way to remove her from all of this. He kept expecting her to turn from him—he'd gotten her deeper into this, after all—but she never took her somber gaze from his face.

"That's why you asked me to be careful," she said presently, her voice little more than a murmur. "You found out he'd been murdered."

He didn't bother to answer that one. It was self-evident. Instead, he did the only thing he could think of. He leaned forward until he lay against her, his face in the curve between her neck and shoulder. Her arms closed around his shoulders immediately, and in their strength he felt her tension and fear. Damn, he thought, at some point she was bound to conclude that he had wanted only to use her as bait. It wasn't true, but there was no way he could prove that. And when she reached that conclusion, she would never, ever forgive him.

"I'm not going to leave you alone for a minute, Jessie," he told her, pressing a kiss on the warm, soft skin of her neck. "Not a minute. I won't let anything happen to you."

She made a noise that sounded suspiciously like a sniffle. "And here I was hoping you were spending all this time with me because you like being with me." As soon as the words were out, she wanted to snatch them back. She couldn't believe she had revealed so much of her hopes, so much of her fears. He didn't want her to care for him. He didn't want to be responsible for her caring or hurting. Funny, he could be so quick to protect her, to take responsibility for her physical safety, but he didn't want any responsibility for her emotional safety. Of course, he didn't want to feel anything himself. No involvement. No emotional risk.

It occurred to him that he had been a fool in more ways than one. If he had any excuse, it was that this was his first affair, too. After all, Lucy had been the only woman he'd dated, and that had been a chaste relationship until their wedding night. Still, he wondered now how he had ever thought that Jessica wouldn't demand a declaration of some feeling other than lust from him. Of course she wanted to know that she meant *something* to him. Hell, he wanted to know the same from her. He just didn't want to mean too much.

"Of course I *like* being with you," he said gruffly. He could say that with perfect truth.

Her arms tightened on him, and her hands began to caress his upper back. She asked nothing more. Instead, with her touches, she let him know she felt the same way.

At length she sighed. "I suppose we have to get back."

"Not until morning." He was taking a risk, but he felt it was a necessary one. Let the watchers wonder where they'd gone, but Jessica would have this time to escape and regroup. "I figure we can get up a little early and go home to dress for work."

"Sounds good to me." Did he, she wondered, realize he had referred to her house as home, as if it were his? Her heart accelerated a little with hope, and Arlen suddenly raised his head to smile into her eyes.

"What did you just think about?" he asked huskily. "Your heart went into overdrive."

Her cheeks heated and she shook her head, too embarrassed to answer. He must never know how much she wanted from him. If he ever guessed how much she cared for him, he would retreat in short order.

"My heart speeds up any time I think about you," she answered finally, feeling terribly, painfully shy. "All I have to do is think about you kissing me or touching me..."

Now *that* was something he felt he could handle, so he did. Willingly, readily, tenderly. Damn, but she made him feel tender.

In fact, she just plain made him *feel.*

Chapter 11

Jessica arrived more than a half hour early for work in the morning, but when she stepped into the section and closed the door behind her, she saw Frank Winkowski coming down the hall with a sheaf of papers in his hands.

"Morning, Frank. Getting a head start on the week?"

Frank was usually a cheerful, pleasant man, but this morning he looked disgruntled. "Well, I'd *like* to," he said almost peevishly.

"What's wrong?"

"The damn cleaning crew," he said irritably. "I've left notes for them before, and they usually listen for a while, but this time it's worse than I've ever seen it."

"Notes about what? What do they do?"

"They rearranged things on my desk! But this time...! I tell you, Jessica, I won't stand for it any longer. This time they were *in* my desk. And I can't imagine what they must have been doing in here over the weekend, but one of Bob's reports was in my desk drawer—" he waved the offending papers beneath her nose "—and one of my folders is missing. I *hope* it's in Bob's desk! All I know is, I'm going down to maintenance right now to complain about this!"

"Wait a minute, Frank." Jessica's heart skipped a beat and then slipped into high gear. "Let's go to my office and talk about this first."

Frank, his face flushed with annoyance, paused in the process of opening his mouth to continue his tirade. "Why?" he asked instead.

"Just come with me and I'll explain." Butterflies fluttered wildly in her stomach as she led the way to her office. How much should she tell him, if anything? And what would Arlen think if she betrayed to the wrong person the fact that the FBI was involved?

She closed her door behind them. Frank took the one extra chair and sat back, papers on his lap.

"What gives?" he demanded. "You can't do anything about the janitors, so why do you want to discuss this?"

"What if it wasn't the janitors, Frank?" she asked baldly. She didn't have any other idea about how to begin this discussion, so she jumped right in.

"Not the janitors?" He repeated the words almost blankly, then abruptly leaned forward as they penetrated. "What are you suggesting? That somebody was looking for something in my office?"

Jessica was thinking as rapidly as she ever had in her life. Arlen, she reminded herself, didn't want anybody to know their relationship was anything but personal. He also didn't want anybody to know that the FBI was investigating her missing document.

And, she recalled with a sudden thud of her heart, Dave Barron had been murdered, possibly because he had found out something. She was being a complete and utter fool if she allowed anyone to guess that she had more than a passing interest in odd happenings around MTI.

Taking a breath to steady herself, she decided she had better be careful. Trouble was, she hadn't gotten much sleep last night, and her mind was a little fuzzy. Frank, however, was still leaning forward, looking at her with a strange intensity. She had said enough to either make him think she was losing her marbles or make him suspicious that something *was* going on. Stupid, Jess, she told herself. Stupid, stupid. Let the pros handle this stuff.

"Uh, no," she said. "I'm not really suggesting anything, Frank. I guess I'm still nervous about that document I mislaid. Maybe a little paranoid."

Frank's lips thinned. "I can understand that. I'm getting a little paranoid about my desk. Damn it, Jessica, you'd think these cleaning people would understand that you don't fiddle around with somebody's desk. Considering the kind of work we do here, I don't think nosy janitors ought to be tolerated."

She nodded agreement. "But we don't keep anything classified on our desks."

"No, of course not, but you know as well as I do that there's plenty of important stuff that isn't classified. Things that would be useful to our competitors as well as to other nations. I'm going downstairs, and I'm going to lodge a written complaint."

"What folder of yours is missing?" she thought to ask as he stood up to leave.

"The design you wrote for the Sure Eye project."

Jessica's heart slammed. She had thought from the outset that the design ought to be classified. The classification guidance provided by the Department of Defense, however, had not permitted it, so she and Bob Harrow had decided to mark it Company Confidential. Theoretically, that designation meant it wouldn't be shown to anyone outside the company and would be treated as a trade secret.

It remained true that, regardless of classification, it delineated the software for the project in a way that would make it possible for someone else to duplicate the project if they had access to the necessary data base of technical information about countermeasures—some of which information was contained in the document that had been taken from her safe.

Troubled, she watched Frank leave, evidently fixed in his determination to complain to maintenance, her own mind still worrying at the problems. A Company Confidential document was relatively easy to steal. People could, and did, carry them off the premises in the course of business. A kind of accountability was kept, a record of everyone who had a copy, but it wasn't difficult for someone else to obtain one or gain access to the information.

The person who was stealing and copying documents could well be someone who didn't recognize the difference between a classified document and a Company Confidential document. Or it could be someone with the technical know-how to realize how the project design fitted into the whole. Well, it had to be the cleaning crew, because everyone in the section already had a copy of her design report. The cleaning crew or security—either one had access over the weekends. And that was something Arlen needed to know.

Picking up her phone, she hesitated. She really should go off-site to call. But then, Frank had left the section, and there wasn't a soul here to overhear her. She dialed.

"FBI."

"This is Jessica Kilmer. May I speak to Special Agent Coulter?"

"Ma'am, I'm sorry, but Agent Coulter is in court this morning. Can someone else help you?"

Jessica glanced at her watch and saw that it wasn't yet eight. Wasn't that too early for court? Something else must be going on. "Will he be back before noon?"

"Yes, ma'am, he's expected around eleven."

Arlen didn't want her to discuss anything to do with the spying on the telephone, so she was left with no alternative. "Please tell him that it's important he meet me for lunch today. I'll be at the Corner Pub a little after twelve. If there's a problem with that, he can call me at work."

The woman who answered the phone repeated the message, and Jessica hung up.

Nearly four more hours. She had the feeling that time was going to crawl.

A movement in the corner of her eye startled her and she spun around, but no one was there. Of course no one was there, she reassured herself, willing her hammering heart to slow down. Frank was the only person in the section who was already at work, and he had gone downstairs to castigate the maintenance people.

"Paranoid, Jess," she told herself aloud, needing the sound in the suddenly uncomfortable silence of the empty office. "Your imagination is running away with you again."

The morning crawled even more slowly for Arlen than it did for Jessica. He was used to the time involved in any kind of legal action, but even ingrained patience couldn't make the waiting go any faster.

Maddy Kazin had dumped the required information for the wiretaps on his desk sometime last evening, and it had been the first thing he looked at this morning. A quick reading told him that Kazin had done her job; this should be enough to get the court order. He had learned a long time ago, however, that attorneys often had a different perspective on such things, particularly U.S. Attorneys. Scooping up the file, he headed upstairs to Carolyn Granger's office, knowing he would probably have to defend his request before she would take it to the judge.

"Intuitively," Carolyn Granger said a half hour later, "I see why you think the tap is necessary. The evidence is slim, though, and mostly circumstantial. As far as I know, it's still not a crime for a U.S. citizen to be acquainted with a Czech, or even with a KGB agent, for that matter. You're acquainted with more than a few yourself."

"Yep," he agreed calmly, maintaining the control that had gotten him through plenty of tense situations in his career. No one would ever have guessed how tired he was of all this legal maneuvering. Of course, a long time ago he had accepted the difference between an FBI agent and a lawyer. He was an agent because he was a man of action. A man of action was bound to get impatient with all the dotting of i's and crossing of t's.

She smiled faintly at him. "No argument?"

"What's the point?" He flashed a quick smile in return. "If there's any way possible, you'll get me what I want, Caro. You usually do."

She shook her head, her smile growing broader. "You take all the fun out of it. I'm supposed to drive you crazy with my nit-picking. You're supposed to do anything short of going down on your knees to get what you want."

"I'll kneel right now if it'll speed things up."

Carolyn shook her head once again. "It would be a mistake to rush, and you know it. It could blow our case out of the water if a defense attorney can argue that the tap was illegal and therefore inadmissible."

"You're talking like a lawyer again," Arlen remarked wryly.

Which was how he came to be standing at the window at the end of the hall outside Carolyn Granger's office while she wove together the necessary threads.

He rocked back onto his heels and shoved his hands into his trouser pockets. Looking up at the blue, blue sky of a sunny Texas morning, he found himself thinking of the velvet darkness of the night just past. The satisfaction he felt this morning went far beyond anything as simple as satisfied passion, though. Yesterday he had been useful to another person on a purely emotional level that had fulfilled a startling need of his own.

It was a need he hadn't really been aware of until now. He had thought—foolishly, it now appeared—that he'd closed a chapter in his life and hereafter would be content with his work, his grandchildren and his other interests. A man who had been the hub of the family for half his life, a man who was accustomed to taking care of others, should have known better. Last night had reminded him that he needed to be needed.

For better than three years now he had closed up on himself and convinced himself that he no longer needed what he no longer had. The folly of that delusion had become eminently obvious to him last night and this morning. And damned if he wanted to sacrifice this morning's utter contentment for some stupid notion that he was too old to be entitled to it. But Jessica was too young for him, too *biologically* young. That youth was going to take her away from him, because she would want children and ...

Children. Another problem. He had missed out on Melanie's early infancy, but he had been around for Andrew's birth and first few months. He could still remember the warm wonder and awe he had felt when he held his son. The small, soft head in the crook of his arm, the fingers and toes so tiny it was impossible to believe they were so perfectly formed. Yeah, he remembered it all vividly. He remembered feeling vaguely embarrassed by the rush of tenderness he had felt for those tiny little children, embarrassed by the soft, warm, utterly unmacho feelings they'd evoked in him. He'd never mentioned those feelings to anyone, but they had tempered his every action ever since.

Jessica shouldn't miss that, wouldn't want to miss it. And he couldn't ... Could he?

"Arlen?" Caro Granger's voice floated down the hall. "Let's go. The judge will see us in chambers in twenty minutes."

He started down the hall to her. "All I want to know is, are *you* confident?"

Caro smiled. "You bet. It's in the bag."

An hour later, stepping off the elevator near his office, Arlen found himself thinking that perhaps the strangest thing about this morning was that he was already looking forward to telling Jessica about it. Another one of those things he'd missed without realizing it. He wouldn't be able to share any official information, of course, but he could tell Jessie about Judge Harris, a surprisingly funny little man with an unabashed interest in war stories.

Did he really want to resume his old life, coming home each evening to an empty, silent apartment?

As soon as he stepped in the Bureau offices, he was swamped by demands and plans. A number of cases appeared ready to come to a head, and in order to set up the kind of constant surveillance he wanted on Stratton and Dobrocek, he needed to request some additional agents. By the time he was finished with all of that it was noon, and he reached for the stack of phone messages Donna had handed him.

By the time he reached Jessica's message it was ten after twelve, and he swore under his breath. He might, if he was lucky, make it to the Corner Pub in twenty minutes. By then she might have given up and left. Nor was the Pub the kind of place you could call and get a message to a guest.

He swore again and grabbed his suit jacket from the coat tree in the corner. "I'm heading out on business," he told Donna as he passed her desk. "I should be back in an hour."

The Pub parking lot was crowded, and he had to park at some distance from the door. He spied Lisa Gonzales parked not too far from a Toyota that looked like Jessie's. *Was* Jessie's, he realized as he scanned the license plate. Good, she was here, and Lisa was on her tail. Everything was all right.

There was a line at the door as people waited to be seated, but he passed it up and went to look for Jessie. The Pub had four different guest rooms, and not until he had walked through them all was he convinced that she wasn't there. Had there been even one empty table, he might have thought she was in the ladies' room, but every table was full.

She wasn't there. The certainty crept into his bones like a winter chill, and the back of his neck prickled. Measuring each step so he wouldn't run, he walked out of the restaurant and headed for Lisa Gonzales. She saw him coming and leaned over to unlock the passenger door for him.

"Have you seen her come out?" was Arlen's abrupt first question.

"Come out? No, her car's still here." Instantly concerned, Lisa frowned at him. "What's wrong, Arlen?"

"She's not in there. Did she come alone?"

"No. She came with a man. Brought him, actually. They looked like they were friends."

The prickling of his neck had become a squeezing of his stomach as tension gripped him. "What did he look like?"

"Thirty-five, I guess, slightly balding, dark hair with thin fuzz on top. Average height, beer bellied. Wearing brown slacks, a yellow short-sleeved sport shirt and a brownish tie. Ordinary, Arlen. You'd never give him a second look."

Leaving Lisa to wait for Jessie in case he missed her, Arlen recrossed the parking lot, faster this time, no longer caring if he was conspicuous. An objective part of his mind—the portion that had kept him sane throughout Vietnam and the interminable months of Lucy's illness—warned him that he was in danger of letting emotion override control.

Arlen hated to lose control. There were a few—a *very* few—times in the past when he had lost his iron control, and the results hadn't been something he was proud of. Warning himself, however, didn't much help. Fear for Jessica rode him like a whiplash.

Once again he checked all the rooms, this time looking for the balding man in the yellow shirt as well as Jessica. Ten minutes later he was convinced. She wasn't here. One last time he scanned the final room, hoping against hope. The last time he'd felt like this was when his daughter hadn't come home from a school football game at the appointed time. Then it had been a simple misunderstanding. This time he knew he wasn't going to be so lucky.

None of the waiters he collared could remember having seen Jessica or her companion come or go. There were so many customers that after an hour people faded into the mists of memory.

By one-thirty it was absolutely certain that Jessica hadn't returned to work or gone home, nor had she called in with an excuse. She had vanished without a trace.

By two o'clock it was certain that one of her co-workers had vanished with her. Frank Winkowski was the man in the yellow shirt and he, too, had failed to return to work or call in.

By seven that evening the Bureau offices looked like the command post of a small army. Extra communications stations had been set up to deal with the growing number of agents who were arriving to assist. Men and women milled around, awaiting their assignments. Operators manned the phones and radios. Several coffee urns had been set up in one corner, and somebody had thought to order a tray of doughnuts from a local bakery.

All the necessities, Arlen thought with a bitterness that shocked him even in his nearly numb state. Excitement. He'd been an agent long enough to know what a welcome event a case like this was. The big ones came so rarely. A double abduction and espionage. All the ingredients for a headline-making case. A chance for young agents to step out of mediocrity.

Taking a slug from his own mug, he turned his back on the confusion and stepped into the relative silence of his own office.

Jessica.

Without evidence to the contrary, he feared she was dead, and each passing hour made it more likely. He really, honestly, didn't think he could survive it. The thought came to him calmly, shrouded in the muffling numbness that had taken over that afternoon, and he pondered it while sipping his coffee and staring uptown toward the lighted beauty of the state capitol.

Well, of course he cared about her. He cared about her as he would care for any close friend, but no more. He couldn't allow himself to care any more than that. Because he couldn't risk the pain again. He couldn't risk *this*. God, wasn't once enough for any lifetime?

He found himself hoping terrible things, hoping that death had come swiftly, painlessly. That she hadn't been raped.... God, not that! She was so young, so innocent, so... Dear God!

He found himself praying for things he wouldn't be able to bear because there were things he would be able to bear even less. Because mercy at this point was a dark and ugly thing, a matter of speed and precision, not a matter of kindness. He'd seen enough death to know the darkest, the worst, the ugliest, that man could do. Imagination didn't even enter into it. He had Dantean memories from hell to paint pictures that shredded his soul.

"She must have discovered something."

Phil's voice drew Arlen out of his morbid thoughts.

"Looks that way." Arlen turned from the window, from the night back to artificial day. *Why* did they have to put these awful fluorescent lights everywhere? "Somebody must have heard her call me, because she told me she'd be at the restaurant shortly after twelve, but Lisa says she got there with this guy at a quarter to."

"Maybe somebody asked her for a favor, so she went early. Most of us can't refuse a favor.

"I guess."

"Anyway, I wanted to tell you, they're ready to trace any calls to us here, any calls to Winkowski's house, and any calls to Kilmer's house. You said you were going to be there? With Mahaffey at Kilmer's place?"

Arlen nodded slowly. "Yeah. I can always hope this is an old-fashioned kidnapping. That somebody thinks they can bargain with us for something."

Phil's expression was concerned. "That's not likely, Arlen."

"I know that." Arlen rubbed the heel of his palm against his temple. "I've got one hell of headache, and I don't think it's going to get any better. Nothing from her co-workers?"

Phil shook his head. "They've been questioned and re-questioned. All they know is that Kilmer and Winkowski were the first two in this morning, and both were hard at work when the others arrived. Security says Winkowski arrived exactly six minutes before Kilmer."

Phil pulled out a pocket pad and checked it. "According to the log entry the security system keeps, Winkowski punched in his door code six minutes before Kilmer punched hers in. She logged onto the central computer at precisely 7:43, eight minutes after she called here. And she logged off the system at 11:30. Winkowski logged off at 11:27. Between those times, everyone claims they noticed nothing unusual at all.

"Front desk security noted the two of them leaving through the main entrance at approximately 11:35. Nobody paid real close attention, though, because they're both readily recognized by the day shift. Jordan, one of the guards, says he noticed only because Kilmer was laughing at something, and he says he's never seen her laugh before."

But I have, Arlen thought. I've seen her laugh, and it's a beautiful sight. A beautiful sound.

"Anyhow," Phil continued, "Lisa saw her come out with Winkowski, looking like two good friends, and they got into Kilmer's car. Lisa tailed them to the Pub and watched them both enter the restaurant by the front door at exactly 11:45. And that's it.''

Just like that, two people had disappeared as if they had never been.

Arlen shook his head grimly. ''I told Jessica Kilmer to trust me, Phil. I was wrong.''

''Maybe not,'' Phil said. ''Maybe not.''

Arlen simply looked at him from hollow eyes.

Ed Marcel poked his head around the corner. ''Arlen? The phone at Kilmer's place has rung three times in the last hour. Mahaffey says they've hung up every time she's answered it.''

Arlen grabbed his suit jacket and tugged it on. ''I'm going. Give me a radio, Ed.''

The numbness was settling over him again, this time more deeply. Coldly. He could almost hear the click as his feelings turned off, one by one. He couldn't afford to care. He couldn't afford the risk. It was as simple as that.

Arlen had spent a lot of time in Jessica's house during the past two weeks, but beyond his first impression of her bedroom, he hadn't really *looked* at it. Wandering through it now, he ignored Colleen Mahaffey's attempts at small talk and looked, really *looked*.

What he saw was an emptiness that seemed to carve a gaping hole in his own heart. Once, when he'd remarked that somebody must have left her a whole houseful of furniture, she had said casually that she'd bought everything in the house, that none of it was inherited. He'd heard it then as a kind of pride. Now he saw it entirely differently.

Oh, God, he thought, and tried to pull another layer of numbness around himself. He'd thought of her house as a nesting thing that women do. Lord knew he'd seen enough of it with Lucy—sudden bursts of frenetic energy during which furniture would be rearranged dramatically, or old curtains would vanish to be replaced by new, or she would do whatever else occurred to her to pretty up their home. Sometimes it would be something as small as a single new acquisition to bring a spot of brightness to a corner. Such storms had barely rippled his existence. It was something Lucy did, just as he drank his beer from a bottle and his coffee from a mug.

And until this moment that was how he'd viewed Jessica's house. Now, each old photo, each doily and antimacassar, every lovingly polished piece of scarred furniture held a different message. Jessica had made her home, and it was empty. She had built her nest, and there was no one in it.

Arlen drew a deep breath, trying to loosen the sudden tightness in his chest. These thoughts were getting him nowhere, accomplishing nothing at all. With an almost conscious inward tightening, he clamped down on the volcanic feelings he couldn't afford.

Colleen Mahaffey's voice intruded. "I made coffee, Arlen. Want some?"

"Yeah." Turning, he tried to give her a businesslike smile. "Just as long as it's not in those flowered china teacups of hers."

"I found some mugs."

The set of heavy brown mugs Jessie had bought when he'd confessed he hated to drink coffee from a teacup. Memory caught him on the cusp between one breath and the next as he recalled the delighted sparkle in her eyes when she'd presented him with those mugs. A coffee mug was a very personal item, to Arlen's way of thinking. It took time to find one with exactly the right feel in the hand and at the lip, and when a mug person found one, he clung to it for dear life. Jessie hadn't understood that, but when he saw the pleasure in her bright brown eyes, that hadn't mattered. He had started drinking out of those damn brown mugs.

"Arlen?"

Again Mahaffey had caught him locked in the grip of a flood tide of memories and feelings he didn't want. Damn it, he'd known Jessica for less than two weeks. She couldn't possibly mean so much. . . .

"Thanks," he said, taking the mug.

"You know Jessica Kilmer pretty well, huh?" Mahaffey asked, retreating to the counter behind her. She lifted her own mug, watching him over the rim.

"Yeah." Damn it all, he thought. Mahaffey had probably picked up on things he didn't want to know himself. "Since she called to report the theft of a classified document a couple of weeks ago."

He turned away and went to look out the window beside the kitchen door. His car was there, parked behind his Harley. Jessica had offered to let him keep the bike here so he wouldn't have to get it out of storage whenever he wanted to ride. It would be safer here than in an apartment-house parking lot, she felt. It was *here,* saying a lot of things he hadn't—couldn't—say himself. Maybe he ought to hang a sign in the Bureau offices, and silence all the speculation. *Agent Coulter has very stupidly gotten involved with someone who came to him for help, and now she's in trouble, and maybe. . .*

An oath escaped him under his breath, but Mahaffey heard it. Suddenly her hand was on his arm, and it didn't matter that he was in charge of this operation and she was a relatively young agent from another field office who hadn't even met him until forty minutes ago.

"I'm sorry," she said. "It has to be hell."

Without looking at her he nodded, grim lipped. He was glad she didn't try to offer any false reassurances. They were both professional enough to know that with each passing minute Jessie's chances diminished.

The phone rang shrilly, as piercing as a gunshot. Arlen's gray eyes briefly met Colleen Mahaffey's blue ones. Just a glance of recognition. Without a word, he went to answer it. If the kidnapper wouldn't speak to a woman, then Arlen knew who he wanted to speak with.

"Coulter," he said steadily into the receiver. Everything inside of him solidified into ice.

"I have her," said a muffled voice. "She's okay."

"Let me talk to her." Calmly. Coolly. Not a tremor.

"No. Start figuring out how to get me out of the country in one piece. And don't make me nervous."

With a click, the kidnapper disconnected, leaving Arlen listening to a hum that suddenly sounded like a death knell. Turning, he looked at Mahaffey. She was on another phone, the one the FBI had had installed, a separate line. She lifted a finger. "The trace got it," she said. "I'm waiting for the address."

Arlen's heart slammed once, hard, and he drew a shaky breath as he hung up the phone. The same technology that made 911 so effective might now save Jessie's life, but he didn't allow himself to hope. Hope was a risky thing.

"It's a phone booth at the corner of Alma and Winter," Mahaffey said. "There's a police cruiser in the vicinity right now. They're going to check it out."

"He'll be gone." Arlen was certain of it with a conviction that sat in his gut like lead.

"Maybe someone noticed him," Mahaffey suggested hopefully. "Maybe someone saw which way he headed, or what he was driving. Maybe we'll find out who he is."

"I know who he is." Arlen spread his city map on the kitchen table so he could look for the intersection of Alma and Winter. "It's Frank Winkowski."

Mahaffey raised both eyebrows. "Winkowski might be a victim, too."

"The more I think about it, the more I doubt it. Winkowski could stick a gun in Jessica's ribs in that crowded restaurant and get her to walk out an emergency exit with him without making a scene. The chances that a man could do that with two unwilling victims in a crowded place are so slender that I doubt any sane person would try it. He'd wait for a more auspicious time to abduct them. No, I really think Winkowski did it. The question is why."

Arrangements to get him out of the country. Well, that was about as clear as you could get, Arlen thought as he bent over the map. Winkowski evidently thought he had been exposed, or was about to be. But how the hell had he gotten that idea?

In the middle of the Corner Pub, Frank Winkowski had suddenly slipped his arm around Jessica's waist and hauled her up tight against him. Startled, she had looked up at him, and then she'd felt the hard poke in her side.

"I've got a gun on you," Frank had said. "Walk toward that exit."

It never occurred to her to doubt him. His hand was tucked against her side in such a way that she easily believed he held a small pistol. He had taken her out to the back parking lot, led her to a car and put her in behind the wheel. Then he'd climbed into the passenger side and pulled a bigger, uglier, meaner-looking gun out of the glove compartment. Pointing it at her, he had told her to drive.

Outside town, on a deserted back road, he'd ordered her out and had made her climb into the trunk. There, the gun pointing right at her head, he had made her put ankle chains on. Then he had locked her in the trunk. Hours later, in the dark, having driven to some other place, he took her from the trunk and shoved her into a dark structure, locking her alone in a barren room.

To be truthful, Frank had terrified her even more than the gun had. There had been something wild in his normally mild eyes, some kind of desperate tension in his words and posture. From being a familiar, friendly co-worker, he had become a dangerous unknown.

Being held hostage—at least, Jessica figured that was her role—was not only terrifying, it was unnerving. Refusing to give in to the terror, she had concentrated on cataloging things, and in the process of cataloging impressions, she had learned some surprising things about herself.

For example, she discovered that it drove her absolutely crazy not to know where she was. In the dark she couldn't read the dial of her watch, and that drove her crazy, too, not knowing how quickly or slowly time was passing. Pondering those two surprises occupied her for a while. Why did she have such a need to know exactly where she was? Was it some kind of human instinct not to get lost? And as far as not being able to read her watch went, she felt there was something distinctly neurotic about being that dependent on knowing the time.

But such cogitations absorbed her only briefly in the yawning space of hours she could not count. She tried to focus on her discomforts—the cold cement floor on which she had to sit and lie, because there was no furniture, the airlessness of the blacked-out, boarded-up room, the lack of sanitary facilities. Oh, there was a bucket, but how barbaric! She wouldn't have thought Frank capable of such things.

But evidently he *was* capable, and she tried not to wonder what else he was capable of. In barren moments, when her mind wandered a little, she would suddenly fear that he couldn't possibly let her live. No way. Because she knew who he was. Just as soon as he got whatever it was he wanted, he would have to kill her so she couldn't identify him.

And that was the possibility she ran from by trying to think about stupid, inane things, like the chains on her feet that let her hobble only a few inches at a time. So she couldn't attack Frank if he ever came back, or run, or really defend herself. Such thoughts were stupid, because she was sure he would never give her the chance to do any of those things even if she wasn't chained. Frank was not dumb. Crazy, maybe, but not stupid.

But finally, fatigued and cold and hungry, she who had never been brave lost the last of her courage. Shivering, with silent tears running down her face, she thought of Arlen and ached, with a longing so deep it seemed to be part of her soul, to be held by him just one more time.

Poor Arlen, she thought as she lay curled up on the cold concrete. He was going to hold himself responsible for this. He was that kind of man. And she wished now that she had told him she loved him, even if it had scared him away. It seemed somehow unutterably sad that she would never tell him something he so clearly needed to know.

Several times sleep tried to claim her, but each time she woke from the nightmare of being stuffed into a car trunk at gunpoint to the living nightmare of her present captivity. A chill crept into her very bones, and she shivered continually, wasting whatever was left of her meager reserves.

Frank Winkowski. Who would ever have thought it?

* * *

Shortly after the kidnapper's first call to Arlen, the phone company finally arranged for Jessica's calls to ring on the phone on Arlen's desk at the Bureau. While he waited for the next call, he and a number of other agents, with assistance from the local police, began to plan. If they could persuade Winkowski they meant to let him leave the country, they might have to let him go as far as the airport before they could move against him. What if he refused to reveal where Jessica was until after he was airborne? Was there anything they could do to increase her chances while preventing Winkowski's escape? All eventualities had to be considered, and most of the night passed in exhaustive discussion.

And with each passing minute, something in Arlen hardened even more. He could not afford to permit emotion or worry to cloud his judgment, or so he told himself, but in reality the hardening was not a deadening, it was a growing, deadly anger. Each minute that passed was another minute of terror for Jessica, and he was by God going to take each and every one of those minutes out of someone's hide.

Near dawn he catnapped in his chair, waiting for the phone to ring. What the devil was Winkowski up to, anyhow? Why was he taking so long? Unanswered, unanswerable questions roiled around in his head, following him even into sleep. One thing stood clear in his mind, like a beacon. Until yesterday at 11:45 a.m., Frank Winkowski could have boarded any plane at the airport and left the country as a free man. What the hell had panicked him into taking a hostage?

The room was not quite dark as Jessica had thought. When she awoke, a small, pale stream of sunlight was pouring through some tiny crack in the heavy window coverings. It was a slender pencil of light, but it caught dust motes in its beam and shed just enough illumination to bring reality to her prison. She could even read her watch and see that it was just before seven in the morning.

That little bit of knowledge was somehow comforting, giving her a sense of connection to the rest of the world. And this window must face east, she thought, for such a strong ray of light to reach her so shortly after dawn. That would explain, too, why it had seemed so dark last evening.

A key scraped in the locked door, and Jessica instinctively edged back into a corner and huddled, shivering wearily from the chill, from fatigue and from fear. Even her shivers were halfhearted, she thought, as she forced herself to look at Frank Winkowski.

"I brought you some food," he said, and set a paper plate down on the floor. On it sat a limp, thin sandwich. Next to it he placed a large paper cup.

"Why are you doing this, Frank?" she asked him, hating the faint uncertain sound of her voice. Yes, she was a coward, but it wasn't something she wanted this man to know.

"You know why, Jessica."

"No, I don't! At least tell me that much, Frank! Are you going to kill me? Why?" Her voice rose in desperation, and he stepped backward.

"I don't want to kill you," he said after a moment. "I won't, unless they don't let me go."

"Go where?" she asked, trying to keep her voice down, trying not to drive him away before she at least had some kind of answer.

"Out of the country. Come on, Jessica. You know what's been going on! Hell, you were working with the FBI on it."

"I was?" Her mind scrambled frantically for some way to deny what he already seemed to know. And then she thought of Leong. "I was working as a double agent, you mean? Because of that Chinese student who kept trying to meet with me?"

"Chinese student?" Frank looked startled. "What Chinese student? I'm talking about that damned missing document you made such a stink about."

"The document? But I reported that to Barron. What does the FBI have to do with that?" Please, God, please let him believe I don't have anything to do with what frightened him. Please!

Frank took another backward step, looking uncertain for the first time. "Don't lie to me, Jessica. You called that Coulter guy yesterday morning to tell him about me. I heard you."

Jessica's heart sank, and hope began to die. "I called to make a lunch date with him," she argued.

"Right. And as soon as you told him your suspicions about me, he would know about Barron, too." He started to turn away. "I'll be back in fifteen minutes, and you can talk to your boyfriend."

An agonizing throb of hope pierced her heart. Arlen. Was Arlen here? "My boyfriend?" she repeated, and hated the hoarse, weak sound of her own voice.

"The FBI guy. Did you think I didn't know?" Frank looked at her. In the faint, dim light, his expression was hard to read, but to Jessica it looked frighteningly like revulsion. "I thought you were a lady, Jessica," he said. "You always seemed like such a lady. But everybody at the FBI office knows you're living with him. Everybody. You can't be much of a lady, after all."

Jessica stared after him as he stomped out and locked the door once again. Everybody at the FBI office knew? Well, that seemed likely enough, she thought.

Funny how her mind wanted to seize on everything except her own impending doom. Her thoughts played hide-and-seek with the intolerable and insisted on thinking about the evidently tattered state of her reputation rather than . . . other things.

And then understanding hit her hard, knocking the wind from her and tearing a short groan from her lips. Frank had spoken of what everybody at the FBI office knew, and there was only one way he could know something like that. She didn't have a chance in hell. Not a chance. She was as good as dead, because somebody at the Bureau had a good reason for not wanting her or Frank to be found.

Chapter 12

The coffee urn held nothing but hot sludge, so Arlen spent a few minutes cleaning it and starting a fresh pot. Most of the agents who had filled the office to overflowing last night had found someplace to crash. Soon they would be returning, and life would fill the silence of the offices.

Walking back down the hall to his own office, he passed by Phil Harrigan's door. Hearing the murmur of Phil's voice, Arlen paused, raising a hand to knock and go in.

"I told you not to do anything," Phil said. "I warned you."

It didn't sound like a good time to intrude, so, mug in hand, he continued down the corridor.

Maddy Kazin showed up moments later and dropped a computer printout on his desk. A small, birdlike woman with huge green eyes, she appeared lost in herself most of the time.

"Everything I've been able to find on Winkowski," she said. She made no secret of her weariness, but pulled off her horn-rims and rubbed her eyes. "I don't think there's a damn thing there to help you, Arlen. If he made any money apart from his job, he hid it. If he knew anybody he shouldn't, I can't find it. He appears to be completely clean."

"He can't be."

"I know." Maddy yawned. "I'm going home for a couple hours of sleep, and then I'll be back."

For lack of anything more useful or active to do, Arlen smothered his own yawn and started flipping through the information Maddy had gleaned.

The phone rang. Every hair on the back of his neck stood up, and his heart slammed into the wall of his chest once, twice. As he lifted the receiver, the attached recorder automatically began to run.

"Coulter," he said.

"Listen," said the muffled voice.

And then, "Arlen?"

The sound of Jessica's tentative, frightened voice smashed into Arlen with all the impact of an out-of-control freight train. "Are you okay?" he barked into the phone.

"Y-yes.... Arlen, why didn't you tell me everybody at your office was talking about us?"

Startled by her direction, Arlen stiffened and frowned. "Jessie?"

"You should have told me," she said with an intensity that sounded almost wild. "Arlen... Arlen, I need to tell you—"

"That's it," interrupted the muffled voice.

There was a click as the connection was cut, and Arlen found himself staring at the humming receiver. An image of his fist slamming into Winkowski's face clouded his vision. He found himself, for the first time in his life, wanting to commit atrocities against another human being.

"Arlen?" Phil Harrigan stood in the doorway of his office. "Was that the kidnapper? Are you okay?"

"I'm fine," Arlen said grimly. "I'm fine. I'd like to kill the son of a bitch. Slowly."

Harrigan shifted uneasily. "Did he make any demands?"

"No, he just let Jessica say a couple of words. That's all. Damn it!" Heedless of the pain—indeed, grateful for it—

he pounded his fist one futile time on the top of his desk. "Damn it," he said again, more quietly. "Damn it."

"I'm going across the street to pick up something for breakfast," Harrigan said after a few moments. "What can I get for you?"

Arlen sure as hell didn't want to eat, but he knew better. "A double order of dry whole wheat toast and orange juice. Thanks, Phil."

"No problem."

Swiveling his chair, Arlen leaned back and looked up at the brightening morning sky. The soft glow of dawn had given way to a harsher, brighter, clearer blue. Behind him, beyond his door, he heard arriving agents. Questions began to swarm around him like bees.

Why had Phil Harrigan hung around all night? He hadn't been assigned to the team that had pulled the night shift. Everybody else had gone home a couple of hours ago, or headed to a hotel to grab some shut-eye.

Why didn't you tell me everybody at your office was talking about us? How did she know that, even if it was true? And Arlen certainly didn't know if it was, because nobody would have the nerve to gossip about it to his face. Who could have told her that? Winkowski? And how the hell would *he* know? And, under the circumstances, why had Jessie considered something that was really so trivial so important that it was all she had managed to say to him? It didn't seem like her, somehow.

I told you not to do anything. I warned you. Phil's mysterious morning conversation.

Arlen snapped out of his chair as if propelled on springs. Striding to the door of his office, he raised his voice. "Who's here this morning?"

Two minutes later he was closeted in his office with Lisa Gonzales, Ted Wilson and Colleen Mahaffey, who had just walked through the door.

At least Frank had been decent enough to leave her with a thermos of hot soup and a jug of water. Jessica considered smashing the insulated bottle, but couldn't figure out what she could possibly use the eggshell shards of glass for.

It wasn't as if she could cut the chains from her ankles, which felt terribly sore from the constant chafing and banging of those steel bands.

The soup warmed her a little, easing the chill that had penetrated during the night, but she still felt cold. She tried hobbling around the room to warm herself, but she couldn't move fast enough to do any good, and the steel rings around her ankles had rubbed her flesh nearly raw, so movement was agony.

Finally, huddled again in the corner, she wrapped her arms around herself and closed her eyes. The present was unbearable, so she resorted to a childhood game. Starting from the moment she had opened her front door to him the first time, she would remember each and every minute of her relationship with Arlen. In sequence, in full detail. It would pass the time.

And time, she realized with a tightening throat, was suddenly something she had both too much and not enough of.

If only she had told him that she loved him.

Phil Harrigan walked back into Arlen's office a half hour later with a foam container of toast and a plastic bottle of orange juice. Halfway across the room, he seemed to notice the silence that had settled over the agents already there. He glanced from Wilson to Gonzales and then to Mahaffey. When his gaze settled on Arlen once again, there was a look of dawning comprehension in his eyes.

"Thanks, Phil," Arlen said, accepting his breakfast. "Have a seat."

Said pleasantly, it was still a command. Phil sat.

"Ted?" Arlen said.

Wilson crossed the room, his young face set in hard lines. "I'd like your weapon, Phil."

"Why?" Phil tried to smile and look relaxed. "What's up?"

"Give him your weapon, Phil," Arlen said grimly, and waited until the pistol was firmly in Ted's hand. "Now. Maybe you'd like to tell me where Jessica Kilmer is."

Phil raised his eyebrows. "You're kidding, right?"

"Wrong." Arlen leaned forward, impaling him with an arctic stare from gray eyes that suddenly looked like shards of steel. "I haven't read you your rights yet, Phil. Nothing you say right now can be used against you. Where the hell is Jessica Kilmer?"

Phil started to rise, but Lisa Gonzales stopped him with a heavy hand on his shoulder. Inexorably, she pressed him back down.

"What the hell makes you think I know anything about where she is?" Phil demanded hotly. "Damn it, I can't believe this!"

"Believe it, you son of a bitch," Arlen said on a low, angry growl. "And right now it's all I can do not to come around this desk and smash your lying face. You were assigned to protect that woman! You, a federal agent! Damn it, *I'm* the one who can't believe this. How does it feel to be only the second FBI agent in history to get involved in spying? Tell me, Phil, where the hell *is* she and what the *hell* did you get out of this?"

"You're crazy, Arlen," Phil argued. "I don't know where you got this insane idea, but you sure as hell can't prove any of it!"

"No?" For just a split second, a pause so brief that it was almost unnoticeable, Arlen considered that he might be wrong. Phil was right: there was no proof. All he had was what Jessica had said and a snatch of overheard conversation. Then he plunged ahead. "Right now, about the only possible way I can see you not winding up with a couple of life sentences is if you cooperate, Phil. We're talking espionage and kidnapping. The Bureau is going to have your skin."

When Phil remained silent, Arlen shrugged. "Have it your way. Lisa, read him his rights."

That was when Phil decided that Arlen wasn't bluffing. If he was going to be Mirandized, then Arlen meant to arrest him, and Arlen wouldn't set himself up for charges of false arrest. Somehow they had gotten evidence against him.

"Okay," he said as Lisa pulled out her card. "Okay. But I didn't have anything to do with this kidnapping, and I don't know where the Kilmer woman is. Honest to God. Winkowski freaked out. I knew he was getting edgy, and I warned him not to do anything, but he didn't listen. I swear, he did this on his own, just like he killed Dave Barron.''

"A loose cannon," Arlen remarked.

"Yeah. Exactly. He's crazy."

"Do you think you can get him to tell you where Jessica is?"

Phil shrugged. "Maybe. Probably. Damn it, Arlen, you've got to believe me. I didn't want to see her hurt."

"You damn well better hope she hasn't been," Arlen said harshly. "I'm going to get Winkowski, at the very least, and maybe Dobrocek and Stratton, and at least one of them is going to tell me all about you, Phil. One of them will, but I'm betting on Winkowski. I'm willing to bet he'll do anything to save his butt. Just like he's doing right now."

Harrigan slumped a little as he faced the truth of that. "Yeah," he muttered. "Probably."

Arlen passed a hand over his face. "Okay. Let's get Caro Granger down here. We're going to Mirandize you, Phil. You just keep in mind that Granger is the person you need to convince that you have some redeeming qualities. She's the one who cuts the deals. Do you want an attorney?"

Phil heaved a deep, unsteady sigh. "What the hell for?" he asked wearily. "An attorney will only tell me not to say anything, and I already know that."

"Get him an attorney," Carolyn Granger said not five minutes later. "Mirandizing him isn't enough to make it stick in court. He's got to have counsel, or a smart defense attorney can weasel him out of this."

Phil muttered an oath. "I doubt that," he said acidly. "I'm a federal agent, for crying out loud. Who the hell is going to believe I didn't know any better? Hell, I don't believe it myself. Look, I'm not going to discuss anything *I* did without an attorney. I'm not going to admit to anything at all except that I know the number of Frank Winkowski's radiophone."

"You do?" Arlen sat up straighter.

Phil nodded.

Arlen's expression was hard. "Why so suddenly cooperative, Phil?"

Phil spread his hands. This time Arlen couldn't doubt his sincerity. "I'm worried he might get nervous enough to hurt the woman. Nobody was ever supposed to get hurt. I never guessed Frank was so unstable."

For the next hour Phil tried to raise Frank Winkowski, without success. Arlen found it increasingly difficult to sit still, and he paced the circumference of his office almost ceaselessly, answering whatever questions came his way, ordering whatever needed to be ordered. Agents were searching Winkowski's home and office yet again, interviewing neighbors and co-workers, seeking any clue to his whereabouts. Maddy Kazin produced the first unusual information about Winkowski—just two days before, he had paid in cash for a new car at a dealership along the interstate. The dealer was only just now getting around to reporting the cash purchase, as required by law.

"And that's something," said Lisa Gonzales. "Most dealers don't even bother."

Well, thought Arlen, now they knew Winkowski was driving a shiny red Accord with temporary tags. Obviously the guy hadn't been planning to run two days ago. Big help. Real big help. If Jessica got out of this in one piece, he was going to... going to... Going to what? Turn his back on her and let her get on with a proper life, that was what. He wouldn't take further advantage of her, that was what. She needed a husband and the next fifty or sixty years. That was what she needed, and he wouldn't stand in her way. Just, dear God, please let her be all right.

And then Phil got through to Winkowski.

"Frank, it's Phil."

Phil's voice brought Arlen pivoting around from the window.

"Look," said Phil, "you haven't hurt the woman, have you?"

Arlen held his breath, then released it as Phil looked up at him and shook his head. Two other agents were listening in on headsets, and Arlen was tempted to grab a pair from one of them. He held himself back, though, knowing he might get upset enough to give the game away. So much for his iron control. It had been a joke, evidently, ever since he met Jessie. Ever since he saw her virginal room and... He hoped heaven could forgive him, but he still wanted to see Jessie clad in nothing but her hair, lying on that satin comforter and waiting for him. Just for him. Smiling, holding out her arms, her long silky hair trailing across her shoulders and breasts.

"Frank," Phil was saying, his tone one of soothing patience, the kind of tone a parent uses with an upset, recalcitrant child, "Frank, listen to me. I've got all the details about the trap that's being set for you. Believe me, you'll never get out of the airport unless you know what they're planning."

Phil listened for a minute, then interrupted. "I know, I know. But I've got a price for this, Frank. I'm not going to tell you what I know for nothing. You know I never do anything for nothing."

Arlen could hear, actually hear, the whining of Winkowski's voice on Phil's handset.

"Just shut up and listen, Frank," Phil said. "I can't tell you over the phone, because somebody might hear me. I need to meet you.... Anyplace, damn it! Just tell me where."

After another space, Phil nodded. "Got it. Okay.... My price? It's cheap, Frank. I want to know where you've stashed the woman."

Phil winced and pulled the receiver away from his ear. "Damn it, Frank, shut up! You're sounding like a crazy man! You can tell me where she is after I tell you what the setup is and how to avoid it. Fine. But you will tell me."

He paused. "Because I want to be the hero in this one, Frank. While you're flying away to Moscow or wherever you're planning to go, I want to be the one who saves the woman. That's why. You get what you want, and I get to be a hero."

Arlen hardly dared believe that Winkowski could fall for anything so transparent, but Harrigan evidently knew what he was doing. In a few more minutes a meeting had been set up.

"Two hours," said Phil after he hung up. "The guy's really cracked. With all the flat, open places he could have picked around here, he chose the hill country out toward Lago Vista. Plenty of cover."

Arlen nodded. That made his job much easier, but it also shortened his time. Two hours. In two hours he was going to have the little crud in his grasp, and if Winkowski wouldn't tell Phil where Jessie was, Arlen was prepared to use whatever means were necessary to get the information. To hell with careers and headlines and what the director thought. All that mattered was Jessie.

It was a day, Arlen thought, for barreling down back country roads on the Harley, roaring around the curves and over hills with the wind in his face. The sky had turned a pure, crystalline blue, the sun was warm and the air was dry. They just didn't come much prettier.

But instead of roaring down roads to oblivion, he was crouching behind a boulder with the sun burning the back of his neck. Fire ants were everywhere, and while he had so far not been bitten, he didn't expect that to last. The thought of rattlesnakes slithered across his mind, too. Probably too early in the spring for them, he told himself. But what did he know about such things? A trickle of sweat rolled down his back between his shoulder blades, and he shrugged to ease away the resultant itchiness. Something sharp poked into his right buttock, but he ignored it. Such discomforts were legion on a stakeout.

All the patience he had learned on past stakeouts was doing him little good on this one, though. Sure, he knew how to sit quietly for hours and ignore all the discomforts—within reason—but the emotional pressure this time was something else.

And where the devil was Winkowski?

They'd had very little time to set the stage for this one. By car it took nearly an hour to get here from town, and then they'd all had to find appropriate hiding places. As a precautionary measure there were two marksmen higher up, hidden in the rugged terrain with their high-powered rifles and sniper scopes. The narrow road leading in and out of here would be sealed the instant Winkowski arrived. Down below, leaning against his dusty caliche-colored Buick, Phil Harrigan waited.

Arlen doubted he was ever going to understand Harrigan. In his youth, Arlen had skirted the law a time or two. Why not admit it? He'd been a hell-raiser at times, wanting to wring more out of life than it had given him. He'd felt bitter and alienated and all those other things that make people cross the street when they see you coming. But never, ever, in his wildest moments or wildest imaginings, would he have considered committing a crime of this type. Hell, wild or not, he had *enlisted* in the marines even though, in those days, as a married man he had an automatic draft deferment. Maybe he'd wanted some of the excitement that boys blindly and foolishly think is war, maybe he had wanted some of the glory and a lot more action than his tame little community could provide, but behind his decision was a blazing patriotism, a belief that no place in the world gave a man more opportunities, more chances, more freedoms. He felt he owed something to his country.

No, he would never understand what led a man to sell out his country this way. Nor would he ever understand how a man could compromise his personal honor and integrity in such a manner. He had never understood it in anyone, but it was far more comprehensible in some of the sleaze he had dealt with over the years than it could ever be in a man like Phil Harrigan—who was evidently a sleaze after all.

All the way out here Phil had been spilling his guts, as if his conscience had finally gone into overdrive and he wanted to appease it. His entire role in the espionage ring had been to warn Carl Stratton if the Feds picked up wind of the spying activities. In return for agreeing to do that, he'd received a monthly cash payment, free and clear, under the table.

Tax evasion, Arlen thought when he heard it. That would get him if nothing else did.

Carl Stratton had evidently been the kingpin of the operation. Phil had the names of everyone involved only because he had to be alert for them being mentioned at the Bureau offices or elsewhere. Otherwise, he probably wouldn't have known about anyone other than Carl. As it was, he knew them all and was in contact with them all. All, that is, except Carl's KGB contact.

Until Dobrocek had been introduced to Jessica Kilmer by Greg Leong, Phil hadn't had even an inkling of the man's identity. He had, of course, known that Carl must have such a contact, but not until then did he guess who it might be. He had, he said, tried to warn Carl that Jessica was acting as a double agent, had tried to prevent the contact from being made, but Carl had been out of town, and at that time only Carl had known Dobrocek's identity. Phil's inability to transmit his warning was the only reason Dobrocek had ever come into the picture. Even after Jessica was introduced to Dobrocek, Phil hadn't been sure the Czech was connected with Stratton, not until Maddy Kazin had made her discoveries.

"What was Dave Barron's role?" Arlen had asked him.

"About the same as mine. All he had to do was provide Carl with the safe combinations. And keep an eye on security, so he would catch trouble as soon as it started. Like it did with Kilmer."

"Who killed him?"

"Winkowski." Phil had passed a hand over his face and looked at the tape recorder microphone Caro Granger held up beside his mouth. He and Caro had sat in the back seat, Arlen and Phil's hastily summoned public defender in the front. The public defender had given up trying to silence Phil. Like the others, he now simply listened in fascination.

"Winkowski's a problem," Phil had said. "A big problem. From what I've been able to gather, Barron told him that Jessica was raising a big stink about that document, and that it wasn't going to die a quiet death. He said he was going to report the theft to the FBI to make it look as if MTI were clean. Winkowski snapped, and I don't think he's unsnapped. I told him not to bother the woman. I told him nobody would ever guess he was involved. Damn, there wasn't any connection except Carl, and Carl left the country—''

Phil had broken off, and Arlen's hands had tightened on the wheel. "Damn it, Phil! When did he leave? He never even came back to his apartment after Maddy..." Arlen's voice had trailed off. When he'd spoken again, his voice had held the sleet of an arctic blizzard. "You warned him we were on to him."

"Hell, yes," Phil had said. "Ever since this thing started going haywire, I've been worrying that somebody would start squealing. As far as I was concerned, it was all to the good if *everybody* skipped the country."

Carl was already gone, having been seen by no one since Sunday night, the night Phil had called him and warned him that Maddy Kazin had connected him with Dobrocek.

Crouched behind his boulder now, Arlen considered one or two unsavory things he might like to do to Phil and Winkowski. Especially Winkowski. Especially the man who had terrified and kidnapped Jessica. God help him if he had hurt her in any way.

It had been Phil who had bugged Jessica's phones, because he was concerned about the kind of information that Jessica might uncover and pass on to Arlen, and he didn't want to be forced to rely on whatever Arlen chose to tell him about it. He had slipped over there that Saturday night after Arlen had told him that Jessica was going to be a double agent. He'd gone over in that small space of time after he left the Bureau office and before Arlen went over to Jessie's to check on her.

The memory of *that* night hit Arlen like a punch to the stomach. Everyone automatically understood that a woman's gift of her virginity was an emotionally charged one for the woman, but he wondered how many people understood that it could be just as emotionally charged for a man. He sure hadn't guessed it himself. Lucy had come to him a virgin because that was the way things were done back then in the small towns of America, and because she really hadn't had the time or experience to find out that it could be otherwise. Hell, he'd been a virgin himself, as most boys had been back then, despite locker-room talk.

Their wedding night had in no way aroused in him the feelings Jessica had evoked with her freely given gift, a gift she had chosen not to give anyone until him.

She hadn't asked for a ring or undying love or guarantees. She had simply given, freely. And he, whether he liked to think about it or not, had received that gift with an awe and wonder he felt to the very roots of his soul.

Static crackled in his ear, and he adjusted the earphone, seating it more firmly, then glanced down at the radio attached to his belt.

"Suspect is on his way," said the voice of Colleen Mahaffey, who was stationed at the junction where this dirt road turned off from the farm-to-market road that was the only way to get here. "He's driving slowly and looking every which way, so duck low. We'll seal the road in three minutes."

Automatically Arlen freed his weapon from its holster and checked it. The automatic was ready, of course. He'd checked the clip before leaving town, but he checked it again, anyway. He was sure every other agent hidden in these rocks and sparse trees was doing precisely the same thing.

A slow toasting over hot coals? Or a skinning? Alive. Inch by inch. Such thoughts bounced around in his head as he watched Winkowski ease his shiny new car around potholes and the occasional large rock. Anything was too good for the scum. Levering himself up a little, he watched Winkowski climb out of the car and face Phil, who remained in a relaxed posture, leaning against the side of his Buick.

Phil was wearing a wire, and conversation began to burst into Arlen's ear, full of static, mixed with the rustle of Phil's clothing, but decipherable.

"Damn it, man," Phil said, "I told you not to do this! You've got the Bureau hopping mad. They're determined to have your skin."

"I didn't come out here to discuss how mad those guys are," Winkowski said shortly. "You're gonna tell me what they've got planned."

"You tell me where the woman is first." Phil held up a hand when Winkowski started to sputter. "Can it, Frank. I don't trust you any farther than I can throw you. You're cracked. You would have been home free if you'd just sat tight, but you didn't have the sense to do that."

"How the hell do I know I can trust you, Harrigan?"

"Simple. I want you out of the country because you can finger me. I don't want you caught any more than you want to be caught. I want you safely away so I can be safe. But you've got this dangerous little bit of baggage hanging around your neck. Think of your future, Frank. We've got a lot of extradition treaties around the world. We can get you back from almost any country if you're wanted for murder, but we can't get you back from most of them if you're wanted for espionage. So it seems to me you need to get the woman off your hands. And I figure since she's gotta be rescued for your benefit, I might as well be the one to do it."

Winkowski paced back and forth, and Arlen found himself holding his breath, wondering if Winkowski would buy the stuff about extradition treaties.

"I'm already wanted for murder," Winkowski said, damning himself on tape. "They've got me on Barron."

"Man, I told you, they don't have any evidence on anyone for that! So he was murdered. It's one thing to know somebody was murdered. It's a whole other ballgame to prove that one particular person did it. They've got nothing on no one for that."

Winkowski hesitated. "You're sure?"

"Of course I'm sure!" Phil drew a breath of long-suffering patience, and even over the poor radio connection Arlen could hear him lowering his tone deliberately. "Look, Frank. It's as much to my benefit as yours to get you the hell out of here. Do you think I want those guys *questioning* you?"

"Okay." Winkowski's capitulation came that quickly and without warning. "Jessica's in the trunk of my car. I put drugs in her water so she wouldn't make any trouble."

That was when Arlen saw red, but he didn't lose his self-control. He couldn't. He couldn't afford to. Instead, while

Phil and Frank had their backs to him as they opened the trunk of Frank's car and looked in at Jessica, he began to creep up behind them. Phil, acting like an agent, thank God, kept Frank's attention on the trunk.

"What the hell did you drug her with?" Phil asked. "Are you sure she didn't get too much?"

"I checked the dosages," Frank said. "It's just some phenobarbital. Even if she drank the whole quart of water at one time, it should just make her sick. Anyway, nobody drinks a whole quart at once."

"I don't know," Phil said. "I don't want to get saddled with any corpses. And look at her ankles. Damn, Frank, what did you do to her?"

"I had to chain her ankles so she couldn't get away. I have to admit, I never thought those cuffs would rub her so bad."

Phil leaned forward. "She doesn't look too good. What if she got carbon monoxide poisoning? Why'd you have to put her in the trunk?"

That did it. Arlen made a flying tackle on Winkowski and found the impact to be one of the most satisfying sensations of his entire life. It appeased a deep, atavistic need to smash the man in ways that civilization wouldn't permit. A few short seconds later he was handcuffing the man and battling the urge to flatten his face.

"I could do it for you," Phil said, as if he could read Arlen's mind. "I'm going to prison anyway."

His knee still on the small of Winkowski's back, Arlen looked up at Phil. "I'm going to remember what you just did. How you helped."

Phil gave a short nod. "Thanks."

Pulling the numbness around him like a shield, Arlen stood up and looked into the trunk. Jessica looked so pale, so fragile, and her ankles were raw and inflamed. Leaning over, he brushed her hair back and felt for the pulse in her neck. Too slow, it was nonetheless strong and steady. She wasn't in any immediate danger.

He turned in time to see Ted Wilson pull Winkowski to his feet. Forgetting all the other agents, not giving a damn, anyway, he stepped up to Winkowski and bent over until he stood nose-to-nose with him.

"You better not have laid a finger on her, Winkowski. You better not have hurt her. Because if you did, I'll find you, and I'll make you pay."

"Arlen..." Ted tried to silence him, knowing the threat could get him into trouble.

But everyone, Caro Granger included, abruptly turned their backs, leaving Winkowski and Arlen facing one another in a circle of people suddenly gone blind and deaf. And, strangely, it was that gesture of support that brought Arlen back to his senses. An agent didn't make threats like that. An agent didn't step outside the law, no matter how he'd been provoked. Not even when others did.

Gritting his teeth, he looked Frank Winkowski right in the eye and saw the fear, mindless and overwhelming, that possessed the man. Fear made men do awful things, stupid things.

And then Arlen turned his own back on Winkowski, and he didn't look at him again.

Chapter 13

Jessica woke in a hospital bed, the night sky clearly visible beyond the open slats of the window blinds. Before she could positively comprehend where she was or what it meant, strong arms closed around her, lifting her from firm pillow to cradle her against a firm chest.

"It's all right, Jessie," murmured a familiar, oddly husky voice. "It's okay, love. You're safe now. You're safe."

Weakly, horrified at herself even as she did it, Jessica turned her face into Arlen's shoulder and began to weep helplessly.

"Shh..." he soothed gently. "Shh...I swear you're safe now, sweetheart." He stroked her hair from the top of her head to her hips, and when his hand slipped into the back of her hospital gown to stroke satin skin, she sobbed even harder, clung even harder.

He knew he needed to leave her, but now was not the time. Another excuse. Just as he'd used the excuse that he had to give her whatever she wanted from him simply because he had deflowered her. And what an old-fashioned term that was. Jessie would probably chuckle over it.

Whatever he called it, it was an excuse. An excuse to cover the fact that he cared when he didn't want to care.

that he was involved when he had sworn to remain uninvolved. God, what would she think if she found out he was having fugitive thoughts of her belly swelling with his child, insane thoughts of starting again at an age when he was about to become a grandfather?

How could he begin to explain to her that in the past two days he had walked through the fire once again, had faced the hell he had sworn never to face again? And that he'd discovered he would risk the terror of loss again and again if only he could have the privilege of holding her one more time?

How could a man of forty-two, who was about to become a grandfather, explain to a young woman of twenty-six that he honestly believed he wasn't too old, that he had a few more sandlot ballgames in him, a few more doll tea parties, a few more years of dirty diapers and first steps and first grades and...

Aw, hell, she'd never believe it. Not after he'd made such a big deal about being finished with all that. She would think he had lost his marbles.

And he had no business telling her such things, anyway. She was entitled to a man her own age and a future that was fifty or sixty years long, not one that was only thirty or forty. She deserved to share her firsts with a man for whom they would also be firsts.

He rocked her back and forth and kissed away her tears, aching for her with a depth that was going to haunt him all his days. But he had to let go.

"I want... I want to go home," she begged unsteadily. "I want to be in my own bed... with you... Arlen, please...."

He wanted it, too. "In the morning, sweetheart. I promise you can go home in the morning."

"I want to go now!"

"They have to watch you. You had some—"

"Now," she said again, a sob breaking the word in the middle. "Now!"

She was irrational, he thought, and didn't find it strange that she should be. And he could certainly understand why she wouldn't feel that all this was over—couldn't feel truly safe—until she was home. That was what being home meant. He understood that because he hadn't been home in years. Not since Lucy got really sick. Not until he had felt Jessie's arms close around him.

"Okay," he said, making the decision instantly. "I'll get a nurse."

The nurse flat-out refused to remove the IV needle, because Jessica hadn't been discharged by a physician.

Arlen had run out of patience. Every last dreg of it had drained away. Jessica had never before heard him use the tone he used now, and she hoped he would never use it on her. It was a tone so soft, so cold, so threatening, that icy fingers skittered up and down her own spine. In that tone of voice, Special Agent Arlen Coulter advised Nurse Benford that she had no legal right whatsoever to detain Ms. Kilmer against her will, and that if she chose to continue in this fashion, he would continue with her in *his* particular fashion. Nurse Benford never asked what that fashion might be. The man was, after all, a federal agent.

"I'll get the house resident," the nurse said. "Really, Agent Coulter, I can't remove the IV without a doctor's order. I'm a *nurse*. I'm not allowed to make medical decisions without a doctor's direction."

The house resident took one look at Arlen's expression and was persuaded, but he didn't give in completely. He was, after all, a doctor, and he wasn't about to make a medical decision that could leave him open for a malpractice suit. He examined Jessica first, before deciding that in all likelihood she would live without medical intervention beyond antibiotics to prevent infection of the abrasions on her ankles. He wrote the prescription himself and told Nurse Benford to discontinue the IV.

Jessie's clothes were filthy, and Arlen wouldn't hear of her putting them on again. Nurse Benford, no longer in the line of fire on this one, became helpful. She brought another hospital gown and put it on Jessica like a robe. A wheelchair appeared, along with an orderly to take her downstairs, but Arlen insisted on pushing her himself.

Jessica was aware of his concern, of his fussing, of his sweet, sweet caring. She wanted to tell him that she loved him because it seemed so important, had been so important throughout her ordeal, that he know, but every time she opened her mouth to say it her breath caught on another sob. What was wrong with her?

It was a nice evening, he thought as he helped Jessie into the car. The air was warm, the breeze gentle, the night soft with moisture from the Gulf. There was more rain coming, he thought, but not tonight. Regardless, he was going to open the windows in Jessie's room and let the breeze wash over her. She needed the openness, the fresh breath of the air.

Reaching out, he pulled her up against his side, under his arm, as he drove. Her sobs had softened, but still they came, soaking his shirt, tearing his heart.

"You need a decent meal," he told her soothingly. "You're just worn down, worn out. You'll feel better soon, sweetheart. I promise."

She clung to his words, to his promise, and hoped he was right. Never in her life had she wept like this, as if her grief were so bottomless and deep that there was no way to plumb it. This was ridiculous, she told herself. She was safe. The danger was over, and Arlen's arms were around her.

"I told you I'm a coward," she managed to choke out brokenly.

But he didn't believe this had anything to do with fear or cowardice. It was a straightforward, honest reaction to intolerable events. Nor was she going to get over this quickly or easily. Victims paid a price for years.

He helped her upstairs and insisted on replacing the hospital gown with a cotton gown of her own. He found it in the dresser drawer just below the drawer she had cleared out for him to use. It smelled fresh, like laundry soap and sunshine, and carried no taint of disinfectants, as the hospital gown did. It was another step away from the nightmare for her.

When he had her tucked safely under the covers, he opened the tall windows on either side of her bed and let the warm breeze glide over her.

"What would you like to eat?" he asked. He perched beside her and took her hand in his.

"I'm not sure I *can* eat," she managed to say tremulously as she dashed away another errant tear. "I . . . seem to be . . . out of control."

"That's to be expected," he said firmly, in a tone that left no room for doubt. "You've been through an ordeal. A terrible ordeal. You cry all you want to, Jessie. But it would sure make me happy if you tried to eat something."

She sniffled. "I can't. . . ." Another sob caught her. "Arlen...Arlen, please...I just need you to hold me...."

So he kicked off his shoes, shucked his shirt, tie and belt, and lay down beside her. Gathering her as close as he could, he held her shuddering, shaking body while sobs racked her. And finally, a long, long time later, exhaustion carried her into a natural sleep.

Arlen didn't sleep. He held her tenderly, every whisper of her breath a caress on his skin, her warmth filling him and soothing him. He knew now with absolute certainty what a future without Jessie looked like, and as the minutes marched by he stared into that abyss.

It was still dark when Jessica opened her eyes. She felt calm now, secure and safe, as if Arlen's sheltering presence had suffused her and driven away the nightmare of the past few days. With a sigh, she snuggled closer and thanked God for Arlen Coulter. Whatever happened, she had been blessed to know him, to share this time with him. And at the first opportunity she was going to tell him how much she loved him, whether he wanted to hear it or not.

Arlen stirred, reaching across her, and then Jessie blinked as he turned on the bedside lamp. Tilting her head back, she looked into flannel-gray eyes and felt as if the wind had been knocked from her. So warm, so intense, so caring.

"How do you feel, Jessie?"

"Much better," she murmured, daring to lay her hand on his bare chest. Afraid he would speak of leaving now that she was safe, she seized on a safer topic. "Who was it, Arlen? Who was the agent who was working with Frank?"

She had wondered so hard and for so many hours that she felt as if only an answer would end the whole affair.

"Phil Harrigan."

"Harrigan!" She was genuinely shocked. "Why? Why did he do it?"

"He says he did it for the excitement."

"Excitement?" Jessie couldn't believe it. "For *excitement?*"

"That's what he says. He's obviously got something screwy in his thinking, but that's the extent of it. He was evidently turned on to the image of himself as a double agent." For a while he talked of what had happened, filling her in on events as if he, too, were reluctant to turn his thoughts to the future.

And then he cupped her cheek gently in his hand and turned her face up to his.

This was it, she thought. He would leave now that she no longer needed his protection. She thought her heart was going to break in two.

"Are you awake? *Really* awake?"

"Absolutely." After all, she thought wildly, you wouldn't want the condemned man to sleep through his execution.

He nodded, and the sudden strain of his face made her hold her breath in expectation of the blow.

"Jessie, I'm a selfish bastard to bring this up now, but I can't stand it another minute."

Her hand curled on his chest until her nails bit into her palm. She waited, feeling as hopeless as she had felt in Frank's clutches.

"I love you, Jessie. I love you, and I don't care how selfish it makes me, but I can't let you go. I've been telling myself for weeks that you deserve someone younger, that I have nothing to offer you. And it's true, Jessie, I don't have a damn thing to offer you—"

Stunned, she had let him plunge ahead with this self-deprecating speech, but now she interrupted with a joy that couldn't be contained another minute. "I love you, Arlen."

"But selfish or not, I can't live without . . ." His voice trailed off as her words penetrated. "You do?" Gray eyes searched her face hungrily. "You've been through a lot. I know you need time...."

"I don't need *any* time, Arlen. I've known for weeks that I love you. I've known for weeks that I can't live without you." Tears prickled in her eyes again, and she couldn't hold them back. She had never dreamed it was possible to feel so much love, so much joy, so much happiness. "Tell me again, Arlen. I never thought...I never hoped...please tell me again."

He was happy to tell her again. It was a *relief* to tell her again, and again, and yet again. And it was absolutely miraculous to hear her make the same avowal in return. He kissed away her tears, held her close to his heart and sent prayers of gratitude winging heavenward.

"We'll work it all out later when you've had a chance to rest, Jess, but you'd better know right now that I want the whole nine yards."

She liked the sound of that and cuddled closer. "Which nine yards?"

"Marriage."

"Mmm. I wouldn't settle for any less."

He laughed softly. "You've been settling for a lot less than you should these past couple of weeks. I can't believe how selfish I've been."

"You haven't been selfish. You were trying to be honest and honorable with me. I don't think you were selfish at all."

"That's because you're so damn generous." He slipped his fingers gently into her hair and pressed her cheek to his shoulder. "How man kids do you want?"

"Kids?" She squeaked the word in disbelief. That was one dream she had been prepared to surrender for him. "You said... But...how many times did you tell me...?" Her voice trailing away, she twisted until she could see his face. The expression she saw there melted her heart.

"I want to give you my children," he said softly. "Because *I* want *your* children. But only if *you* want them, Jessie." He kissed her gently on the lips and then on her damp eyelids. "I know what I've been saying," he said gruffly. "I've been a complete and total ...

Never mind. I'm sorry it took nearly losing you to bring me to my senses, but I *am* in my right mind at last. The whole nine yards, Jessie. All of it, including the dog, the cat and the station wagon."

Oh, how she liked the sound of that. "But what about Melanie and Andrew?" she asked as a different kind of fear stabbed her.

"Melanie will be thrilled. She's been trying to persuade me to remarry for years. Andrew will resent it, but he'll get over it, and it doesn't matter a damn anyway, because *I'm* the one marrying you, and he's not a kid any longer. This is between us and only us."

She turned into him, wrapping her arms around him and hugging him close. "Two," she said. "A boy and a girl."

He laughed and squeezed her. "I'll try."

It had all been worth it, she thought. Every fear, every worry, every risk.

* * * * *

SILHOUETTE·INTIMATE·MOMENTS®

IT'S TIME TO MEET
THE MARSHALLS!

In 1986, bestselling author Kristin James wrote A VERY SPECIAL FAVOR for the Silhouette Intimate Moments line. Hero Adam Marshall quickly became a reader favorite, and ever since then, readers have been asking for the stories of his two brothers, Tag and James. At last your prayers have been answered!

In August, look for THE LETTER OF THE LAW (IM #393), James Marshall's story. If you missed youngest brother Tag's story, SALT OF THE EARTH (IM #385), you can order it by following the directions below. And, as our very special favor to you, we'll be reprinting A VERY SPECIAL FAVOR this September. Look for it in special displays wherever you buy books.

Silhouette Books®

Silhouette Special Edition

presents

SONNY'S GIRLS

by Emilie Richards, Celeste Hamilton and Erica Spindler

They had been Sonny's girls, irresistibly drawn to the charismatic high school football hero. Ten years later, none could forget the night that changed their lives forever.

In July—
ALL THOSE YEARS AGO by Emilie Richards (SSE #684)
Meredith Robbins had left town in shame. Could she ever banish the past and reach for love again?

In August—
DON'T LOOK BACK by Celeste Hamilton (SSE #690)
Cyndi Saint was Sonny's steady. Ten years later, she remembered only his hurtful parting words....

In September—
LONGER THAN . . . by Erica Spindler (SSE #696)
Bubbly Jennifer Joyce was everybody's friend. But nobody knew the secret longings she felt for bad boy Ryder Hayes....

Take 4 bestselling love stories FREE

Plus get a FREE surprise gift!

Special Limited-time Offer

Mail to
Silhouette Reader Service™
3010 Walden Avenue
P.O. Box 1867
Buffalo, N.Y. 14269-1867

YES! Please send me 4 free Silhouette Intimate Moments® novels and my free surprise gift. Then send me 4 brand-new novels every month, which I will receive months before they appear in bookstores. Bill me at the low price of $2.92 each—a savings of 33¢ apiece off cover prices. There are no shipping, handling or other hidden costs. I understand that accepting the books and gift places me under no obligation ever to buy any books. I can always return a shipment and cancel at any time. Even if I never buy another book from Silhouette, the 4 free books and the surprise gift are mine to keep forever.

240 BPA AC9Q

Name	(PLEASE PRINT)	
Address		Apt. No.
City	State	Zip

This offer is limited to one order per household and not valid to present Silhouette Intimate Moments® subscribers. Terms and prices are subject to change. Sales tax applicable in N.Y.

MOM-BPA2DR

© 1990 Harlequin Enterprises Limited

Coming Soon

Fashion A Whole New You.
Win a sensual adventurous
trip for two to Hawaii via
American Airlines®, a
brand-new Ford Explorer
4 × 4 and a $2,000
Fashion Allowance.

Plus, special free gifts* are yours to
Fashion A Whole New You.

From September through November, you can take part in
this exciting opportunity from Silhouette.

Watch for details in September.

* with proofs-of-purchase, plus postage and handling